PRAISE FOR MICKEY FRIEDMAN'S

RIPTIDE

"A ripping good yarn . . . Friedman deftly weaves these diverse strands into an exciting tale."
—*Publishers Weekly*

"The greatest mystery about Mickey Friedman's mysteries is that they haven't achieved the popular and critical acclaim they deserve. . . . Another winner."
—*The San Diego Union-Tribune*

"Lots of local color and a carefully knotted plot."
—*The Orlando Sentinel*

"*Riptide* surges with tense, complex characters. . . . Friedman's continued mastery at integrating energetic, realistic characters with vivid settings and turn-the-page plots is attested to by her growing number of dedicated readers."
—Book-of-the-Month Club

"Provides an engaging heroine, an offbeat supporting cast, and just enough mystery to keep them occupied."
—*Kirkus Reviews*

"Friedman, a New Yorker who grew up on the Panhandle, describes the hot, salty air of a summer day, the sound of the wind through the palms, the groan of a porch swing in a gale with the authority of memory burned into the brain at an early age. . . . Fun for lovers of suspense and intrigue."
—*USA Today*

RIPTIDE

MICKEY FRIEDMAN

HarperPaperbacks
A Division of HarperCollins*Publishers*

This is a work of fiction. The characters, incidents, and dialogues are products of the author's imagination and are not to be construed as real. Any resemblance to actual events or persons, living or dead, is entirely coincidental.

HarperPaperbacks *A Division of* HarperCollins*Publishers*
10 East 53rd Street, New York, N.Y. 10022

Cover illustration by Joe Berleson

A hardcover edition of this book was published in 1994 by St. Martin's Press.

First HarperPaperbacks printing: April 1995

Printed in the United States of America

HarperPaperbacks and colophon are trademarks of HarperCollins*Publishers*

10 9 8 7 6 5 4 3 2 1

To Victoria Dearing
Once my neighbor
Always my friend

riptide: *n.* a tide running against another or others, creating turbulent waters

—*Oxford American Dictionary*

acknowledgments

FOR INVALUABLE ASSISTANCE IN WRITING THIS BOOK, I AM indebted to: Virginia Barber; Alan Friedman; Sheriff Al Harrison, of Gulf County, Florida; Herman Jones; Frances Kiernan; Sergeant David King, of the Marine Patrol; Captain Jimmy Lumley; Jerry Milanich, of the Florida State Museum of Natural History; Jim Miller, of the Bureau of Archaeological Research of the Museum of Florida History; Isadore Seltzer; and Dan Wharton, of the Bronx Zoo/Wildlife Conservation Park.

They are not responsible for my mistakes or for the use I have made of the material they so generously provided me.

The French fairy tale "The Children from the Sea" can be found in *French Folktales* (Pantheon Books).

prologue

EARLY-MORNING FOG HUNG OVER THE BAY, DAMPENING the heavy-headed sea oats on the dunes. No birds cried. Milky dull green waves broke and spread with no more noise than water makes slopping in a bucket.

The lighthouse was set back from the beach, on a gentle rise sketchily covered with scrub palmetto and clumps of coarse grass. Its top was lost in whiteness. Standing at the base of the skeletal metal tower was a man wearing a lightweight windbreaker in a red lumberjack plaid. The man had been standing there a long time, leaning back on one of the structure's supports, bending a knee to rest first one foot and then the other against it.

When the muffled drone of an outboard motor reached his ears, the man straightened. He walked toward the beach and stood at the end of the dunes.

The motor cut off, its cessation intensifying the hush. A moment or two later, the man in the plaid jacket heard splashing. A figure in a hooded black wet suit came in view, pulling a blue boat with a ragged canvas top through the shallows. The diver beached the boat in the listless surf. His back was turned and he didn't hear the lumberjack approach. He reached into the boat and pulled out a burlap sack. The sack seemed heavy, and when he placed it on the packed sand, it made a faint clatter. The diver flexed his shoulders and turned to see the lumberjack a few yards away. He stood still on bare feet as the lumberjack came closer.

The two looked at one another. The diver's clenching toes dug in the sand. When the lumberjack shifted his weight, the diver could see the gun clipped to the belt of the man's jeans.

"Reckon I better have a look in the sack," the lumberjack said. He stepped forward.

The diver bent sideways. He picked up the damp sack, which was now encrusted with sand. Instead of giving it to the lumberjack, he swung it with all his strength.

The heavy part of the sack caught the lumberjack in the face with a clashing noise and knocked him backward, down on the sand. The lumberjack shook his head and blood spurted from his nose. When he tried to sit up, the diver smashed the sack into his face again. The lumberjack pushed himself sideways into the softly spreading waves. He lurched to his hands and knees, his head hanging, a string of mucus and blood dripping into the water. The diver hit him once again, and as he listed forward, the diver dropped the sack and pushed the lumberjack's head down into the swirling water and mushy sand.

When the lumberjack had stopped struggling, the diver sat back on his haunches. His body was heaving, his face wet with tears. "Don't you come at me," he whispered to the lumberjack's corpse. "Don't you come at me."

The diver splashed salt water on his face and dropped the heavy sack in the blue boat. He gripped the lumberjack under the arms and hauled him over the side of the boat. The lumberjack flopped into the bottom like a red plaid fish, but heavy and gone already, without gasping and thumping or arching death throes.

The diver splashed his face again and blew his nose

into the water, a nostril at a time. Blinking rapidly, he turned toward the dunes and saw the old lady.

She stood skinny and still as an egret, her white hair ruffled on top. She clutched a gray sweater around her. He could feel her accusation moving toward him, sharp and clear.

Tears spurted to the diver's eyes again. He glanced at the boat where the lumberjack lay and said, "I didn't—" But it was no use. "Oh hell," he said, and surged up the beach toward the old lady.

She ran faster than he would have credited, her blue-veined legs scissoring, her battered sneakers and crew socks churning through the sand, but of course he caught her. He clasped her shoulders and shook hard, her head jerking back and forth, but still she glared at him, a look so unyielding, he got carried away and clipped her a good one with his fist. Her mouth fell open, her eyes turned up, and she fell out of his grasp, disjointed as a handful of loose Tinkertoys.

He hadn't had more than two seconds to contemplate her sprawled there among wire grass and dollar weeds when from down the beach he heard a child's voice, thin and piercing, singing:

He's got the whole world
In 'is hands
He's got the whole wide wor-hurld—

The diver left the old lady where she lay and ran back to the boat. His body was slick with sweat inside his wet suit. He pushed the boat out, guiding it, scrambling in when the water was thigh-deep. From here, the old lady looked like a log, a pile of seaweed—like nothing at all.

He found the lumberjack's boat on the other side of the lighthouse, at the mouth of the slough. The mist was still heavy as he towed it out, the waves curling and falling lazily, buoys looming up and defining themselves as he passed.

He dumped them out past the shoals. The lumberjack made barely a splash in the dead air as he went over the side. When the diver pulled the plug on the lumberjack's boat, he stood in it a minute or two, feeling the water start to take it, feeling it start on its long trip down.

PART ONE

1

ISABEL ANDERS HAD BEEN UNEMPLOYED FOR TWO months when the letter arrived. Somehow being fired in March, a cold, mean month in New York but a month when it is reasonable to hope for spring, had seemed an additional cruelty.

Spring, with its supposed promise of renewal, had arrived late and chill. Isabel monitored it from the window of her apartment while she refined her portfolio and honed her resume. The leaves on the chestnut tree in the garden below unfurled as she made endless follow-up phone calls. The bushy, undisciplined privet became a haze of green, and now Isabel could look down and see it busy with finches and sparrows, tough little New York survivors.

Unlike, Isabel was beginning to fear, herself.

Isabel was an artist, or so she fancied on good days, but she had no desire to be a starving artist. Thin, pale, and leggy, with abundant unruly dark hair and green eyes, she harbored a streak of practicality behind an ethereal, even eccentric, facade.

For ten years, since shortly after her twenty-fourth birthday, Isabel had been happily and productively employed in the art department of a small publishing house. She had loved every aspect of it—designing books, selecting typefaces, doing jacket illustrations. She had been good at it, too, or so she forced herself to believe. Publishing fell on hard times, though, and her employer was not spared. First the fat was cut, and then the lean, and after a while Isabel herself was sliced away.

During a determinedly manic period right after she was laid off, Isabel made much of welcoming the crippling blow as an opportunity. At animated lunches with her former colleagues, she rhapsodized about the projects, long deferred, she would now have time to tackle. "I always wanted to try a children's book," she would say. The skin on her face felt taut, hot, as if it might split open with enthusiasm. "I started one once, based on a French fairy tale. I can't wait to get back to it." Her companions, fearful they might be next to get the chop, cheered her on and picked up the check. The French fairy tale, *The Children from the Sea,* remained on the closet shelf.

Some years before, boosted by luck and creative financing, flush with extra money from some big freelance jobs, Isabel had bought a co-op on a quiet street in Greenwich Village. A studio on the top floor of a ramshackle brownstone, the apartment was small, all but devoid of storage space, wretchedly inconvenient, the kitchen a converted broom closet, but it had a skylight and a tiny balcony. The place oozed charm. It also, and this was the nub of the matter, was extremely expensive. Even in good times, Isabel was house-poor. She bought winter coats in the thrift shops on Bleecker Street and underwear on the Lower East Side. She was constantly strapped to make her payments. Now, unemployed, she was in arrears.

When she was first cut loose, Isabel had eagerly descended the four flights of stairs between her apartment and the mailboxes on the ground floor, making the trip the instant she thought the mailman had arrived (and often making it several times, since the delivery schedule was erratic). In recent weeks, however, she had become less eager. She had learned that good news, of which she had had precious little, comes by telephone; bad news, of which she had had gracious plenty, comes by mail.

Some days, if she had no other excuse to go out, Isabel didn't check the mail until four or five in the afternoon. She didn't bother until 5:30 on the day the letter came.

The envelope was a businesslike white, the printed return address a law office in St. Elmo, Florida. Isabel stared at the blurry gray postmark. The imprint seemed to be coming toward her through fog, the kind of fog that hung low and smelled like salt and then coalesced and trickled from the porch railing.

She put the letter from St. Elmo on the bottom of the stack and, trudging upward again, riffled through a coupon offer, a brochure about season tickets to an Off-Broadway repertory company, and an upscale housewares catalog. In the back of her mind, a vibration had started. By the time she reached the third floor, it had formed into words: *Merriam is dead.*

So Merriam was dead. It wasn't Isabel's fault. She closed the apartment door behind her and opened the envelope.

Dear Ms. Anders:

I am sorry to tell you that your aunt, Miss Merriam Anders, recently had an accident and is incapacitated. She is in the hospital here in St. Elmo. As her attorney, I am in the process of making arrangements for her future care.

I thought perhaps you would like to know.

Sincerely,
E. Clemons Davenant
Attorney-at-Law

Isabel dropped the letter and the other mail on her dining table. E. Clemons Davenant. Isabel thought she remembered him, sitting on the front porch with Merriam, a tall man with thinning white hair, wearing a seersucker suit and fanning himself with a straw hat.

Isabel had made an effort. She had sent Christmas cards, a note now and again but she had gotten very little response. Some gulfs couldn't be bridged.

Your aunt, Miss Merriam Anders, recently had an accident and is incapacitated. Isabel went and stood at the window. No doubt as a rebuke to Isabel, Mr. Davenant had been stingy with information.

Well, Isabel had been rebuked by people more expert at it than E. Clemons Davenant. Merriam herself, for one. Rebuking Isabel had been one of Merriam's frequent activities.

So Merriam wasn't dead. *It would have been easier if she were,* Isabel caught herself thinking. After a brief flush of shame, she stood by the thought. It would have been easier. Below in the garden, birds fluttered in the privet. The sound of their quarrel drifted up through the open windows.

Isabel's lover, Zan, was in town. That night, they went out for barbecue. Zan, the most European of Eurobusinessmen, loved everything he considered authentically American—baseball, tap dancing, Mickey Mouse, Dixieland jazz. He was the most pro-United States person Isabel had ever known. His uncritical fervor had led to many heated arguments during the years of their disjointed and improbable affair.

Zan's job for a multinational conglomerate brought him to New York from his base in Paris for several days nearly every month. He and Isabel had met when Zan took Isabel and his daughter, one of Isabel's art school classmates, to a Mets game. Although Zan was twenty-five years older and a couple of inches shorter than Isabel, their mutual attraction had been so explosive, it had taken Isabel several years to wonder whether seeing a married man every now and then, and no other men at all, was a healthy format for her love life.

Naturally, she had decided it was not. She made efforts to meet more suitable men, and had some success. These were troubled times for romance, however. Zan had staying power, and she was comfortable with him. Besides, he could never be hers. For Isabel, this had been an argument in his favor.

Zan was sixty now. His salt-and-pepper hair was completely white at the temples. Isabel was no longer consumed with lust at the sight of him, but she was usually glad to see him. Lust could still blaze up, too, if the conditions were right.

This evening, they weren't right. Isabel was thinking about Merriam and the letter from E. Clemons Davenant. Zan seemed distracted, too. They had eaten their baby-back ribs and french fries in relative silence. When Isabel finally asked Zan what was wrong, he said, "Elena isn't well."

Isabel sat back. She toyed with a bone on her greasy plate. Elena was Zan's wife, and Zan almost never mentioned her. If he was telling her Elena wasn't well, Elena had more than a head cold. "I'm sorry."

Zan bent over his coffee cup. "It's serious, I'm afraid."

"I'm sorry," Isabel repeated.

Steam from Zan's coffee swirled toward his face. He looked careworn and old. "It isn't good for me to leave her," he said. "I've had to ask for a transfer—a job that won't require me to travel."

There it was. Although she had always known it wouldn't last forever, and indeed never wanted it to, Isabel had a moment of raw panic when she wanted to grab and cling, to beg Zan to tell her what she was going to do, having already lost her job and now losing him.

She conquered the urge. Zan was holding her hand, saying how much their relationship had meant to him. She responded warmly, with similar sentiments. In a surprisingly short time, there was nothing left to say. Zan pulled a cigar out of his breast pocket and a young maître d' in a cowboy shirt and faded jeans rushed up to prevent him from lighting it. Soon they were walking up Bleecker Street toward Isabel's apartment, a trail of smoke wafting behind them.

Isabel had told Zan about the letter. Zan was endlessly fascinated by Isabel's childhood years at Cape Cache with Merriam. He had claimed to want to visit the northwest Florida panhandle some day, listening eagerly to her descriptions of swamps and pine woods, wide white beaches and barrier islands. "Will you go to Florida to visit your aunt?" he now asked.

It had been a long evening. "Of course not. Why should I?" Isabel snapped.

Zan, in his way, was a great believer in family ties. "I thought perhaps since she's ill—"

"To go would be hypocritical," Isabel said. "She never asked me to come, never made any effort to communicate. Why should I pretend?"

He put his arm around her shoulders. "I'm sorry you're upset."

"I'm not upset."

They walked on. The sidewalk glowed dully under the streetlights. A chilly wind blew. How could it be so cold in May? "I can't even afford the airfare," Isabel went on after a minute. "Even if I could, there's no reason for me to go."

Back in her apartment, Isabel poured two glasses of cognac. She and Zan slipped their shoes off. This had been their routine for years. Tonight, the comforting ritual was suffused with sadness. Isabel sat on her end of the sofa, her feet tucked under her.

"Any luck with finding a job?" Zan asked.

She shook her head.

He asked a few questions about her financial situation. She answered reluctantly. Outside, a car alarm whooped.

Zan sipped his cognac. "I can help you, Isabel."

"Help me how?"

"Money. I can lend you money. I can make the payments on this apartment, if you like, until you're able to take them over again."

A broad road was opening in front of her. If Isabel went down it, everything would be changed. "No thanks, Zan."

"Please think it over first. I'd be happy to do it."

"No thanks. Really." Isabel put down her glass. "I've got a plan," she said. She did have a plan. She'd just thought of it. "I'll find a tenant. I'll sublet this place and go live cheaper somewhere else for a while."

Zan nodded. "Live cheaper? Where?"

"I don't know." She waved a hand, indicating the rest of the known world. "Out of the city. Maybe upstate."

"Maybe Florida?"

Isabel stiffened. "I *told* you," she began, and he laughed. They dropped the subject and made love.

Isabel woke, or thought she woke, early the next morning. She was in the house where she and Merriam had lived, the old house on Cape Cache. A gale was blowing, lashing the palms along the drive, making the chain that held the porch swing creak and groan. The house was cold, and Isabel was searching for Merriam, flinging the doors of the upstairs rooms wide, the curtains flapping and cracking like flags. Only one door was left, and from beneath it oozed a thick purplish liquid like the juice of rotten plums, and the door began to swell like a wound, and she knew Merriam was in there, but before it could burst, she tossed, shuddered, and opened her eyes.

2

RECKON YOU HEARD THEY FOUND THE MARINE PATROLman who disappeared," said Mr. Small.

"Found *part* of him," Daisy Lewis said. She closed her coin purse with a snap and started separating her envelopes into St. Elmo and Other.

"Found his arm," Mr. Small agreed. "Some old boy fishing over at Westpoint caught a shark. Slit its belly open and there was the arm. Or maybe part of the arm."

Daisy's tightly permed blue-white curls bobbed in agreement. She licked a stamp and affixed it to a corner, lining the edges up neatly. "I never heard how they knew it was his arm, though. Was it fingerprints?"

"What I heard, it was some kind of plaid shirt he had on," said Mr. Small. "What was his name again? Kelly?"

"Darryl Kelly," Daisy said. "Awful for his family."

Bill Grogan, who had just checked his box, said, "His boat never turned up, did it?" He pushed a creased piece of pasteboard across the counter to Mr. Small. "Package notice, Tiny."

"Never found the boat," Daisy said. "They reckon he came up on a floating log or something, stove in the bottom."

"That's what they say," said Mr. Small. He took the notice to the back and sorted through a mound of parcels. "Any idea what it is?" he called to Bill Grogan.

"Something the wife ordered, probably," Bill said. He turned to Daisy. "I wonder, myself."

Daisy put on her last stamp and tapped each pile of envelopes smartly on the counter. "What about?"

"Whether Kelly ran over a log or whether some of Buddy Burke's cronies got him."

Daisy clucked and shook her head. "Buddy Burke deserves everything that's coming to him. He ought to be ashamed of himself." She crossed to the mail slots under brass letters reading U.S. POST OFFICE, ST. ELMO, FLORIDA, EST. 1892 and dropped her two piles of envelopes in the appropriate slots.

Mr. Small returned with a glossy volume in his hand. "Catalog. Couldn't fit it in the box," he said, handing it to Bill.

Bill took it. "Just what I need."

Silence fell. Bill Grogan squinted out the window, watching a lawn sprinkler scatter brilliant drops on the patchy grass of the post office lawn. "Is it supposed to rain this afternoon? I'm umpiring the Little League game."

"Chance of showers," said Mr. Small. "Did you hear Isabel Anders is back?"

Daisy snorted. "Reckon she heard Merriam is poorly. Wants to get her share."

Mr. Small shook his head. "Merriam disinherited her is what I heard."

"I hope so . . . after the way Isabel treated her."

Mr. Small settled himself against the counter. "Ran off with a boy from the air base," he said. "Merriam was fit to be tied."

"Merriam was well rid of a girl who would do such as that."

"Isabel was a pretty girl, though," said Mr. Small, watching Daisy for a reaction.

She bristled satisfactorily. "Beauty is only skin-deep, Tiny." After a moment, she added, "Poor Merriam."

Mr. Small nodded. "Doctor has to keep her drugged up or she's screeching to beat the band."

"Poor soul. She ought to be in the home." Daisy settled her pocketbook over her shoulder. "Well, I got groceries to buy, and a hair appointment, and I don't know what all."

"Best to your old man," said Mr. Small.

Daisy waved and in a moment passed the window. Bill Grogan was still looking out. "Did they say what percent chance of showers?" he said.

At dusk on the same June evening, Harry Mercer pulled his pickup into Elmo Texaco, on the corner where the state road dead-ended into Beach Road. Leaving the truck to be gassed up, he walked over to Margene's MiniMart to get a soft drink and some peanuts. Moths and bugs danced around the incandescent lights on the poles at the filling station.

Margene was sitting on a stool, leafing through *USA Today.* On his way back to the refrigerator case, Harry waved and called, "Hey, hon."

"Harry." Margene turned a page. She was liberally freckled and on the hefty side. When Harry returned with his Cherry Coke and put it on the counter with the peanuts, she said, "I bet you remember Isabel Anders."

Harry had been digging in the pocket of his khakis. He stopped digging. "Hell yes."

"Was she in your class at school? I was trying to think."

Harry rolled his eyes to show that he, too, was trying to think. "Year behind."

"I thought it was something like that." Margene punched numbers into the cash register. "That's a dollar twenty-nine."

Harry paid. He popped the top of his drink and said, "What about her?"

Margene's eyes had strayed back to *USA Today.* "Who? Isabel?"

"Who else are we talking about?"

Margene looked up and said, "She was in here today." She folded her arms.

Harry blinked but mastered any further indication of surprise. "Naw," he said.

Margene nodded. "She was. Buying groceries. Cereal, milk, bananas—"

"Are you sure it was her?"

"Am I sure? I asked her. I said, 'Isn't that you, Isabel?' "

"She said yes?"

"Sure she said yes. It was her."

"Did she know you?"

"No. I was a few years behind you all in school."

Harry took a swallow of Coke and bit open the top of his cellophane peanut bag. Once he got it open, he shook out a handful of nuts and tossed them in his mouth. "Humpf," he said, chewing.

"She looked different, but I knew."

Harry swallowed. Harry had deeply tanned skin and sun-bleached brown curls. He looked like what he was, an outdoorsman gone soft in the stomach. He wore deck shoes without socks, a knit shirt. "How different?"

Margene raised her eyebrows. "Way too skinny, and white as a ghost. No tan at all."

"She never did have a tan." He took another swallow. "She say where she was staying?"

"She didn't say, but she headed off toward the Cape. She was driving Miss Merriam's old Ford." Not much got by Margene.

"No kidding." Harry stifled a burp. "I'll be damned."

"Yep." Margene turned a page.

Harry nodded. "See you, Margie."

Harry walked slowly back toward Elmo Texaco, feeling the heat from the parking lot warming the soles of his shoes and rising up his pants legs. He finished his drink, tossed the can in the oil drum the station used as a recycling bin, and paid for his gas. When he pulled away from the pumps, he sat for a while as if considering something before finally turning right on Beach Road.

Night hadn't quite fallen, but it was dark enough for headlights. In a few minutes, Harry was out of town. The smell of salt water filled the truck. On his left were rolling dunes covered with sea oats, and beyond the dunes, waves curled and broke. Cottages, interspersed with strips of town-house apartments, dotted the roadside.

After a few miles, Harry reached the Beachcomber Boatel and Restaurant, a long dock with gas pumps and boat slips attached to a two-story frame building with plate-glass windows, its roof ringed with blinking multicolored lights.

Beyond the Beachcomber, civilization thinned to an uneven row of widely separated cottages on the beach side and woods on the other. Amid the tangle of palmetto, scrub oak, and pine, an occasional magnolia was visible, with pale blossoms luminous in the dusk. Up ahead, the Cape Cache lighthouse flashed rhythmically.

When Harry reached a nearly obscured track leading off to the right, he pulled onto the shoulder and turned off his engine. Moving over in his seat, he craned out the passenger window. He could barely see the dark bulk of the old Anders place through the cabbage palms bordering the overgrown drive.

Harry got out of the truck and walked down the drive, the palms overhead rustling in the hot breeze. The big house loomed in front of him. Off to one side, some twenty-five or thirty yards away, sat a small mobile home. Light shone through its curtained windows. An old Ford was pulled up nearby.

Harry stood with his hands in his back pockets, looking at the trailer. Every now and then, a shadow moved behind the curtains. After a while, he returned to his truck and drove away.

3

THE PALMS WOKE ISABEL AT DAWN. SHE SAT UP STRAIGHT, listening to the sound that was both alien and dreadfully familiar.

The palms along the drive. She had forgotten the racket they made in the wind. The dry rustling was so loud, it almost drowned out the ineffectual churning of the air conditioner.

Isabel leaned back against the carved oak headboard of Merriam's bed. The air in the bedroom was tepid and stale. The room was almost filled by the massive bedstead and matching dresser with its tarnished mirror. These two pieces were the only furniture Isabel recognized from the house. The living room suite, rattan with tropical print cushions, must have been included with the trailer.

Merriam had never told Isabel she had moved out of the house.

Isabel got up, picking her way around her suitcase. She had not yet figured out how to unpack, since every drawer and closet shelf was jammed with the detritus of the Anders family history. There were starched linen tablecloths, old shotguns, crocheted runners, photo albums, cutwork baby garments.

In the shower, lukewarm water slid over her body from a nearly corroded shower head. Headachy and unrefreshed, she pulled on shorts and a shirt and went to the kitchen to make coffee. The dented aluminum coffeepot she had found there could well be the same one she remembered from her childhood.

Here she was. New York and her life there might as well be on another planet. She had sublet her apartment to a young record company executive, then said farewell to her friends and good-bye to Zan. She was back at Cape Cache, which she had once hoped never to see again.

She wasn't sure why she had changed her mind. Being able to live cheaply was, she recognized, a wan excuse for this major upheaval. She wasn't convinced she owed Merriam anything, and it was too late in her life to start bowing to convention. Still, she had found herself determined to come.

Isabel wandered around the tiny, shadowy living room, waiting for the coffee to drip. Although cluttered, and dusty from lack of occupancy, the place had been perfectly clean when she arrived. Knowing Merriam's ways, Isabel would have expected no less. The magazines were neatly stacked on a shelf under an end table, the standard-issue seascape on the wall hung straight. There was a portable radio but no television set. Merriam had always considered television an unnecessary, possibly even sinful, indulgence.

Yes, the place was much as Isabel might have imagined, including the shrine in the corner.

What else could you call it but a shrine? The photograph hanging on the wall, sepia-toned in its heavy frame, was one Isabel remembered well. It depicted a dark-haired man, handsome but running to jowls. He was staring out of the picture, a surprised expression in his bulging dark eyes. The man was John James Anders, Merriam's father and Isabel's grandfather.

Isabel felt Merriam's fingers digging into her shoulder, anchoring her in front of the portrait. She heard Merriam's voice: "You know who this is?"

"Yes, ma'am." Of course Isabel knew. They had been through the catechism before.

"Who is it, then?"

"My grandfather."

The fingers tightened. "What was his name?"

"John James Anders."

The sainted John James, dead before his time. His photograph had had the place of honor in the front parlor of the big house. Now it dominated this tacky little room. Beneath it, sitting on a tall, spindly-legged flower stand, was a porcelain bottle. The bottle was square, about six inches high, with an airy blue pattern of flowering branches and flying birds on a white background. In the old days, it sat on the mantel under John James's portrait. Isabel used to dust it very carefully every Saturday.

The bottle was part of John James's shrine. Merriam told the story like an incantation.

"He gave it to me the very day he went away," Merriam would murmur. Isabel, clutching the feather duster, had watched her warily. It was always best to be still and quiet.

"I walked with him through the woods to the dock," Merriam said. "Mama and I begged him not to go. The storm wasn't even over. I walked with him, and when he was fixing to leave, he pulled this bottle from under his jacket and said, 'Here's a play-pretty for you, Merriam.' Then he took off."

John James Anders had taken off in 1922. He never came back. He had left behind failed business schemes, angry creditors, and a shell-shocked family. After his lumber and turpentine businesses were sold to meet his debts, his wife, Polly, daughter, Merriam, and infant son, Johnny, were left with the laughably grandiose house and the few acres of swampland surrounding it. That and a blue-and-white porcelain bottle.

The coffee must be ready. Isabel walked into the kitchen area, separated from the living room by a waist-high counter. Merriam must have sold the china. The dishes in the cabinet were pink plastic. Isabel poured a cup of coffee and pushed back the curtains on the kitchen window. There, across an expanse of sandspurs, yucca, palmetto, and coarse calf-level grass, was the house.

The upstairs veranda sagged dangerously and a broad-leaved vine grew out of the tumbled chimney. Windowpanes were broken; drainpipes leaned away from their moorings. The flaking paint was dirty gray. The porch swing had been taken down and shoved into a corner, but the rusting chains that had attached it to the ceiling still dangled.

The downstairs windows were shrouded by curtains. Some had boards nailed across them, as did the front door. The upstairs windows were blank, shaded.

From an artist's viewpoint, the colors were muted, subdued: dull gray, dull green, dull brown—except for a spot of red on the front steps. A red metal can sat there, a gasoline container perhaps. The single brilliant blob made the overall spectacle even more depressing. Isabel thought of Merriam standing here, day after day, watching the place disintegrate while she washed dishes.

Today, Isabel would go to the hospital. She would see Merriam. The thought made her breathe faster, as if she were still a girl who could have a switch taken to her if she disobeyed.

She made toast and had another cup of coffee while she ate it with grape jelly. Isabel and Merriam used to eat grape jelly. Isabel never ate grape jelly in New York. She would go to the hospital to see Merriam this afternoon. Tonight, she had been invited to have dinner with E. Clemons Davenant and his sister.

E. Clemons Davenant, the attorney who had written the letter about Merriam, had been a surprise. Although he wore, as he had in her memory, a blue seersucker suit, he was not the elderly man Isabel remembered, but his son. Clem Davenant—as he had introduced himself when he met her at the airport—was in his forties. He had sandy hair, a neatly trimmed beard, a sprinkling of freckles on his nose and the backs of his hands, and a somber demeanor. He had arranged for Isabel to stay in Merriam's trailer and use her car. He had met Isabel at the airport and driven her to Cape Cache. He had done these generous deeds without a flicker of warmth or welcome. Isabel didn't think he had smiled once during the couple of hours she had spent in his company.

Not that there was much to smile about. Merriam was in bad shape. On the trip from the airport to the Cape, Clem Davenant had filled her in: Merriam had been found wandering on the beach, dazed and incoherent. She had had a slight concussion, and her doctor speculated that she had fallen. Although the physical damage was healing, she continued to be agitated and out of touch with reality.

"She's being medicated to keep her calm," Clem had said, his eyes on the road. "I don't like it much, but they've convinced me it's necessary."

It was hot in the car. Isabel's long-sleeved silk shirt was much too warm. She unbuttoned the wrists and began to roll up the sleeves. She was so overwhelmed by being here that she was finding it hard to concentrate. "Where did she fall?"

"Somewhere on the beach, I assume." He glanced over at her. "She used to take a walk in the mornings. Six o'clock or earlier."

Yes, Merriam's morning walk. Isabel remembered her energetic gait, her feet crunching on the crushed oyster shells as she strode up the drive.

After the meager information had been imparted, the drive wasn't nearly over. Clem, with punctilious courtesy, seemed determined to make conversation if it killed him. "When did you come to live with Miss Merriam?" he asked.

"When I was nine. My parents were killed in a car accident. My father was Merriam's brother, Johnny. He was ten years younger than she was."

"Awful shame," Clem said vaguely.

He could have been referring to the death of her parents, with her hell-raising father drunk at the wheel, the general misery of her years with Merriam at Cape Cache, or Isabel's running away at the age of sixteen with Airman First Class Ben Raboski of Nutley, New Jersey. In any case, she could only agree. "Yes, a real shame."

Silence. She studied his profile: sharp nose, haggard around the eyes. "I've been trying to remember you from school," she said.

"I was years ahead of you. I was probably already in law school by the time you . . . left."

Isabel suppressed a wry smile and studied her hands. Moths had wheeled in the headlights of the car, splattering on the windshield, as she and Ben Raboski sped away from Cape Cache. They must have been driving eighty-five or ninety, although nobody was chasing them and nobody ever would. "Well, I left in a bit of a rush, and I haven't been back," she said.

He looked surprised that she'd mentioned it. "Whatever happened to . . . to the man—"

"To Ben? Last I heard, he and his brother were partners in a Pontiac dealership in Teaneck. New Jersey, that is." She sat forward as they rounded a curve. The gleaming bay and a curve of white beach came into view. "There it is," she said softly. An unfocused sensation rushed through her. *Yes! There it is!* The sand, the water, the dunes. Had she really missed it so much?

"Not a great deal has changed, really," said Clem.

"No."

But of course a lot had, starting with the house, that sad wreck. Clem was already apologizing as they jounced down the drive. "She didn't have the money to keep it up," he said. "It was too big for her, there all by herself." Not for the first time, Isabel sensed his condemnation. He didn't think she had treated Merriam right.

Whatever his opinions, he had helped her unload her bags, given her keys to the trailer and the car, and, a hospitable Southern gentleman to the finish, invited her to dinner at his home. If he could be believed—and what Southern gentleman ever could be?—his sister Eve was eager to meet her. No Mrs. Davenant had been mentioned.

Isabel stood up and put her coffee cup in the sink. Today she would go see Merriam, but not yet. She wasn't ready. It was still too early. She would reorient herself, go for a walk on the beach.

She put on sandals, stepped out on the concrete block that served as the trailer's front step, and was engulfed by hot, muggy air. A dirt track led through the weeds to the drive. She walked under the palms up to the road. It was deserted, oily ripples of heat rising from its surface. To her right, the black metal frame of the lighthouse rose above the trees. She crossed the road and wandered through the dunes. White sand stretched to pale green water. Far out, pelicans, ten or fifteen of them at least, were diving for fish, making mighty splashes. Waves nudged a line of seaweed on the damp sand.

She heard singing, a child's voice:

He's got the whole world
In 'is hands

Not far away, right at the waterline, a little girl, seven years old perhaps, was twirling a baton. She wore red shorts and a yellow T-shirt. She pranced through her routine, tossing her yellow hair, kicking her bare feet with abandon.

He's got the whole wor-hurld
In 'is hands

The child was good. She tossed the baton upward and caught it without missing a beat. When she finished, she curtsied deeply to the waves and ran away down the beach toward the nearest cottages.

Isabel started to stroll along the beach, but the image of an injured Merriam stumbling beside her made her tense, and as the sun rose higher, the light was almost blinding. After a short while, she turned back.

Going to the hospital was not, after all, the ordeal she had expected. Merriam was asleep, motionless, her beaky nose protruding above the curves of the pillow. She looked small, wrinkled, frail. The past fifteen years had aged her considerably, which was only to be expected. "She's eighty years old," said the doctor standing at Isabel's elbow. "Remarkable shape, but you don't come back so easily at that age."

Dr. McIntosh didn't look far from eighty himself. His nose was bulbous, his face deeply lined. A sparse brush of white hair was scattered thinly over his scalp. He had given Isabel vaccinations, treated her when she had strep throat at the age of thirteen. He smelled faintly of cigarettes.

Isabel wiped her hands on her skirt. She had had an absurdly difficult time deciding what to wear. She had finally settled on a dark print sundress that now seemed rather too bare, although she had considered it demure back in New York. "What's your prognosis, exactly?" she asked.

He shoved his hands in the pockets of his white jacket and studied Merriam's inert form. "She's getting better physically, but whether she'll ever be the same, I don't know," he said. "I doubt she'll be able to live on her own again. She was an accident waiting to happen anyway, out there all by herself. If you're asking if she's about to die, well . . . I'd have to say no. But at her age . . ." He lifted his shoulders.

Isabel stared at Merriam's sunken face. Her lips were slightly parted. Here was Isabel's oppressor, reduced and subdued. "Merriam, it's Isabel," she said.

"I don't imagine she'll wake up. She's had her medication."

"I'll wait for a while."

Sitting in a chair beside the bed, Isabel waited. Merriam did not wake up. She did not even move. When it was time to go to dinner at Clem Davenant's, Isabel left.

The Davenant house, just inside the St. Elmo city limits, was red brick, two-story, magnolia-shaded. A rangy, freckled woman with a toothy smile answered the door. She said, "Hi, Isabel. I'm Eve, Clem's sister. He's out back getting the coals on." Isabel followed her through a dim, cool interior to a back patio where Clem, looking buttoned-down despite his cotton slacks and sports shirt, was emptying coals into a barbecue pit. His greeting to her was only slightly less formal than it had been when he met her at the airport, and by the time the coals were lighted and gin and tonics provided, he had fetched his briefcase and was sitting opposite her in a lawn chair, broaching the subject of Merriam's condition.

"Let Isabel have her drink before you get down to business," Eve protested.

A furrow of displeasure appeared between his eyes. "I expect Isabel would like to get this out of the way."

Eve raised her eyes to heaven. "I'll go make the salad, then."

Clem plowed on, taking papers from his briefcase. "I imagine Dr. McIntosh told you Miss Merriam will need constant care, at least for a while. I've applied for a place in Sunny Haven, a facility in Bay City, but they're full at the moment. What I propose is this—"

What Clem proposed, it developed, was that Merriam be released from the hospital and live at the home of a local practical nurse until space became available in the nursing home. As he talked, Isabel realized that his plan was less a proposal than a fait accompli. "She'll have individual care, and Bernice Chatham is experienced. The atmosphere will be more conducive to recovery." He droned on, filling her in on details of Merriam's modest financial situation.

Isabel took a swallow of her drink and wondered why he was bothering to consult her. She had given up the right to any say over Merriam years ago, and vice versa. Isabel ran away; Merriam disinherited her. That's all there was to it.

When she got a chance to put in a word, she said she thought Clem's idea was fine. He gave a brisk nod, wiped his brow, and got up to put the steaks on.

Eve Davenant was easier to talk to. As smoke billowed above the barbecue pit, she asked Isabel questions about her life in New York and how she was managing at Cape Cache. Eve, it developed, was a schoolteacher. She stretched her legs luxuriously. "School's out, and am I glad," she said. "I'm exhausted. The first year on a new job is so hard."

Isabel had pictured bachelor brother and spinster sister as longtime fixtures here, growing into middle age together. "You just started teaching?"

"Oh, I taught for years in Atlanta. I moved back to St. Elmo last summer. To be here and help Clem."

To help Clem? Clem, standing over the steaks, seemed a capable, if taciturn, grown-up. Why his sister should give up another job to move back home and look after him was not immediately clear.

Thanks mostly to Eve, dinner, which they ate at a backyard table, passed pleasantly enough. Clem, Isabel noticed, occasionally zoned out of the conversation. His eyes became fixed, his expression melancholy. When this happened, Eve would raise her voice, or direct a question to him, and alertness would return to his face.

Mosquitoes drove them inside to have coffee. By this time, Eve and Isabel had discovered a common interest in children's literature, and Isabel had warmed up enough to confide that she was working on a picture book. "I brought it with me. I'm planning to finish it this summer."

Eve was glowing. "How exciting! Tell me about it."

In the warmth of Eve's reaction, Isabel's enthusiasm began to stir. Maybe it had been worth digging out her sketches, after all. "It's a retelling of a French fairy tale. I had to revise the original story drastically."

"Why was that?"

"It was really gory and violent. I toned it down, and I think it has possibilities now."

"What's the title?"

"The Children from the Sea. It's about twins, a brother and sister named Marin and Marinette. They're castaways. They nearly drown when their ship sinks, but they wash up on a beach where—"

Something was wrong. Eve's smile had faded. In the shadows, Clem sat motionless. "It sounds just great," Eve said in a strained tone. She stood up. "I'm going to have more coffee. Anybody?"

Isabel dropped the subject of *The Children from the Sea.* Silence fell. It was, in any case, time to leave. She asked where the bathroom was and escaped down a hall, fleeing the uncomfortable atmosphere.

She stayed in the bathroom longer than necessary, staring in the medicine cabinet mirror, fiddling with her hair, which had, predictably, become completely unmanageable in the humidity. She would give Clem and Eve time to regain their composure and then say a swift good night.

When she emerged, a light was on in a room across the hall. Clem was standing inside the door, gazing at something. Here was her chance to take her leave. She stopped in the doorway. "Thanks. It was a lovely evening."

He started, as if he hadn't heard her approach. The room was a library, book-lined and hung with old maps. Clem, she saw, was standing in front of a mounted glass display case containing a collection of seashells. He gestured, inviting her in to look. She recognized conchs and cowries, shark's eyes and whelks. She pointed to an array of unfamiliar ones with long, delicate spines. "What are those?"

"Murex and spiny oysters. You have to be careful cleaning them or they'll break and be spoiled." His voice was almost inaudible.

"Cleaning them? You mean you found these on the beach?"

"Oh, no." His lips actually curved. His first smile. "Not on the beach."

"They're beautiful."

He nodded. "These with the spines, you can't boil. You have to leave them outside until the ants strip out the flesh. Take the algae off with muriatic acid."

"Where did they come from?"

"Out in the bay. Deep water."

"You go scuba diving?"

He didn't answer right away. When she glanced at

him again, she saw that his eyes had reddened. "Not anymore," he said.

"*Here* you are, for heaven's sake!" It was Eve. She went on with forced cheerfulness. "I keep telling Clem to donate those shells to the school. They'd make a wonderful display for the students, and then we'd have the space they take up."

Isabel looked at Clem. He seemed to have forgotten she was there. She hurried through her final thank-yous and said good-bye.

4

HARRY MERCER, IN SWIMMING TRUNKS AND UNBUTtoned shirt, sat on the roof of his boat, the *Miss Kathy,* watching out for his afternoon dive party. They should be surfacing soon. The married couple had already come up once, in a flurry, to tell Harry they'd seen a barracuda down there. Six feet long, they said, which probably meant three or four. The husband had looked nervous, but Harry could tell the wife was excited.

"He won't bother you," Harry had called down, talking to the man.

The woman wasn't even listening. "I'm going to find him again," she said, and down she went. Her husband hadn't had much choice but to follow her.

People from the air base. Harry had never seen them before, probably wouldn't again. Over here diving to pass the time. Of the three, she was the only one who knew what she was doing, but Scooter was down there with them. They would be all right. Harry was left with very little to do, which was fine. He hadn't slept so good last night.

He had lain there, his wife, Kathy, practically smothering him the way she did, thinking about Isabel Anders. If all his thinking could have been boiled down, it would have amounted to this: Isabel had been gone all this time; why didn't she stay gone?

Harry had good reasons for wanting Isabel out of here. It was nothing personal against Isabel, although, God knows, years ago she had cut him off at the socks and damn near killed him with grief. None of that personal stuff was important now.

The orange anchor buoy bobbed on the glistening swells. Clouds were building on the horizon and it might rain later, but right now the glare was fierce, and it was hotter than hell on the roof. Harry settled his brimmed Beachcomber Boatel cap lower on his brow. When the party got back on board, he would suit up and go down to cool off.

Kathy would never leave him. She couldn't get enough of him, even after all these years of marriage. Kathy would not take off with some Yankee dude from the air base and leave without one goddamned word.

Harry had cried when Isabel did that to him. A big old boy of seventeen crying like an infant. And he couldn't say a word to a soul, because everything between him and Isabel had to be secret so Miss Merriam wouldn't find out and make Isabel memorize chapters from the Bible.

They had been cunning, Harry and Isabel. Meeting on the beach, or going out after choir practice, but not leaving together. Putting notes in each other's locker at school with times and places. You had to be a crazy teenager to carry on like that, making love in abandoned beach cottages, rowboats, the backseats of cars. Even now he could remember Isabel's small white breasts, the sounds she made. The thought made his body quicken, and he shifted position.

He had just about time to get himself a drink. He climbed down from the roof. The deck of the boat was a tangle of towels, discarded clothing, masks and fins. In the shade of the roof overhang, he wiped his face with the tail of his shirt and took a Cherry Coke from the cooler. The first deep swallow made the back of his nose prickle. He'd better get back up there before they surfaced. As much of an amateur as the husband was, he was likely to come up under the bow of the boat and get his brains, if he had any, knocked out.

Why couldn't Isabel stay gone? Harry didn't need that complication.

These days, Harry resented the time he spent taking out dive parties. You always imagined things would be fun. That's why you did them in the first place. It would be fun to be married. It would be fun to have a boat and run dive trips for a living. It would be so much fun.

Until you had a couple of daughters who wanted everything they saw on TV and then some, and a wife who didn't appeal to you the way she used to, and on top of that you realized the business you really were in was kissing the asses of idiots and making sure they didn't kill themselves.

On his perch again, Harry studied the coastline. He could barely make out the lighthouse, all but lost in the shimmering brilliance. He squinted, but he couldn't see the Anders house.

When Isabel took off, it was in the middle of Harry's senior year. Afterward, he felt like his body had turned into a repulsive lump. He couldn't study, and he almost didn't graduate. His parents couldn't figure out what was the matter with him.

His daddy had taken him freshwater fishing up the river. They tied up near a stand of cypresses and the hooks were hardly wet before Harry's daddy said, "Son, let me ask you something."

"Yes, sir."

Harry's daddy's eyes were fixed on his cork floating out in the current. "Are you sick or something?"

Harry swallowed. "Naw, sir."

"I mean any kind of sick at all. Any kind."

"I'm fine."

"I'm glad to hear that, because you ain't acting too—"

The cork went under, and Harry's daddy pulled in a good-sized shellcracker. Harry hoped by the time they got it strung that would be the end of the conversation, but Harry's daddy came back to the point. "Your mother says you don't eat. You always used to eat."

Harry couldn't figure out what to say, so again he said, "I'm fine."

"If you were in trouble, Harry, I would want to know about it."

"I'm not in trouble, Daddy," Harry said, and the slow water, drifting corks, and cypresses had seemed like messages sent to torment him with what his life used to be.

He had been a fool, but there was no use dwelling on it. He had graduated, after all, and by the end of that summer he had met Kathy. Kathy was soft, where Isabel was bony; placid, where Isabel was restless; faithful, where Isabel was a betraying bitch.

Out in the water, heads started to appear. Idiot number one. Idiot number two. The woman. Scooter. Harry climbed down from the roof.

Helping the woman up the ladder at the stern he said, "Careful when you sit down," but she paid no attention and whapped hell out of the ledge with her tanks. Without acknowledging Harry at all, she started talking to the two men about her barracuda, which she had found again.

"Good dive?" Harry said to one of the men, the one that wasn't the husband.

"Super," the man said. In a louder tone, so the woman would be sure to hear, he said, "Betsy met up with her twin sister down there."

The woman—Betsy, it must be—threw one of her diving booties at him, and a look passed between them that told Harry all he needed to know about what was going on in *that* trio. "Everything all right?" he said to

Scooter, the deckhand. Scooter nodded, unzipping his wet suit.

Harry didn't like this woman. She treated him like the waiter in some restaurant where she was eating. Wondering if he could shake her up, he said, "You talk about barracuda. A while ago, a fisherman over at Westpoint caught a shark. Know what they found in its stomach? A guy's arm."

The woman wrinkled her nose. "Ugh," she said, but Harry could tell she wasn't especially impressed. She probably ate men for breakfast herself.

"Do they know whose arm?" the husband asked.

"They reckon it belonged to a Marine Patrolman who went missing."

The woman wasn't even listening anymore. "Gross," said the guy. Stupid comment.

Harry stripped off his shirt and went into the small forward cabin to retrieve his wet suit. To Scooter, who had followed him to the door, he said, "I'm going down for a few minutes, cool off."

"I told you everything was all right, Harry." Scooter looked at Harry with edgy defiance.

"I believe you. I'm going down to cool off. Let them have a drink and comb their hair." Harry zipped his wet suit and moved past Scooter to get his tanks.

When he was ready, he somersaulted backward off the side of the boat and felt the water close over him. His world was a cool, shadowy, infinite blue. His breath was loud and harsh in his ears.

Isabel had come here to see about Miss Merriam. She wouldn't stay long. She might be packing up now. She might be gone by this afternoon. The thought sent a tremor through Harry Mercer's gut.

5

ISABEL SLEPT LATE THE NEXT MORNING. SHE WAS GETTING used to the sound of the palms, the scraping of the undergrowth against the back wall, the animal scrabblings that filled the night. She was still at the breakfast table when the telephone rang. It was Eve Davenant.

"I owe you an apology," Eve said.

"You do?"

"Yes." Eve rushed on: "You see, it hadn't occurred to me that you've been out of touch with St. Elmo, and you probably hadn't heard about Clem, and—"

She broke off. Isabel waited.

"I'm lying, damn it," Eve said. "I used you as a guinea pig. I wanted to see if we could get through a normal evening with somebody who didn't know. It was close, but the answer was still negative."

Isabel sat down on the sofa, wishing she had brought her coffee with her. "What are you talking about?"

"I'm sorry. I'm calling to explain." She hesitated. "A year ago, there was a—the only word for it is *tragedy*. Clem and his son, Edward, were scuba diving in the bay. There was a freak accident, and Edward drowned. Twelve years old. Clem went to pieces. We all did."

This explained a lot about Clem Davenant. "I'm so sorry."

"It was in no way Clem's fault, but he blamed himself," Eve went on. "So did Andrea, his wife. She left him three months later, filed for divorce. So you see"—her voice wavered—"you see why Clem acts strange sometimes."

Isabel was horrified. "Oh God. And there I was, talking about *The Children from the Sea.*"

"Look. In the first place you didn't know, and it was my fault for not telling you. In the second place, Clem has to get used to it. He can't be protected all his life from people talking about drowning or accidents at sea."

"I guess not, but still—"

"I really think it would've been all right, except there's been a lot of talk recently about a Marine Patrolman who drowned and was eaten by a shark."

Isabel's breakfast toast seemed to have congealed into an acidic mass beneath her breastbone. "What happened?"

"A young patrolman from Westpoint named Darryl Kelly took a boat out early one morning and didn't come back. A few days later, a fisherman caught a shark, and part of Kelly's arm was found inside it. Everybody has been buzzing. I know it bothered Clem."

"When did this happen?"

"Two weeks ago, maybe? I guess they're continuing to investigate, but the excitement has died down."

Merriam's accident had happened two weeks ago—an unfortunate time for both her and Darryl Kelly.

"So anyway, please forgive me. I hope you'll come see us again."

"Of course I will."

"Good. I'll call you."

The coffee was cold. Although Isabel liked Eve, the phone call had left her feeling dyspeptic. Clem Davenant's melancholy face hovered in her mind. Listlessly, motivated by a need to give the morning a purpose, she took out her portfolio and spread the sketches for *The Children from the Sea* on the dining table.

She had done these sketches at least a year ago. She had labored hard and, as well as she remembered, enthusiastically. Now, she decided she didn't like them much. Maybe it was an unpleasant aftertaste from the upsets of the phone call and the previous evening, but she didn't think so. She studied each one in turn. She had tried for a medieval style—glowing borders of flowers and vines, antique ships, iconlike faces. The drawings were pretty enough, but remote, unrelated to the emotional impact of the story. After a while, she hunched over the table and buried her hands in her hair.

She was still sitting there when someone knocked at the door.

A sharp-faced, grubby-looking little girl was standing on the step. The child had lank yellow hair and wore red shorts and a yellow T-shirt. Her legs were dust-streaked from her knobby knees to her sandaled feet. She was, it took Isabel a couple of seconds to realize, the early-morning baton twirler she had seen on the beach singing "He's Got the Whole World in His Hands."

The girl regarded Isabel with suspicion. "Where's Miss Merriam?"

"She's—sick. She's in the hospital."

The girl nodded impatiently. "I knew *that.*" She pointed at the Ford parked beside the trailer. "That's her car. I saw it go by yesterday. I thought she came back."

"That was me. I was driving her car."

"Did she say you could?"

Who in the hell was this child? "Yes, she did," Isabel lied firmly.

The girl peered past Isabel into the trailer. "Miss Merriam gives me a banana. With peanut butter."

"I don't have any peanut butter."

"Just a banana, then." Showing no doubt of her welcome, she walked in.

Isabel closed the door behind her. She didn't know many children. She wondered whether they were always this brassy. She detached a banana from a bunch on the counter and handed it to the girl, who had noticed Isabel's sketches scattered on the table. "What's your name?" Isabel asked.

"Kimmie Dee Burke." Still studying the sketches, Kimmie Dee Burke peeled the banana and took a bite. "Who drew these?" she asked through the mushy mouthful.

"I did."

"Really?" Kimmie Dee bent closer.

Unable to stand it, Isabel asked, "Do you like them?"

Kimmie Dee shrugged, took another bite, chewed, swallowed. "I can draw," she announced.

Isabel gritted her teeth. Kimmie Dee Burke could easily get on a person's nerves. "Can you?"

"Yes. I'll show you."

Kimmie Dee went to an end table in the living room, pulled out a drawer, and there, sure enough, was a collection of crayon drawings on newsprint. A house and an apple tree. A horse, or possibly a dog. Isabel saw no evidence of outstanding talent, but to be nice she said, "Very good."

Kimmie Dee nodded. "I did those for Miss Merriam."

Isabel noted with some bewilderment that Kimmie Dee Burke seemed to adore Merriam. Perhaps Merriam never made Kimmie Dee sweep the back porch before she could have dinner or lectured her for half an hour about there being no excuse for carelessness.

Kimmie Dee wandered around as if checking the trailer to make sure Isabel hadn't done any damage. "When is Miss Merriam coming back?" she asked.

"I don't know." The answer sounded too stark. Isabel added, "She isn't feeling very well."

Kimmie Dee's shoulders drooped. She studied the framed portrait of John James, touched the blue-and-white porcelain bottle with a careful fingertip. "Well, guess I better go," she said.

Isabel was not sorry to usher her out.

Kimmie Dee was outside on the dirt path, Isabel seeing her off, when the girl said, "You never told your name."

"My name? Isabel."

The child's face contorted with shock.

Isabel stepped outside. "What's wrong?"

Kimmie Dee didn't speak.

Isabel said, "I'm Merriam's niece. I lived with her years ago. Did she ever talk about me?" Possibly Merriam had told this child that her niece, Isabel, was some sort of monster.

At last, Kimmie Dee said, "She called me that."

Insects were buzzing. The palms rattled in a gust of warm wind. "Merriam called you Isabel?"

"Yes." The girl took a backward step. "I got to go."

"Kimmie Dee—"

But Kimmie Dee Burke was running up the drive, leaving motes of dust whirling in the sunlight behind her.

6

CAME INTO TOWN BIG AS YOU PLEASE, DRIVING MERriam's car and all," said Daisy Lewis. "Ouch, Kathy!"

"You got to hold still, hon," said Harry Mercer's wife, Kathy. She planted a roller on top of Daisy's head.

"Had dinner with Clem and Eve Davenant. Reckon they felt an obligation because he's Merriam's lawyer."

Kathy, humming breathily, didn't reply.

The air in Kathy's Beauty Place, located in the converted "Florida Room" of Kathy and Harry Mercer's house, was fragrant with shampoo. A dryer droned over the head of a woman reading a back issue of *People.*

"She could probably use a good haircut. Maybe she'll come in and let you give her one and you can get a look at her," Daisy said.

Kathy Mercer, a buxom, pleasant-faced woman wearing a pink smock, black stretch stirrup pants, and aerobics shoes, seemed to be concentrating hard on winding up strands of Daisy's damp hair. Normally, she loved to gossip.

"Probably thinks she'll get something out of Merriam. There's no justice if she does," Daisy continued.

The customer under the dryer pushed back the metal helmet and craned toward Daisy. "Who's that y'all are talking about?"

"Isabel Anders," Daisy said.

"Oh, *her.* I heard she was back," the customer said. To Kathy, she said, "I think I'm dry."

"Not yet. Go on back under, now." When the

customer retreated, Kathy said, "How are your grandchildren doing, Daisy?"

"Fine. But like I was saying about Isabel—"

Kathy put her comb in the pocket of her smock. She said, "Excuse me a minute, Daisy. My throat's tickling. I need a Coke."

Daisy narrowed her eyes at Kathy's reflection in the mirror. "You do look a little off. Hope it isn't a cold coming on."

Kathy turned and went out the door to the kitchen. When she had gone, the customer under the dryer peeked out again. "I know I'm dry. My whole head feels like it's burning." She got up and crossed to Daisy's chair. "Feel."

Daisy patted the curlers. "Feels dry to me." She loosened one and unwound it, feeling the hair between her fingers. "Why, I think you're perfectly—" she was saying when Kathy returned.

Kathy's face turned pink. "You're *not dry*. Didn't I tell you?"

"I only—" the customer began as Daisy let go of the loosened hair and clasped her hands in her lap.

"You want to spoil your set, I guess it's your business," Kathy said. She buried her face in her hands. "Oh *hell.*"

"My head was too hot," the customer said, but Kathy had run out of the room, leaving the customer and Daisy Lewis staring at one another.

At Cape Cache, at the Beachcomber Boatel, Harry Mercer was having a discussion with his deckhand.

"I'll tell you, Cap'n, I'm thinking about going on strike," said Scooter.

Harry, studying a bill for engine work on the *Miss Kathy,* didn't reply. He and Scooter were in the office of Captain Harry's Charters, a minuscule room next to the

Beachcomber Restaurant's kitchen. Ropes, floats, buoys, flippers, and tanks festooned the walls or leaned against them. A cork bulletin board displayed sheets of marine regulations, along with a couple of postcards from satisfied customers. The door was open on a weathered pier. From where he stood in the doorway, Harry could see, past the gas pumps and bait tanks, the *Miss Kathy,* a twenty-seven-foot inboard, moored in her slip. He knew she was going to need even more work before very damn long.

Scooter was sitting at Harry's paper-strewn desk, in a wooden swivel chair on casters. He was barefooted, wearing his usual ragged cutoff jeans and a white rib-length T-shirt. "You hear me?" Scooter said. Scooter's voice vibrated in Harry's ears and gave him a sharp taste in his mouth.

"I hear you." Harry tossed the bill on his desk with the others and turned his back on Scooter again.

"Maybe I should've stayed in business for myself." A rumbling sound had started up. Scooter, Harry knew without looking, had hooked his long and remarkably flexible toes on an open desk drawer and was pushing himself back and forth in the swivel chair.

Harry asked himself why it had to be Scooter. Scooter was the curveball life had thrown him. Harry said, "Did you refill the tanks yet?"

Rumble, rumble, rumble.

"I asked you a question, Scooter."

Rumble, rumble, whack! Scooter must have bumped hard and deliberately into the desk. "You don't believe me?" Scooter said.

Harry turned around. Scooter had that look on his face, like a kid who's going to push to the limit to prove he can. "What's the problem?" he asked.

"You know what it is." Scooter studied his knee. Scooter was always concerned about his body, and now he was caressing his knee in a way Harry found almost sickening. In Harry's mind, this attitude went along with the fact that Scooter was a vegetarian, never touched alcohol or drugs, and had a headful of shoulder-length yellow ringlets that made him look like some degenerate rock singer. Harry wished Scooter had, in fact, chosen that line of work. Except that without Scooter—

"Like taking that party out today," Scooter said. "What a waste of time." There was a nasal edge on the word *time* that could cut glass.

First Isabel came back. Now this. Harry folded his arms and tried to concentrate on the sound of the water sloshing around the dock pilings, a soothing sound he had always loved. "I have to keep up the business. If I quit taking parties out, people will notice."

"Yeah, but—"

"Besides which, I have a family to support. We haven't made any money on the other thing."

"Harry, I think you just heard what I'm saying." *Rumble, rumble* with the goddamn chair again.

High clouds drifted overhead. The afternoon sun was mellowing to deep gold and the bay winked with thousands, maybe millions, of wavelets. "What do you want me to do?" Harry said. "I can't just—"

But he had asked the wrong question. "What do I want you to do? I want you to put your ass in gear. The longer this drags on, the easier it's going to be for us to land in the shit."

The words wound around Harry's throat like a wire. "All right. I get the point."

"I didn't tell you so we could piss around wasting time. I told you because—"

"I said I got the point, Scooter, so you can shut up."

Scooter shut up. For five full seconds, motionless, he stared at Harry. Then, pushing off with his feet, he sent the chair careening across the floor to crash into the wall where the bulletin board was mounted. At the impact, several pieces of paper swirled down. *"Don't tell me to shut up,"* Scooter hissed.

"All right. Don't shut up." Harry was disgusted. He walked out of the office, past the gas pumps, and along the pier to the *Miss Kathy.* He leaned on the wooden railing and gazed out over the water. Scooter would either follow him out here and harass him some more now or he would stomp off, come back, and harass him some more later.

Harry heard a door bang. Scooter was going to stomp off. Harry fixed his eyes on the dark blue horizon. This is the price you pay, he said to himself. This is the price. This is the price.

7

AFTER KIMMIE DEE BURKE'S VISIT, ISABEL'S CONCENTRATION was shot. She wanted to know why Merriam had called Kimmie Dee Isabel. She wanted to know why Kimmie Dee was so fond of Merriam.

Merriam had been in her fifties, a solitary local eccentric, when nine-year-old Isabel came to live with her at Cape Cache. Merriam and her brother, Johnny, Isabel's father, had been estranged for years. When Isabel became Merriam's responsibility, Merriam's primary concern had been making sure Isabel did not become an irresponsible ne'er-do-well—in other words, making sure Isabel didn't take after her father. Isabel's mother, Johnny's third wife, had been generally beneath mention as far as Merriam was concerned.

So Merriam had cracked the whip, and Isabel labored; Merriam lay down the law, and Isabel obeyed; Merriam lectured, and Isabel learned. Until Isabel, inevitably, rebelled and did everything Merriam had tried to prevent her from doing and then some.

Isabel leaned against the sink, gazing across the weeds at the house. It was a hell of a scene, like something out of a horror movie. What a strange man John James Anders must have been to build that ambitious structure, with its deep porches and elaborate gingerbread trim, in such an inhospitable spot. Now that Isabel thought of it, the gesture smacked of recklessness, even arrogance. According to Merriam's history lessons, John James had gone to a lot of trouble and expense to do it: "He came here with nothing but the shirt on his back, and first thing you know he had a sawmill and a turpentine business and decided to build himself a house. There weren't even any roads around here to speak of. Every stick of this place had to come in by steamer. Every stick."

It was a pity that Merriam had let the place fall to pieces after working so hard through the years to keep it up. Merriam had cut dead fronds from the palms, chopped palmettos out by the roots, painted the front porch—

The gasoline can was gone.

A red gasoline can had been sitting on the front steps. It was gone.

Isabel put on her sneakers and stepped out into the blazing forenoon. The house seemed to hover, almost to lean toward her. She walked along the dirt track to the palm-shaded drive. She should have worn a hat. Merriam's sun hat was hanging on a peg by the door and she should have taken it. The sun was dazzling.

The pulverized oyster shells of the drive had been ground almost to the consistency of sand. They did not crunch under the soles of her shoes as they used to. Sandspurs grew in huge clumps in the oval clearing in front of the house.

Isabel stood at the front steps. A circle of rust showed where the gasoline can had been. She looked around. The can was not on the porch. It was not in the palmetto thickets encroaching on the steps. Somebody had moved it. Somebody had been here without Isabel's knowledge. The thought made her uncomfortable. She would ask Clem Davenant if anyone else had a reason to come to the house.

The air was motionless, the only sound the hum of dirt daubers at their mud-colored nests under the porch roof. Stupefied by brightness and heat, Isabel stared at the boarded-up front door. She could go in, see what was left. She pictured the wide hall and the staircase, the front parlor with its marble mantelpiece. The door was nailed shut. She imagined her younger self inside, trapped.

She wasn't going in. She had no reason to go in. She turned away.

That afternoon, Merriam was awake. She sat on the side of her hospital bed, a flowered nightgown voluminous around her shrunken body. Her eyes were fixed on a point beyond Isabel's shoulder, and from time to time her mouth worked soundlessly.

"She's better today," said Dr. McIntosh. "If she keeps up this way, we can move her to Bernice Chatham's."

"I guess so." Isabel's heart was laboring. The reunion was worse than she had anticipated.

When Dr. McIntosh stepped out of the room, Isabel took Merriam's hand. The skin was mottled and rough. Isabel said, "Merriam? Merriam, it's Isabel."

Merriam's body stiffened. Her hand closed on Isabel's like a vise. "Don't do it," she said. She rounded on Isabel. *"Don't do it! Don't do it!"*

Isabel tried to pull away, but Merriam was flailing, clutching at Isabel's sleeve, at Isabel's hair. Isabel struggled silently, unable to escape the thought that Merriam was trying to destroy her. Merriam's screams rose into an agonized, wordless howl.

In seconds, Dr. McIntosh was back, and a nurse had rushed in with a hypodermic. Isabel extricated herself and Merriam was subdued, her cries becoming more languid, modulating to dreary sadness.

Soon Isabel left the room, weak with relief at her escape. She talked with Dr. McIntosh on the hospital porch, where empty cane-backed rocking chairs sat in even rows. "You can see it's a difficult situation," the doctor said. "The slightest thing agitates her. She has medication all right, but it takes time to adjust the dosages."

Merriam's fingernails had raked Isabel's neck and left a stinging scratch. She touched it gingerly.

"The skin is barely broken," Dr. McIntosh said. "Clean it with hydrogen peroxide and put antibiotic ointment on it. It'll be all right."

Isabel was still shaking when she said good-bye to Dr. McIntosh. She walked across the parking lot. Merriam's car had been sitting in the sun and the door handle was almost too hot to touch.

The drive back to the Cape was sweltering. Isabel's thoughts kept returning to the scene with Merriam. She thought she must have done something wrong. Maybe she shouldn't have taken Merriam's hand.

Isabel couldn't stop wondering why Merriam had called Kimmie Dee Burke by Isabel's name. She wanted to talk with Kimmie Dee again. Since the girl was in the habit of visiting Merriam, she must live close by. After Isabel doctored her scratch, she would take a walk and look at the names on neighboring mailboxes.

Finding Kimmie Dee Burke proved absurdly simple. Across the road from Isabel's driveway, straggling through the dunes toward the Beachcomber, was a line of stucco cottages. Their backyards, bordering the road, displayed sagging clotheslines and spool tables. Deflated beach balls and rusting motor-oil cans lay half-hidden in wire grass. Open carports sheltered upturned boats, motorcycles, Jet Skis. The name Burke was on the closest mailbox. The house was a flat-roofed bungalow like the others, painted a fading turquoise. Squatting under the carport near the screened back door, stirring in a red plastic bucket with a toy shovel, was Kimmie Dee Burke. A diapered toddler stood beside her, looking on.

Isabel walked a few steps up the driveway. "Kimmie Dee?" she called.

The girl looked up. Isabel couldn't read her expression. "Has Miss Merriam come home yet?" she asked.

"No. No, she hasn't." Closer now, Isabel could see that the bucket was half full of wet sand. Several circular patties of sand had been deposited on the concrete. "Are you making mud pies?" she asked.

Kimmie Dee looked incredulous. "Mud pies? No!"

Isabel pointed to the blobs of sand. "I thought those were mud pies."

Kimmie Dee snorted. "They're *sand cakes.*"

So much for chitchat. The toddler crowed loudly. "That's my brother, Toby," said Kimmie Dee. Toby plunged a chubby hand into the bucket, pulled out a fistful of sand, and flung it at Isabel.

Isabel sidestepped and pushed on. "I wanted to ask about something you told me. You said Merriam called you Isabel."

Now, the girl did look uncomfortable. "That's right."

"Well, I wanted to know—when did she call you that? What did she say?"

After a slight hesitation, Kimmie Dee said dismissively, "She was just mixed-up." She picked up the shovel. With a sweetness Isabel could not believe was customary, she said, "Now we'll make sand cakes for *you,* Toby."

Merriam *was* mixed-up, and the question wasn't crucial, but it felt crucial. Isabel said, "If you could tell me when she did it. Tell me what she said."

Kimmie Dee sighed. "Miss Merriam would get mixed-up and say, 'Here's your banana, Isabel,' or 'That's a mighty pretty drawing, Isabel,' and I'd say, 'I'm *Kimmie Dee!*' and we would laugh. That's all."

That wasn't all. Isabel could tell by looking at the

girl's face. She didn't want to push much harder, though. "There wasn't another time?"

Kimmie Dee shook her head. Her hair fell along her cheeks.

"All right, then." Isabel half-turned to leave.

"Just that day," Kimmie Dee said.

Isabel stopped. "That day? What day?"

"The day I saw her down yonder." Kimmie Dee pointed in the general direction of the lighthouse. "The day she got sick."

Isabel tried to remember what Clem and Dr. McIntosh had told her about Merriam's accident. Merriam was found wandering on the beach, dazed and incoherent. Nobody ever said who found her. "Were you the first one to see her?"

Kimmie Dee nodded. "Yes'm. I had been practicing my routine, and I saw her. She was holding her head. Walking funny. I said to her, 'What's wrong, Miss Merriam?' and she looked at me like she didn't see me at all. And that's when she called me Isabel."

Isabel's throat was tight. "What did she say?"

Kimmie Dee squirmed, as if trying to wriggle away from the memory. "She said, *'Help me, Isabel! Help me, Isabel!'* " She shivered. "I tried to tell her I wasn't Isabel."

Isabel stared down the beach at the lighthouse. *Help me, Isabel.* Merriam had called on her for help. Kimmie Dee went back to stirring the wet sand. Toby, meanwhile, had pulverized several sand cakes and was depositing their remains in his wispy brown hair.

Isabel smelled cigarette smoke. Standing inside the screened back door of the Burke house, a cigarette in his hand, a man stood watching her.

She was embarrassed, as if she had been caught intruding. She said, "Hello."

"Hidy." The man was about fifty, with graying blond

hair and a weathered face. He wore an open-necked shirt that exposed white chest hairs. On his wrist was a complicated-looking black watch.

"I'm Isabel Anders. I'm staying across the road at my aunt's trailer."

"Ted Stiles." The man turned and called, "Joy! You got company!"

Isabel glanced at Kimmie Dee. The girl seemed intent on her sand cakes.

A woman with tousled bleached hair appeared beside Ted Stiles. She had an attractive, sulky face and a well-formed body shown off by pink-and-white-checked shorts and a matching halter top. She came out the screen door, looked at Toby, and said, "My God, Kimmie Dee! Look at the mess you let him make."

Ted Stiles said, "Joy, this is—um—"

"Isabel Anders."

"—Isabel Anders. Looks like she already met Kimmie Dee."

Joy Burke said, "Hi," and returned to Kimmie Dee. "Turn on the hose this minute and rinse him off. You know better than that."

Stiles said, "Would you like a beer or something, Isabel?"

"No thanks." Isabel felt a need to explain what she was doing there. To Joy Burke, she said, "I'm Merriam Anders's niece. I was just talking to Kimmie Dee about Merriam's accident."

"Oh yeah," Joy Burke said. "Give me a cigarette, would you, Ted?" When the cigarette had been donated and a light provided, Joy said, "Kimmie Dee found her. She sneaks out early in the morning to practice her baton. I've told her not to. She'll get a whipping for it one day."

The prediction didn't seem to faze Kimmie Dee, who had turned on the hose as requested and was dribbling water over a delighted Toby. "I'm going to be in the talent contest July Fourth," the girl said.

"Hush up. The lady doesn't care about that." Joy Burke expelled smoke. "Kimmie Dee came running in all upset and got me. Poor Miss Merriam wasn't making any sense at all. I called the ambulance and they took her off."

Stiles, leaning in the doorway, said, "May I ask what you all are talking about?"

Joy Burke smiled at him, teasing. "Nosy, aren't you?"

Stiles grinned, but Isabel didn't think he was amused. "Yes, I'm real nosy."

Isabel said, "My aunt had a serious accident. The doctor thinks she fell and hit her head. Kimmie Dee found her wandering on the beach."

"You don't say," Stiles said. "When was this, exactly?"

"About two weeks ago."

"She in the hospital?"

"She is now. She's about to move in with a nurse named Bernice Chatham."

Stiles picked at his bottom lip as if removing tobacco, although he was smoking a filter tip. "You never told me this, Joy."

Joy simpered, "I don't tell you every little thing." To Isabel she said, "Miss Merriam was off her head, hollering and all. It was terrible."

Ted Stiles seemed engrossed. "*What* was she hollering, Joy?"

"Oh, craziness."

"What craziness?" Stiles persisted.

"I don't remember, Teddy! A bunch of words like *Help* and *Don't.*"

"She said, *'Help me, Isabel'* to me," Kimmie Dee offered.

"Huh," Stiles said. He took a long drag on his cigarette.

"I don't really remember," Joy said. She yawned and stretched. The tops of her tanned breasts strained at the halter.

Isabel said she had to leave, and Joy Burke did not urge her to stay. She started up the driveway toward the road, but before she got there, a voice cried, "Isabel!" She turned to see Kimmie Dee running after her, bare feet slapping the pavement.

"I want to tell you," the girl gasped, out of breath.

So there was more, after all. "Tell me what?"

"That Mr. Stiles? Ted Stiles?"

"Yes?"

"He is *not* my daddy." Kimmie Dee shook her head adamantly. She repeated, "He is *not* my daddy."

"I understand," said Isabel, but there was a lot she didn't understand at all.

8

PEERING THROUGH A TATTERED WINDOW SHADE IN AN upstairs bedroom of the old Anders house, Harry Mercer watched Isabel walk toward the trailer. From this distance, she looked just the way she used to—tall, almost gawky-looking. Flyaway dark hair that was always coming loose from the elastic band or barrette.

So now he'd seen her. Big deal.

"Who is she?" Scooter asked, his voice pitched low.

Barely moving his lips, Harry said, "Her name's Isabel Anders. She's the old woman's niece."

"Fabulous." Scooter's hiss seemed to fill every corner of the room.

Isabel glanced up at the house, and Harry's stomach lurched. He stepped back from the window. Although he was sure she hadn't seen him, he felt as if their eyes had met. She used to know when he was looking at her, feel it all the way across the lunchroom, but that was a long time ago.

"What's she doing here?" Scooter asked.

"She must have come to see about the old lady."

Scooter made a sound of disgust. Harry looked out again. He watched Isabel continue to the trailer and go inside.

The air was stifling and only murky light penetrated the shades. The room was unfurnished. Scattered around the floor were an ice chest, a plastic tackle box closed with a combination lock, a red gasoline can, and a wadded-up sleeping bag. Along one wall, makeshift shelves, constructed from concrete blocks and unfinished boards, held an assortment of objects: bottles of chemicals, a collection of brass nails, a length of corroded chain, a battered pewter pitcher, several small rust-encrusted cannonballs, a white enamel dishpan.

Harry hated to admit it, but when he and Scooter first got into the house, he had walked around the whole place, running his hand over the banister rail, opening the kitchen cabinets, fingering strips of rotting wallpaper. As many times as he had made love to Isabel, he had never been in the house where she lived. Miss Merriam wouldn't let her have company or go anywhere except school and church.

Scooter had sat down on the floor. He looked up at Harry, his eyes narrowed. "How long will she be here?"

Harry raised his shoulders.

"Great," Scooter said.

Pretty soon, Harry knew, Scooter would work it out to be Harry's fault. Harry said, "Don't blame me. I didn't invite her." He hadn't invited her. He wanted to be rid of her at least as much as Scooter did. More.

"She could screw us up, Harry." Scooter's tone was casual, but Harry wasn't fooled.

"Not unless we let her. And we aren't going to let her." Harry was not about to let Isabel Anders mess him up again.

"I could take care of her. Easy."

"Sure you could."

"I could. No problem."

Harry caught the challenging look Scooter gave him. He ignored it and walked to the bedroom door. It opened on the landing, which was ringed with closed doors. Harry went to the door at the head of the stairs, which was the bathroom. He opened it a crack and peered in. "Did you feed Sis?" he called softly to Scooter.

"Yesterday. Frogs."

Harry peered at the big tub. Through the chicken-wire screen over the top, he could see part of the water pan and a curve of Sis's greenish brown coils. She seemed quiet, drowsing. She got active sometimes, slithering up and down the length of the tub. That mostly happened when she got hungry.

Scooter and Harry had trapped Sis, a cottonmouth moccasin, out back near the slough and carried her to the house in the extra ice chest. It had been a crazy thing to do, which fit in with Harry's recent mood. He watched a minute longer, then closed the door. When he returned to the bedroom, Scooter had opened the tackle box and was crouched on his knees in front of it, fingering the coins.

It made Harry uncomfortable to see Scooter doing that. He didn't like the sight of Scooter's long fingers moving over those gleaming surfaces. He averted his eyes and said, "I heard the forecast. Rain."

Scooter's expression was remote. He didn't answer.

Rain was good news. Bad weather meant no dive parties. It also meant Harry and Scooter could go out to the wreck with less chance of snoopers spotting them and wondering what they were up to. There was a trade-off, though. In bad weather, visibility was terrible. There was more chance of getting tangled up in the lines, and the water was rough and you had to fight the surge. You were likely to get thrown into things if you weren't careful, and you could get scraped badly. None of it was what you'd call fun.

Still— Harry crossed the room and picked up the enamel dishpan from the shelf. He took it back to the window and knelt down where the most light came in.

The dishpan was half full of fragments of blue-and-white porcelain. Some of the pieces were big enough to reveal a pattern of flowering branches and birds in flight.

Harry picked up a rounded piece of a bowl. He

remembered finding this one, thinking it might be whole, and fanning the sand away gently while his breath rattled through the tube. It was only half a bowl, though—broken, like the rest.

Chinese porcelain. Who would imagine Harry knowing about porcelain? But he had gotten interested.

K'ang-hsi, this kind was called. K'ang-hsi was the Chinese emperor when this porcelain was made and shipped out from Canton and finally came to rest on the shoals off Cape Cache. Around the early 1700s, it would have been.

Canton to Manila, they sailed. Manila to Acapulco, then overland to Veracruz. The plan would have been to sail from Veracruz to Havana and then on to Spain. But a storm blew them off course, more than likely, and the Cape Cache shoals finished them, and all the pretty porcelain ended up in the drink.

There it lay for more than two centuries, it and all the rest, at the mercy of salt water and sand.

Harry wished, God how he wished, he had found the wreck himself. Harry wasn't a treasure hunter. Not then. Harry was a dive captain, trying to make house payments and support a family. He wouldn't have known an eight *reales* silver piece if he'd found one in his jockstrap.

The experience took hold of you. It wasn't only the possibility of getting rich or keeping it all secret so the state and the archaeologists didn't push in. It was being down there and finding something—and because you found it, you started to love it.

Harry remembered his first gold doubloon. Gold doesn't tarnish. It shines like new, and you know it's been shining for years, beautiful, unspoiled. You see that glimmer, and right away your body goes chilly and you say to yourself that it can't be real gold, but in fact nothing else looks the same. When Harry pulled that coin out of the sand, he thought he would never be able to let go of it. Dumb as it seemed, he wanted to hug and kiss it.

This was what he had needed so badly all his life, even when he didn't know he needed it. He wouldn't let anything spoil it now that he knew.

9

THERE'S NO REASON THAT I KNOW OF FOR ANYBODY TO hang around the house," said Clem Davenant. "Where did you say the gasoline can was?"

"On the front step. It was there one day, and then I noticed it was gone." Isabel could feel the effort he was making to show interest.

"Hmm." Clem studied the pile of uneaten french fries and barely touched tuna-salad sandwich on his plate. He said, "Sometimes the teenagers get up to things. They may have been hanging around there after Miss Merriam went to the hospital. I don't think you should worry about it."

Maybe he was right. She could wait and see if anything else developed. Isabel drank the last of her iced tea. She had eaten all her lunch—popcorn shrimp, fries, coleslaw—while Clem toyed with his. Isabel and Clem had been, it was impossible not to realize, the featured attraction for the lunch crowd at the Coffee Time Café in St. Elmo. Many of their goggling fellow diners had made excuses to stop by the table to chat. Had Clem been a different person, the two of them might have chuckled about it together.

The café had emptied out by this time, frigid gusts from the air conditioner had cleared some of the cigarette smoke, and the waitress was desultorily clearing tables and removing the remaining collard greens, fried chicken, and creamed corn from the steam table. Outside, the sky was dark. Intermittent rain spattered the plate-glass windows.

Merriam was leaving the hospital this afternoon, moving to Bernice Chatham's for custodial care. Clem had taken Isabel to meet Bernice this morning. Bernice had struck Isabel as not overly bright, but her small house was clean and she seemed capable. "About the best we can do in St. Elmo," Clem had said with a trace of apology after they left. Then he had suggested that they have lunch before picking up Merriam.

The invitation must have been for politeness's sake. As she struggled to keep the conversation afloat, Isabel began to wish he hadn't bothered. When things quieted down, though, she had taken the opportunity to bring up the gasoline can. Now she launched into another concern. "I've been wondering about what actually happened to Merriam."

The look he gave her was uncharacteristically keen. "Dr. McIntosh told me she fell."

"He assumes she fell because she had a concussion, but as far as I've heard, nobody saw her fall."

He had been fiddling with a french fry. He put it down. "What do you imagine happened, then?"

His blue gaze made her uncomfortable. "I don't know. It worries me to see her so violently upset. She's totally out of control."

"The doctor says it isn't unusual for her to be disoriented."

"Disoriented, yes. But she seems terrified."

"Terrified," he repeated. His eyes wavered. "Yes, she does."

"She never used to be afraid of anything."

To her surprise, he laughed. The sound was brief and bitter. "I guess fear is something we can all learn." He signaled for the check.

They drove toward the hospital in silence, through downtown, past the redbrick courthouse where the mimosa tree on the lawn showed a few pink tufts. Beyond the courthouse, the road swung toward the bay. Rain was now falling in earnest and the water was choppy. Isabel watched the sweeping downpour obscure the horizon.

Clem said, "Nobody really knows what happened."

"To Merriam, you mean? I guess not."

"It can be so fast, so confusing, and before you know it, something terrible has taken place. Something irrevocable."

His hands were tight on the steering wheel. He wasn't talking about Merriam, was he? He seemed to have veered to the subject of his son's fatal accident. Isabel tried to get the conversation back on track. "Maybe Merriam will get better. Be able to tell us what happened."

He turned in at the hospital. "It's something to think about."

Merriam was dressed, sitting in a chair beside her bed. Although her eyes widened when Isabel walked in, she didn't respond to Isabel's remarks. It took a few minutes to pack her suitcase and go through the formalities of checking out, and then the two of them walked slowly down the hall to the front door, where Clem was waiting with the car. As he stowed Merriam's suitcase in the trunk, Isabel decided to risk conversation again. "I'm Isabel, Merriam. Remember me?"

No answer. Merriam seemed to be looking at a stand of pines across the lawn.

"We're taking you to a sort of—nice place where there's somebody to look after you."

Clem came up the steps with an open umbrella. "Okay, Miss Merriam, let's go for a ride."

Merriam's grip on Isabel's arm tightened. "Isabel," she said.

Isabel's breath caught. "Yes, it's me."

Merriam's fingers dug in. "Isabel. Isabel."

During the short drive to Bernice Chatham's, she did not speak again.

Bernice Chatham's house was in an older neighborhood where spreading oak trees dwarfed the modest homes beneath. When they pulled up in front of the aluminum-sided bungalow, Bernice appeared on the screen porch. "Well, looky here," she called. "Have you come to see me, Miss Merriam?"

Bernice was a fleshy woman in her sixties, with gray hair and the wispy shadow of a mustache on her upper lip. She showed them to a bedroom with windows opening on a verdant backyard. "Here's your room, sugar!" she said to Merriam.

Merriam clutched Isabel's arm. "Isabel."

"Yes, that's Isabel. It sure is."

"Isabel. Isabel."

"Now, do you need to go to the bathroom?"

As Merriam allowed Bernice to lead her away, Isabel looked over the room. Modest furniture of pale wood, three big windows, a ceiling fan. It seemed comfortable enough, but still there was something fundamentally terrible about this occasion.

When it was time for Isabel and Clem to leave, Merriam, seeming dazed, did not make a scene. Bernice saw them on their way with a cheery "Don't you all worry about anything! We'll be fine!"

Back in the car, Isabel leaned back against the seat and closed her eyes.

"So that's that," said Clem. He sounded as wiped out as she felt. The rain had let up, but drops still sprinkled the windshield and made the view of Bernice's house an oozy blur. "It's hard," he went on. "You're doing the best you can."

Isabel opened her eyes. He actually seemed to be talking to her. "Merriam and I weren't exactly best friends. I keep asking myself why I'm here."

"Have you come up with an answer?"

"I have excuses but no answers."

"Excuses are worthless. They look solid, but they crumble and then you're left without any props." He started the car.

As they drove through the drenched streets, Isabel, on impulse, said, "I've heard about your son."

The corners of his mouth jerked. "Name me one person who has spent twenty-four hours in St. Elmo and *hasn't* heard."

"And I'm sorry."

"I appreciate that." He sounded unmoved. They had wound their way to town. "I'm going through the motions, that's all. Therapy? Hell, I've had therapy. One of my therapists quit seeing me after I bloodied his nose. There's only one thing they can't make me understand."

"What?"

"Why *I* should be alive."

The windshield wipers slashed back and forth. Isabel said, "I imagine a lot of people have argued with you about that. Anything I could say, you'd have an answer ready."

"Probably." He smiled and his face came briefly to life.

They had reached Clem's office, where Isabel had left her car. Before she got out, Isabel said, "Do you think Merriam really recognized me?"

He considered. "I couldn't tell."

"I think she knew who I was," Isabel said, but when she thought back on it, she couldn't be sure.

Back at the trailer, Isabel changed into shorts, lay down, and fell instantly asleep. She awoke an hour or so later, hearing tapping on the door. Groggily, she splashed water on her face and opened the door to Kimmie Dee Burke.

The rain had stopped and the vegetation was steaming. Isabel was not thrilled to see Kimmie Dee, but Kimmie Dee didn't seem to care how Isabel felt. "Maybe you can do me a favor," the girl said without preamble.

"What favor?"

"I need to borrow a pencil and some writing paper."

"A pencil, some—"

"And an envelope and a stamp. I know where Miss Merriam keeps them."

There seemed little to do but stand back and let Kimmie Dee in. The girl opened a drawer in an end table and brought out a pad of paper, a pencil, a package of envelopes, and a book of stamps. She carried them to the dining table. "I'm going to write a letter," she said. She pulled out a chair and sat down.

"Make yourself at home," said Isabel, but the irony was lost on Kimmie Dee. She had already opened the pad and bent over her work, her hair brushing the tabletop.

Unneeded for the moment, Isabel picked up her sketch pad and a pencil and doodled a couple of studies of Kimmie Dee. The girl was all angles: sharp elbows, sharp knees—

"Could you do me another favor?"

Isabel sighed. "What is it?"

Kimmie Dee raised her T-shirt and extracted a crumpled envelope from beneath the elastic waistband of her shorts. She held out the envelope to Isabel. "Write the address for me. I can't do real writing yet."

Isabel took the envelope. It was addressed to Mrs. Joy Burke at Cape Cache. "This letter is to your mother," she said.

"No, the other address. My daddy."

The return address was a Buddy Burke, at the

Regional Correctional Facility in Tallahassee. Kimmie Dee said, "It's the Regional Correctional Facility. That's a jail."

The girl's tone was matter-of-fact. Isabel tried to match it. "I see." She decided not to ask what crime Kimmie Dee's father had committed.

She sat at the table. Kimmie Dee's letter, the lines sloping down the page, was lying in front of her:

Daddy can I have boots. Please. I dont like Mr. S.
Love Kimmie Dee

I don't like Mr. S. Mr. S., surely, was Ted Stiles. Looking over Isabel's shoulder, Kimmie Dee said, "I need the boots before the contest. July Fourth." She touched the letter. "Can you mail it for me?"

Isabel hesitated. She wasn't sure what she had wandered into. "Does your mother know you're writing this?"

Kimmie Dee's jaw jutted. She didn't answer the question. "I thought *you* could mail it."

Isabel had given Kimmie Dee a pencil, paper, an envelope, and a stamp. She had addressed the envelope. Was she going to refuse to mail the letter? "All right," she said, and the girl's face pinkened.

Together, they folded the letter, sealed it, and put the stamp on. Kimmie Dee went home and Isabel took a walk down the beach, past the Beachcomber to the Cape Cache postal substation. There, she dropped Kimmie Dee's letter in the mail.

I don't like Mr. S. Who was Ted Stiles, and what was his relationship to Kimmie Dee and her family? If Isabel got to know Kimmie Dee better, which looked highly likely, she would ask about Ted Stiles. Isabel could see that there was a lot of upheaval in Kimmie Dee's life. She had begun to understand that Merriam—critical, censorious Merriam—had provided a haven for the girl.

And who, when Isabel had needed one, had provided a haven for Isabel? Isabel's anger at Merriam, never far from the surface, flared, as it had flared over and over in the past.

At dinner that night, at the Beachcomber, Isabel saw Harry Mercer.

The sky was darkening to violet as she walked along the damp beach after mailing Kimmie Dee's letter. Waves broke with a foamy slosh, and out on the water buoys flashed to mark the channel. The lights at the Beachcomber winked through the dusk. It was time to eat, and her refrigerator held nothing of interest. She could see people sitting at tables by the window and heard a faint twang of country music. She climbed the steps to the dock and went inside.

Paintings of shrimp boats and fishnets festooned with seashells hung on the walls of the dining room. There was a strong smell of beer, and the jukebox was just short of painfully loud. A waitress in a denim skirt and rubber thongs led Isabel to a table wedged between two others at a window with a panoramic view of the bay and the dock. The laminated menu offered fried grouper, fried oysters, fried shrimp, fried mullet, fried crab claws, french fries, and a "Capeburger Deluxe: Quarter pound of ground round on a sesame bun with lettuce, tomato, and our own Special Sauce."

She ordered the Capeburger and a beer, sat back, and eased her feet out of her sandals. The jukebox wailed about wanting to go back home. Her thoughts ranged over the events of the day— Merriam, Kimmie Dee and her letter, Clem Davenant.

Her thoughts lingered on Clem. She felt daunted by his despair. Yet today he had spoken to her frankly, almost as a friend.

Her burger arrived, a rock-hard knot of greasy meat

on an untoasted nonsesame bun. The "Special Sauce" was suspiciously akin to tartar. She gnawed at it, looking out at the dimly lighted dock. The line of tied-up vessels bobbed with the movement of the water. Through the near dark, she saw the yellow lamp of an approaching boat. It pulled into a berth and a shadowy figure jumped out to tie up. She watched idly as two people unloaded gear and an ice chest. After a while, one of them, carrying diving equipment, walked toward her. When he was close enough, she saw that it was a lean man, tanned golden, with frizzy shoulder-length hair. He unlocked a door, went inside for a minute, and returned empty-handed to the boat. Soon, he and another man came back, carrying an ice chest between them. The other man was Harry Mercer.

Isabel sat with the unappetizing burger suspended in her fingers. Harry was not looking her way. He wore a black wet suit top and swimming trunks, and he was bending sideways with the weight of the chest. His curly brown hair was wet and unruly, falling over his forehead.

Yes, it was Harry. The last person she had expected to see here. If there was anything Harry Mercer had been clear about, it was that he did not intend to spend his life in St. Elmo and environs. He was going to join the Coast Guard, maybe, or get a job with an oil company and go to Saudi Arabia. Harry planned to search for adventure.

So he had told her, in the whispered conversations they had had after they made love.

Isabel put down the hamburger. Harry was close now, passing the window. She averted her face. She wasn't ready to greet him with a friendly "How've you been?" And she wasn't at all sure how he would greet her.

She and Harry had been insane, both of them. Surely

some of their intensity had come from putting one over on the ever-vigilant Merriam, yet in the end it had been more than that.

They had rarely spoken to each other at school. Isabel could remember watching Harry in the lunchroom, tracing the curve of his ear and the cords of his neck with her eyes. Sometimes he had turned toward her, and her blood had surged and she'd felt a sheen of moisture on her face like the one she felt now.

He had passed by, gone through the door. Time to pay up. He wasn't supposed to be here. Time to pay up and go.

10

HARRY HAD SEEN ISABEL. HE SAW HER TURN HER FACE away.

In the office, he unzipped his wet suit and hung it up and pulled on khakis over his swimsuit. His hands were shaking, but that was from tiredness. He and Scooter had busted their tails today, working against the swells, barely able to see, half the time one of them undoing what the other had just done. On top of it, Harry had gotten seasick, or at least queasy, and had to sit on the bottom with a rock in his lap to hold him still until it passed off. Sitting there with muddy water swirling past him and the current pulling at his body, Harry had questioned how long this could go on. They had found a brass lantern today, and some barrel hoops and a few pieces of broken crockery. Where was the gold?

It was down there. It had to be. They had found enough already to know the big strike was there somewhere.

The stories you heard: barrels of gold, bricks of gold, medallions, chains, figurines, rings. So far, Harry and Scooter had found twenty or thirty cob coins they kept in a tackle box, and a few chunks of silver conglomerate.

Things had to pick up. Harry had read documented stories of people pulling hundreds of coins out of a wreck in a day, finding seventy-pound chunks of silver made up of a thousand *reales*. It wasn't necessarily the people with the high-tech equipment who had done it, either. It could be small-timers like Harry. Locating the wreck was the hard part, and they had already found the wreck.

Scooter had found the wreck.

After a day like this, to walk past that bitch Isabel Anders and see her turn her head away.

"I got to go home. I'm late," he said to Scooter. Scooter grunted, and Harry walked out. Not looking toward Isabel's table, he went to the parking lot and got in his truck.

Harry lived in a subdivision on the outskirts of St. Elmo, just past Margene's MiniMart. His house, a two-bedroom ranch-style, was cramped for space, especially since Kathy had taken the back room for her beauty salon. Although it was late in the dinner hour, when Harry drove up he saw only one dim light burning—in the girls' bedroom. An unfamiliar car was parked in the driveway.

When Harry saw the car, he muttered, "Shit." He pulled up and parked at the curb. As soon as he walked through the front door, he could smell the smell, all the way in the living room.

Harry wandered into the kitchen, where there was no sign of supper. He checked the refrigerator for beer and didn't find any. He could hear voices coming from behind the door to the salon. Although the door was closed now, it had been open sometime recently. He knew because of the smell.

Harry peeked into the salon. He saw Kathy in her pink smock, sweeping hair off the floor while a woman with pink curlers all over her head sat reading the *Reader's Digest.*

The smell here was strong enough to make Harry sneeze, and Kathy looked up at the sound. She smiled. "Hi, hon. I didn't hear you come in."

"Can I see you for a sec?" Harry said.

Kathy's eyes swiveled to the customer.

"Just for a sec," he insisted.

Kathy checked her watch, said, "Be right back" to the woman, and came out into the kitchen with Harry. When Harry closed the door behind her, she said, "Wow, what a day! And a late perm on top of everything. Give me a sweet, yummy kiss."

Harry pursed his lips and bent down, but at the last minute he moved so she got his cheek instead of his mouth.

Kathy didn't settle for his cheek. She grabbed his ears and planted a juicy kiss on his mouth. Harry pulled away. "For Christ's sake, Kathy."

She looked hurt. He ignored it. "Who's parked in the drive?" he asked.

Kathy put a hand to her mouth. "Oh no! She's a new customer, Harry. All the regulars know better."

"Yeah? Did she leave the salon door open, too? The whole house smells like a—"

"The girls left it open. I didn't notice until a few minutes ago." She patted his shoulder. "I'm really sorry, Harry."

Who did she think she was, being so sweety-sweet? He folded his arms. "All I ask is a few simple things. No customer cars in the driveway. Keep the door closed, so we don't all choke—"

Kathy put a finger to her lips. "Don't yell, Harry. She'll hear you."

"I'll say what I want in my own goddamn house."

He watched Kathy's eyes puddle up. Exactly what he needed. She blinked a couple of times and said, "I've got some chili to put in the microwave as soon as I'm finished."

Harry usually liked chili. "I don't know. I've got an upset stomach."

"Oh no! Should you take some—"

He nodded at the door. "Don't you have to get back?"

She checked her watch. "Oh gosh." She gave him a worried look. "Harry—"

"Go on. See you later."

When the door closed, Harry walked through the house to a back bedroom, where he found his daughters, Jennifer and Cissy, lying on their twin beds like rag dolls. Their eyes were glued to their very own television set, which Harry should never have bought them.

Harry leaned in the doorway. "Hey there."

"Hey." Their heads didn't move.

"You girls hungry?"

This time, Cissy glanced his way. "We had a snack. Mama's doing a perm."

"Right." He remained in the doorway, watching them while they watched the tube. Jennifer's mouth was half open and a shock of hair fell to the top of her glasses frames. Cissy, the prettier one, had her mother's creamy skin and curly hair. As far as Harry knew, for the last year or more he, their father, had not said one word they thought was worth listening to or done anything they admired.

Harry's stomach did feel upset. "Cissy. Jennifer. Listen," he said. Although he couldn't tell whether they were actually paying attention, he went on: "I'm going out to get myself some supper. I don't feel like eating chili. Tell your mother. All right?"

"Okay."

All the way back to the Cape, Harry was lightheaded. He had walked out. He had gotten away.

At the Beachcomber, though, the kitchen was about to close and all Harry could get was lukewarm gumbo and hush puppies. A couple of strangers, almost through eating, were sitting at Isabel's table. She was long gone.

11

ISABEL STARED INTO THE DARKNESS, LISTENING TO THE grating rustle of the palms. She wished she had not seen Harry Mercer. She did not want to relive those days. She didn't want to argue with herself about the way she had treated Harry.

All right, she had treated him badly. On the face of it, her behavior was indefensible. Harry had loved her, and—

And, damn it, she had loved Harry. There you had the problem, and a sad glimpse into Isabel's psyche. The sickening truth was, she had run away from Cape Cache with Ben Raboski because she hated Merriam, all right, but she had also run away because she loved Harry. She had been afraid of being consumed by her own feelings.

Oh baloney.

Well, she had been afraid of never getting away if she didn't go then. She was afraid she'd never get another chance.

Or maybe Merriam had held her too tightly, and she couldn't stand being held.

Or all of the above.

Isabel tossed. She sat up and punched her pillow with her fist. Who knew why she had done it? She had been a mixed-up sixteen-year-old. Harry had probably forgotten the whole episode by now.

Isabel was having exactly the argument with herself she had intended to avoid. She was determined to stop it. She would not allow herself to be thrown for a loop by something that happened way back in high school. She closed her eyes and emptied her mind. Eventually, she fell asleep and had a dream about Harry that was so searingly, throbbingly, gut-clutchingly sexy that she woke up vibrating and bathed in sweat.

As she searched Merriam's medicine cabinet for aspirin, Isabel told herself her irrational response to Harry had to be a displacement of her feelings about Zan and the end of their affair. The explanation was calming. She fell asleep again, this time dreamlessly.

The next morning was overcast. Hoping to obsess about something besides Harry Mercer, Isabel dragged out her drawings for *The Children from the Sea.* She couldn't imagine what had ever appealed to her about the project. Her own voice rang in her ears: *It's something I've always wanted to do, and now I have the time.* Right.

She picked up her sketchbook and a pencil and went to sit on the front step of the trailer. As the sky lowered, she drew, with intense concentration, a leggy and ugly sandspur plant growing nearby. The sandspur was laden with the spiny, cruel burrs that had been the bane of Isabel's childhood, and she rendered each tiny needle. When she finished with the sandspur, she looked around and focused on a Georgia thumper, an immense multicolored grasshopper sitting obligingly motionless on the path.

Isabel liked to draw from life. Although she had often used photographs, she felt the sketches she did while looking at the actual object were usually better, more vital.

When the grasshopper hopped away, she tried a palmetto. She was in the groove now. This was what she had always loved, creating a world resembling the real world but at the same time all hers. She continued happily until it was time to drive into town and see Merriam.

It had started to rain lightly, a misty curtain sweeping over the car. At Bernice Chatham's, she found Merriam sitting in a metal lawn chair on the front porch. Azalea bushes crowded against the screen, raindrops sliding off their dark green leaves. After saying hello to Bernice, Isabel pulled up another chair and sat beside Merriam.

Merriam's spiky white hair had been brushed. She wore a clean dress and bedroom slippers. She made occasional fishlike movements with her mouth. After some minutes of silence, Isabel began to chat about whatever came into her head—Kimmie Dee, the trailer, the weather. Merriam studied her lap, then began smoothing her skirt. She made no response.

After a while, Isabel ran out of steam. She stopped talking and turned her attention to the dripping azaleas. There was something almost hypnotic in the sight of the drops sliding off the wet leaves. She had almost lost touch with her surroundings when Merriam spoke.

Merriam said, "You ought to cut off some of that hair, girl. You look like a haystack."

Isabel gritted her teeth. Despite herself, her hand strayed to her hair. She said, "So you do know me, Merriam."

Merriam's eyes were bright. She said, "We got to cut those fronds back. They'll be falling and making a mess. We got to do it this afternoon."

She half-stood, but Isabel caught her arm. "Wait. It isn't time yet," she improvised.

"Wait! They'll be all over the place. We got to—"

She was getting agitated. Isabel said, "Merriam, listen. I want to talk to you. Do you understand me?"

"We got to go now!"

"I'm Isabel. Isabel."

Merriam gave her a look of withering scorn. "I know who you are. Do you think I'm cracked?"

The thought had crossed my mind. "Merriam, sit down

a second. I want to ask you. Do you remember being on the beach, walking on the beach? And you saw Kimmie Dee?"

"Kimmie Dee." Merriam's face grew sober.

"Yes. You hurt your head somehow. I wanted to know if you remember—"

Merriam had deflated. Her shoulders sagged and her head hung forward. In her lap, her fingers twined and untwined aimlessly. "No," she whispered.

"I want to know how you hurt your head."

Merriam began making the fish motions with her mouth. Isabel waited, but she wouldn't speak again.

On the way back to the Cape, Isabel stopped to buy groceries. She pushed into the trailer laden with bags. She had put everything away and poured herself a glass of club soda before she noticed the envelope on the floor.

It was a sealed envelope, plain white, with nothing written on it. Judging from its position near the door, someone—Kimmie Dee?—had slid it underneath while she was gone. She tore it open and took out the folded paper inside. The message was printed in block letters with a red felt-tip pen:

GO AWAY YOU WHORE. WE DON'T NEED YOU HERE.

No signature, naturally.

Oh please. *Please.* Surely Isabel had enough problems without this kind of garbage. She tossed the note on the counter and beseeched the powers that were to give her a break.

Whore. A generic insult or a calculated reference to her youthful peccadilloes? The image of Harry Mercer presented itself. *Go away, you whore.*

Grimly, Isabel folded the note and replaced it in the envelope. She didn't want to look at it anymore. She would be watchful, in case the person came back. She would—this inspiration gave her pleasure—put weather stripping along the bottom of the door so nothing could be slid underneath.

If it continued, she would have to go to the police. Undoubtedly, they would ask whether she had any idea who had done it. She thought of Harry again. She imagined the police asking Harry Mercer whether he had written a note calling Isabel a whore.

She did not want to go to the police. She put the envelope in a zipper compartment in her handbag, where it would be out of her sight.

The rain had stopped. She once again installed herself on the concrete block front step with her sketchbook, but she couldn't recapture her absorption of the morning. Either the note, her frustrating visit with Merriam, or something else had stalled her. She was doodling meaningless shapes when the sound of sandals slapping down the drive announced Kimmie Dee's daily visit.

Kimmie Dee came into view and got right down to business. "Did you mail my letter?"

"I certainly did."

"Good." She gave a nod of approval. "What are you doing?"

"Working."

"No you're not. You're drawing."

Isabel didn't argue. She turned back to her sketchbook. Kimmie Dee found a dried magnolia leaf, freighted it with pine straw, and began to sail it on a mud puddle by the steps.

After a few minutes, Isabel said, "Let me ask you something, Kimmie Dee. Did you slip an envelope under my door while I was gone this afternoon?"

"Nope."

The reply was offhand, without hesitation. The girl

seemed to be telling the truth. "Did you see anybody else come down here?"

"Nope. Toby and I were watching TV." Kimmie Dee pushed the leaf, which wobbled and capsized. "Oh shoot." She retrieved it and said, "When do you think my daddy will send those boots? I need them pretty soon."

"He couldn't have gotten the letter yet."

"Fourth of July. The talent contest. My old ones don't fit." She stood, kicked off a sandal, and stuck out a mud-streaked foot for Isabel to inspect. "My toes are too long."

The light dawned. "It's majorette boots you want?"

"Well, sure."

Kimmie Dee knelt to play with her leaf boat. She made a charming picture, squatting there by the puddle with her bony knees in the air. Isabel turned to a fresh page. "Has your father been . . . gone for a long time?"

"Pretty long. He'll be coming back, though."

"When?"

"When they let him out." She picked up sand and added it to the leaf's freight. "He did something stupid and wrong, so he had to go to jail for a while. That's what he told me. Stupid and wrong."

Isabel was sketching, her pencil flying. "Sounds like he's sorry for what he did."

"Oh, he is. Real sorry." The girl crossed her arms on her knees. "They took his boat away and everything. They aren't even going to give it back."

"That's a shame."

"Yeah. He brought some marijuana over from Westpoint in it and they caught him." Kimmie Dee gave her a suspicious look. "Are you drawing my picture?"

"Yes. Do you want to see?" It was rough, just a few lines, but Isabel was pleased.

Kimmie Dee looked. The sketch showed her

crouched by the puddle, her hair falling forward. "You can't even see my face," she said, sounding disappointed.

"You want your face in it? I'll do another one. Go back over there."

Kimmie Dee returned to the puddle and posed, her face stretched into an unnatural "Say cheese" grin. To dissipate it, Isabel said, "You can go ahead and talk to me. I'll tell you when to be still."

"Talk about what?"

Isabel had meant to ask Kimmie Dee about Ted Stiles. *I don't like Mr. S.* "Oh, about your mother, Toby, Mr. Stiles . . ."

All semblance of a smile had vanished. "It's *our* house, not his," Kimmie Dee declared. "He bothers us all the time."

"Bothers you how? What does he do?"

"He comes over and eats, and drinks beer and smokes cigarettes. He piled a bunch of diving stuff in our utility closet and broke Toby's train."

"Does he go diving?"

"No. And he asks me questions."

Isabel studied her sketch. "Questions about what?"

"What I've seen on the beach. Who's coming and going. I don't like to talk to him, but Mama gets mad if I won't."

Kimmie Dee moved, and Isabel gave up. She didn't like the second sketch as much as the first. Doing it had given her an idea, though. Kimmie Dee, with her sharp little face, would be an ideal model for Marotte. Marotte was a villain, the evil foster sister, in *The Children from the Sea.* If Kimmie Dee would pose, it could give the book some needed vigor. Isabel said, "Let me ask you a favor. Would you let me draw your picture for a book I'm working on?"

Kimmie Dee wrinkled her nose. "What kind of a book?"

"It's a kids' book. A fairy tale." No need, at this point, to tell her she'd be the model for an equivalent of Cinderella's stepsisters. "I was thinking—if you'll pose for me a few times, I'll buy you the majorette boots."

The girl shook her head. "I already asked Daddy. He'll send them."

Her faith was touching, but privately Isabel wondered. "I'm worried he won't get the letter in time, or won't be able to find them. This way, you'll have them for sure."

Kimmie Dee hesitated, but Isabel could see it was no contest. "Okay."

"Good. You have to get your mother's permission, and then we'll start."

Kimmie Dee's face fell. "Get her permission? Why?"

"Because she has to know what's going on."

"She won't care."

"You have to ask her. If you don't, I will."

"I'll ask her! Promise." Although Kimmie Dee crossed her heart, Isabel wasn't sure she'd ask. Isabel was meddling in a sticky situation, but this way Kimmie Dee would get her boots. And the girl would be a perfect Marotte.

After Kimmie Dee left, Isabel went inside. For a while, she had forgotten Harry Mercer. She had forgotten the anonymous letter. She would have plenty of time to think about them during her long evening alone.

12

HARRY MERCER WIPED HIS HANDS ON A RAG AND LEANED over the *Miss Kathy*'s engine again. A drop of sweat from his forehead fell into the works. Maybe that would do some good. Nothing else he tried was helping.

Harry and Scooter had headed out at daylight, but the engine trouble developed before they even reached the site. Maybe they could have carried on, but as Harry had pointed out, all they needed was to have the boat die on them out there. If they had to radio for help, they might as well put up a billboard to advertise what they were doing.

So they had lost the morning. Back at the Beachcomber, Harry was still tinkering, barefooted and shirtless, in the noon blaze. He had to get the sucker fixed. He couldn't afford to hire somebody to do it. He had spent a lot of extra money on the salvage operation, figuring he'd get it all back tenfold. Which he would, but at this point things were tight.

"Try it again," he said to Scooter.

Scooter cranked. Harry didn't like the sound. He knew his boat, and he knew the problem was still there somewhere, underneath.

"Sounds all right. I think you fixed it," Scooter said.

"Not yet."

"Harry—"

"I said not yet, Scooter. Give me another minute or two, okay?"

Leaning over the engine, screwdriver in hand, Harry felt his resolve crumbling. They didn't have time to waste. They ought to be out working the wreck, not lolling around here. Every day that went by, every hour, increased the risk that somebody would get suspicious.

Harry stared at the engine. To figure out what the underlying problem was, he'd have to dismantle the damned thing. He'd have to take off a couple of days, and he couldn't.

To show he wasn't giving in to Scooter, he spent another ten minutes tinkering, tightening screws and so on, before he said, "All right. Let's get the cover back on." He wiped his hands on the rag again, dropped the screwdriver in his toolbox, and looked up, to see Isabel Anders standing on the dock.

Isabel was shading her eyes, looking at him. She was wearing white slacks and a loose white shirt. She looked cool and clean. She also looked nervous. She said, "Harry? I asked in the office and they said I'd find you out here."

Harry was outraged. He was aware of Scooter standing nearby, aware of his own greasy hands and sweaty torso, and, more than anything else, aware that Isabel had felt free to waltz over here and seek him out as if she was entitled to.

He crossed his arms. "They were right. Here I am."

"I wondered—do you have a minute?"

"For what?"

He saw her eyes cut toward Scooter. "I wanted to talk with you."

This was a moment out of Harry's dreams, a moment he could never realistically have hoped for. He made the most of it. He gave her a long poker-faced stare. "Talk with me?"

He could see she didn't care for his attitude. She took a step backward. "That's what I said. But it looks like you're busy."

She had a hell of a nerve, getting snippy with him.

Harry said, "I'm kind of busy, yeah. But you know what else? I haven't got anything to say to you, Isabel, and I'm not interested in anything you have to say to me."

God, it felt good. Like lancing a boil. Harry went on: "I can't stop you from being here, but I'm telling you to stay out of my way. I don't know what you think you're—" But Isabel had turned and was walking down the dock away from him, her back straight and stiff.

Harry's chest was heaving. He leaned next to the engine and tried to catch his breath. He wanted to run after Isabel and say more, shout more. He wanted to get her told.

"What was that about?" said Scooter. Scooter was in the shadow of the roof, beside the instrument panel.

"There was bad blood between us from a long time ago," Harry said.

Scooter didn't say anything right then. He and Harry put the boat back together, got the equipment on board, and headed out for the wreck. They had dropped anchor and were suiting up to go in when Scooter said, "We've got to get rid of her, Harry."

"Who?" Harry asked, even though he knew.

"Isabel. If you talked to her, you might find out when she's leaving."

Sitting on the ledge, Harry put on his flippers. He said, "I don't want to know anything she has to tell me."

The two of them somersaulted over the side.

Conditions were better than they had been the past couple of stormy days, but their luck hadn't changed. Scooter made the only interesting find, a spike with a coin stuck to it. Harry found another spike. They uncovered broken crockery, porcelain shards, a wine bottle.

As they worked, Harry thought about Isabel standing there on the dock in her white outfit, asking him to talk to her. She must be nuts. She must think he was some kind of patsy who'd clap his hands and jump up and down at the sight of her.

Harry watched Scooter through the haze of sand the equipment was kicking up. He wished Scooter hadn't said that about talking to Isabel. Because in a way, he was right. It would be useful for them to know Isabel's plans: how long she would be in the trailer; how long she would be in their way.

Harry rested and watched the plume of bubbles from his breathing gear swirl toward the silvery surface above. Scooter could forget it. There was no way he would go back and talk to her now.

When the light started to fail, they stowed their meager take in the tank on deck and chugged back to the Beachcomber. As they approached the dock, Harry said, "I guess I could go ask her when she's leaving."

"It better be soon," Scooter said, his voice flat and cold.

Harry drove Scooter past the Anders driveway and on to the sandy palmetto-covered knoll where the steel tower of the lighthouse pushed up above the pines. The road dead-ended at the base of the knoll, which was bounded by a bar fence with a sign at the gate:

CAPE CACHE LIGHTHOUSE U.S. GOVERNMENT PROPERTY
KEEP OFF

Scooter jumped out of the truck and got the ice chest from the back. "You can carry it all right?" Harry said.

"Yeah. It's not heavy this time." With the chest, Scooter crossed the pavement, ducked between the bars of the fence, and disappeared into the woods. They had a boat with an outboard motor moored not far away, at the mouth of the slough. Scooter would load the chest in it and putt along through the weed-choked water to an old dock that was part of the Anders place. There was an overgrown path from the dock to the house. They went in and out of the house through one of the tall dining room windows on the side hidden from the trailer.

After Scooter was out of sight, Harry lingered. He should get moving. He didn't want to be caught hanging around here. It was time to go talk to Isabel. He put the truck in gear and rolled off. He'd go now, get it over with.

He left his truck at the top of the drive and walked down. Mosquitoes whined in his ears. There was a light on in the trailer and the curtains were open. When he got closer, he could see in the window. Isabel was sitting at a table, bent over something. He could guess what she was doing—drawing.

She always loved to draw. She had done lots of pictures of him and had given him some of them, but he'd thrown them away. All her class notes used to have drawings all over them, more drawings than notes sometimes. He took a couple more steps and saw her head jerk up. She had heard him. She stood and peered out, and he raised his hand. In a minute, the door opened and she stood silhouetted against the light.

Isabel had changed out of her white outfit and now was wearing a pair of baggy shorts and a T-shirt. No shoes. Her hair was pulled back at the nape of her neck, but escaping from the band as it always did. She didn't look thrilled to see him, but he hadn't imagined she would. She said, "What are you doing here, Harry?"

He waited, then took a step forward. "Can I come in or not?"

She seemed to be thinking it over, but finally she stepped out of the doorway to let him by. She left the door open. She didn't sit down or invite him to. Harry said, "What was it you wanted with me this morning?"

She half-smiled. "I wanted to see if things were all right between us. I found out the answer to that."

"Well, what the hell did you expect?"

She seemed calm, but he could tell she wasn't. "I didn't know you'd even remember who I am."

It was too late now to pretend he didn't remember her. He wished he'd thought of it.

He did remember, though. He remembered how dark her eyebrows were against her skin and the way her lips curled at the corners. He remembered, but none of it could touch him now.

She said, "I didn't think you'd still be here."

Harry wasn't going to discuss the shape of his life with her. He asked his question. "How long will you be staying?"

"I'm not sure."

He had humbled himself and crawled for an answer, and he had gotten it: *I'm not sure.*

"Anyway," Harry said. He shoved his hands in his back pockets. This had been a useless exercise. As he drew breath to say good-bye, he noticed the bottle.

There, over against the wall, was a blue-and-white porcelain bottle.

It was sitting on a spindly wooden table under a photograph in a heavy frame. A Dutch bottle, or gin bottle, those square ones were called. Even from where he was standing, he recognized the pattern of blue flowering branches and birds against a white background.

Harry crossed to the bottle like a sleepwalker. It was whole, not a fragment—completely intact, not even chipped. The pattern was identical to the pattern of the fragments they were finding at the wreck. "Where did you get this?" he asked.

"It's sort of a family heirloom."

She had stayed by the door. Her tone told him she thought he was acting strange. He lied. "I think my grandmother used to have one like it." He slid the tip of his forefinger gently over the surface of the bottle.

"My grandfather gave it to Merriam when she was a little girl, right before he disappeared."

Harry had to act normal when nothing was normal. "When was that?"

"Back in 1922."

"Huh." Harry pinched the bridge of his nose. "And—where did your grandfather get it?"

"I don't think anybody knows." After a moment, she asked, "Are you all right, Harry?"

With an effort of will, he forced himself to turn away from the bottle. "How is Miss Merriam?"

"Not very well. She's moved in with a woman named Bernice Chatham. A practical nurse." Isabel was looking at the bottle. "I just thought of something. I wonder how Merriam would react if I took the bottle next time I visit. It might stimulate her, don't you think?"

Good. Good. He wanted to know what Miss Merriam had to say. "I guess it might."

"I think I'll do that tomorrow."

There was an awkward silence. Harry said, "I better go. My wife will have dinner on the table."

Isabel saw him out. Harry wasn't as eager for her to leave Cape Cache as he'd been before. She might as well stay until he found out where that bottle had come from.

13

MERRIAM TOOK THE BLUE-AND-WHITE PORCELAIN BOTTLE out of Isabel's hands. Tears rolled down her cheeks. Unchecked, they dropped from her chin and spotted the front of her dress.

Isabel dug in her bag, brought out a tissue, and blotted Merriam's face. The two of them were sitting on the screened front porch at Bernice Chatham's. Bernice was out grocery shopping.

"I didn't mean to make you cry," Isabel said. It was too bad. Her idea of bringing the bottle to show Merriam had seemed the one constructive outcome of her reunion with Harry Mercer.

Seeing Harry again, talking to him, had been disturbing. Harry's anger was one reason, certainly, but, to be honest, her motives in seeking him out had not been pure. She'd told herself it was because of the anonymous note, but she had been curious, too. Possibly even titillated. In the end, reluctant to disturb their fragile truce, she hadn't mentioned the note.

To be honest, she had felt afraid, even though it was only Harry. Harry, her first lover.

He had looked much the same. More lines around the eyes, heavier in the gut. And a wariness—was it wariness?—in his face that she didn't remember. A sense of something guarded, hidden.

She couldn't figure out his reaction to the porcelain bottle. She hadn't bought his explanation about his grandmother owning a similar one. Possibly he recognized it as a valuable antique. It could be, for all she knew, although she could hardly imagine Harry as an expert.

Anyway, he had given her the idea of bringing the bottle to Merriam, and now it was lying in Merriam's lap while Merriam wept. Isabel put her hand out. "Why don't you let me put it away?"

Merriam came alive. Jerking the bottle out of Isabel's reach, she cried, "It's mine!" She pushed her chair back, making a grating noise on the concrete floor. "Daddy gave it to me!"

The azalea leaves pressed against the screen, oppressive and suffocating. The metal arms of Isabel's chair felt sticky. "Fine, Merriam. Fine. Keep it."

Merriam cradled the bottle. "Then he went off," she said more softly.

Best to stay on this familiar turf. Isabel could recite the story by heart. "There had been a big storm," she prompted.

"All night, it blew," Merriam said dreamily. "We stayed down in the back parlor the whole night long. The wind was howling, the trees cracking, and along about midnight you know what happened?"

Of course Isabel knew. "No. What?"

"Somebody came knocking at the window. I was so scared. Daddy pushed the curtain back, and River Pete was out there."

River Pete had been a local character, a sometime hunting and fishing buddy of John James. He occasionally figured in Merriam's stories of her youth. "So River Pete came in out of the storm?"

"Came in and spent the night. You know, he used to live in a driftwood shack down on the beach. Did odd jobs at Pursey's store. That night, his shanty blew clean away." Merriam fell into silence.

To keep her talking, Isabel said, "What happened the next morning?"

Merriam's lips moved, then stopped. Her eyelids half-closed. After a minute, she continued: "Daddy and Pete went out about daylight to look at the damage—trees uprooted, branches blown down. I watched from the upstairs veranda. Waves were breaking practically in the front yard, salt water running down the drive."

Merriam must have used these same words on the afternoons she and Isabel stood in obeisance in front of John James's photograph. The story was as ritualized as the Apostle's Creed. In Isabel's role as listener, all she had to do was put in a question now and then. "The house was all right, though, wasn't it?"

Merriam nodded. "It was God's mercy. The only thing that happened was, we lost the wash pot. We had an old iron wash pot out in the back, where Mama boiled the clothes, and it was gone. I reckon it washed away. I wouldn't have credited it, the pot was so heavy, but I reckon that's what happened."

As a child, Isabel had been intrigued by the disappearing wash pot and by the idea of boiling clothes over a fire in the backyard. She said, "It was never found? Not even out in the woods later?"

"Never. Mama had to get a new one to boil Johnny's diapers." She grimaced. She was approaching the nub of the story. "Johnny had colic the whole day, wouldn't hush at all."

That colicky baby had been Isabel's father. As she had so many times in the past, she imagined his cries, the tearing wind, the fallen trees, the encroaching sea.

"Daddy and Pete were cutting up fallen trees," Merriam said. "We could hear them sawing. Toward afternoon, when the water went down some, Daddy crawled under the house to check the foundation. He came out covered with mud. Afterward, he cleaned up and told Mama he was taking his boat to St. Elmo that very afternoon. Mama didn't want him to go. She said it was blowing too hard, that the seas were too high. He said he had business to do."

That stubbornness wouldn't be credible in some men. In John James Anders, who had constructed his dream house in the wilds of Cape Cache and driven his family to ruin with schemes for railroads and amusement piers, it was completely in character. He would go out in the wake of a hurricane if he took a notion, and he had taken a notion.

"River Pete was still in the yard," Merriam said. "I saw him stick his head under the pump and rinse off his hair and beard and scrub the mud off his hands, but after that, I didn't see him anymore. Daddy said he'd best get on, and he said to me, 'Merriam, walk along with me a ways,' so I went out with him."

"That was when he gave you the bottle."

"We got on toward the landing." Merriam's voice was remote. "He said, 'You better go on back to Mama now,' and he pulled this bottle out of his coat pocket and said, 'Here's a play-pretty for you, Merriam.' I took it and hugged him good-bye. He never got to St. Elmo, and he never came back."

That was it. Rest in peace in the briny deep, John James Anders.

Isabel heard a lawn mower. She smelled fuel oil and cut grass. Merriam picked up the bottle and looked at it for a long time. Then she held it out. "Take it, Isabel."

Isabel didn't move. She said, "It's yours."

"No. You take it."

Isabel sat still.

Some months after Isabel ran away from Cape Cache with Ben Raboski, Merriam had tracked her down and written to say that Isabel was disinherited. The letter had been brief, and Isabel remembered it well. "My goods and chattels are none of yours," Merriam had written. "You turn your back on me, Isabel. So be it.

Now I turn my back on you." Under the signature—a stark, upright *Merriam*—was a reference to the Bible: "See Psalm 41, verse 9."

Hating herself for doing it, Isabel had looked up Psalm 41, verse 9, and read: "Yea mine own familiar friend, in whom I trusted, which did eat of my bread, hath lifted up his heel against me."

Isabel's fingers closed on the bottle. Merriam let it go.

Merriam pushed herself to her feet. "I want to lie down now."

"All right." Isabel replaced the bottle in the canvas bag she'd brought it in. She walked with Merriam to the back bedroom, shook out the pillows, and turned on the ceiling fan.

Merriam stretched out. Breeze from the fan stirred the hair on her forehead. She said, in a voice almost lost in the fan's gentle whir, "I lost his letter."

Isabel returned to the bedside. "What letter, Merriam?"

"The letter. He gave me a letter." The sides of Merriam's mouth had pulled down in a mask of misery.

"What are you talking about?"

Merriam's eyes bulged. *"Don't be so careless!"* she screamed. *"Look what you've done!"*

Isabel recoiled. She had heard this too many times in her life already. "Stop it! *Stop it!*" she cried. There was an assortment of pill bottles on the bedside table. She wasn't sure which one would calm Merriam down.

"Look what you've *done!*" Merriam howled. She thrashed on the bed, flinging her body from side to side. "You idiot! You stupid, careless girl!"

Isabel grasped at Merriam's arms, trying to hold her down. "I am not!" she cried. "I am not!"

They wrestled grotesquely for a few seconds, and then Merriam broke free and sat up. Panting, she said, "I lost the letter. I lost it."

Isabel tried to fight back to rationality. "What letter, for God's sake?"

"Daddy gave it to me." Merriam's voice had dropped to a whisper.

This was not part of the recitation ritual. "When? That same day?"

"Yes." The sudden hysteria had dissipated. "When he gave me the bottle, he gave me a letter for Mama. I lost it, Isabel."

"I don't—"

"I wanted to pick a flower to put in the bottle. There was Queen Anne's lace by the path. I let go of the letter and the wind blew it away."

"Merriam—"

"I went after it, into the deep woods. Everything was wet; the wind was blowing. I couldn't find it. And he never came back. Never came back."

You careless, irresponsible girl. "It's all right," Isabel said.

"No. No."

"Yes. It doesn't matter now."

Merriam slumped against the pillows. "I didn't tell. I couldn't tell," she said. Her eyelids drooped.

After a few minutes, Merriam seemed to doze off as Isabel sat on the edge of the bed. So John James had left a letter, and Merriam had lost it. If the episode had really happened. If it had, Isabel began to see a connection: Merriam once lost an important letter; to atone for her mistake, she spent years making hapless Isabel toe the line.

Merriam's breathing became regular. Isabel returned to the front porch. She found Clem Davenant there, his tall frame folded into one of the metal lawn chairs.

"I knocked, but there was some commotion going on," he said. "Is Miss Merriam all right?"

Isabel sat down. "I don't know."

"What happened?"

It was too complicated to explain. "She was talking about something that happened years ago." She thought about it. "Actually, I think she's getting better. Her memory is coming back, and a lot of the time what she says makes sense."

"Is that so? I never thought she'd get that far."

"She's definitely better." Isabel was sagging with exhaustion.

From the back of the house came a low, anguished wail. Goose bumps rose on Isabel's arms. Her eyes met Clem's. "Oh God," she said, jumping to her feet.

He followed her to Merriam's bedroom. Merriam was sitting up in bed, wild-eyed, her hair standing in tufts as if she had been pulling it. "Watch out, Isabel!" she shrieked. "Watch out!"

Merriam scrambled away from them, toward the wall, while Isabel fumbled with the pill bottles.

Clem reached out. "Calm down, Miss Merriam!"

She shrank away, pressing herself into a corner "Watch out! Watch out!"

Clem grasped her arms as she howled and fought, screaming hysterically. He held on, his face taut.

After a while, Merriam's eyes unfocused and her strength ebbed. She took her pill meekly. As Clem lay her down, the back door slammed and Bernice called, "I'm back! Everything all right?"

Isabel's eyes met Clem's. Neither of them answered.

14

YOU WENT TO SEE HER. I KNOW IT," KATHY MERCER SAID.

Still in his swimming trunks, his body sticky from salt water, Harry Mercer stood in his bedroom. Kathy was sitting in the middle of the gold quilted bedspread. Her nose was red. Fortunately, the girls had gone off to camp for two weeks.

"With who?" Harry had more than a suspicion that this wasn't his night.

"You know who."

Harry started unbuttoning his shirt. He had ferried a boatload of assholes out spearfishing, worried about the engine some more, locked horns with Scooter as usual, and hauled his butt home for this? His shirt hanging open, he untied his sneakers and took them off, scattering sand on the wall-to-wall carpet, but to hell with it. "I don't know who, so you better tell me."

Kathy's eyes narrowed. "Isabel Anders, that's who."

Harry felt a deep rumbling of fear. "I don't know why you think that," he said, a response so lame, he might as well have kept his mouth shut.

"You don't?" Behind her glasses, Kathy's eyes looked like huge brown accusing blobs. "I think it because I know it's true."

Harry needed to work up some righteous indignation, but he wasn't sure he could. He dropped his shirt on the floor and said, "Kathy, tell me exactly what you think is going on."

"I *know* what's going on!"

"Well, fill me in."

Kathy's face and neck were blotchy, almost as if she had a rash. Her nostrils were flaring in a way that Harry did not like. She drew an unsteady breath. "You went to see Isabel Anders yesterday evening. You parked your truck right there in her driveway."

Goddamn this gossiping town. Yes, he had gone to see Isabel yesterday. Yes, he had parked in her driveway. And it had been as pure and innocent as the driven snow, but he might as well have been screwing his brains out with her, for all the good his virtue had done him.

Miraculously, righteous indignation began to seep into Harry, after all. "Well, did any of your nosy friends tell you she came looking for me? Came to the Beachcomber and said she wanted to talk to me?" He could see by her face that this was news to her. He pressed his advantage. "Yes, she said she wanted to talk to me, so I did stop by her place a few minutes—"

"Just because she wants to talk to you doesn't mean you have to go to her place!"

Harry had sand between his toes, his trunks were scratchy and dry, and he wanted to take a shower. Most of all, he wanted Kathy to shut her mouth. "That's right," he said in the most scathing tone he could manage. "I wouldn't have done it if I'd known it was a mortal sin."

She wasn't giving up. "Why didn't you tell me you went there?"

"I sure don't know, Kathy. I guess I thought I was a grown man, not a snot-nosed shirttail kid you had to keep watch over."

"What did she want to talk about?"

He exploded. "What is this? I'm telling you nothing happened and it wasn't important. Now back off!"

Kathy seemed to shrink. She looked pathetic with her blotchy face and blobby eyes. In a hushed tone, she said, "You were in love with her."

"Oh my God Almighty." Harry thought about throwing something, but there wasn't anything handy. He settled for clenching his fist and bonking himself on the forehead. The problem was, all those years ago when he and Kathy were courting and he was still smarting from the way Isabel had treated him, he had told Kathy things. He had told her what a bitch Isabel was, how badly she had treated him, how much nicer Kathy was than Isabel. "Kathy, that was high school. Do you know how long ago that was? I don't even want to think about it."

He could hear her hiccuppy breathing. When she didn't come back with anything, he said, "I'm going to take a shower."

Once he was in the shower, thoughts of Kathy and her accusations melted in the steam and he returned to the topics that currently preoccupied him—Isabel and the porcelain bottle.

All day, all this crummy day, Isabel and the bottle had faded in and out of Harry's consciousness. He wondered whether Isabel had taken the bottle to show Miss Merriam, as she'd said she would, and what Miss Merriam had said. According to Isabel, Miss Merriam's father had given her the bottle in 1922. How had he come by it? was what Harry wanted to know. It could have washed up on the beach, he guessed, but Harry had not found one unbroken piece of porcelain out at the wreck. If the bottle had bumped along on the sea bottom and was finally tossed ashore by a wave, how had it stayed whole, not even nicked?

It could be that this was all a coincidence and John James Anders had bought the bottle at the dime store. It could be, but Harry didn't think so. He wasn't ready yet to speculate about what the answer was. He had debated telling Scooter but had decided not to tell him quite yet.

Harry stepped out of the shower and dried off. When

he came out of the bathroom, the towel around his waist, he had actually forgotten all about the scene with Kathy and was surprised to see her sitting on the bed.

Kathy gave him a tragic look. She whispered, "I'm so sorry, Harry."

"Yeah. Me, too."

She got up and came close to him, putting her arms around him, resting her face on the damp hair on his chest. Harry forced his arms to slide around her shoulders.

"Do you forgive me?" she said.

"Sure."

Harry knew they'd have to make love later. He prepared himself mentally, and it went all right. After Kathy was asleep beside him, he didn't drift off for a long time.

The next day, Harry had an early-morning dive trip with some people from Atlanta. He had planned to drop by Isabel's place in the evening, when they could have a chat and he could take another look at the bottle. When he saw her on the dock as they pulled in about noon, Harry felt cheated. He suspected she had shown up on purpose to deprive him.

She was on a bench by the bait tanks, drawing in her sketchbook, her hair tucked under a beaten-up straw sun hat. He helped the Atlantans off the boat and waved them good-bye, then crossed the warm tar-smelling boards to where she was sitting.

"I came to tell you I talked to Merriam yesterday about the bottle," she said. Her face was covered with bright specks from the sun shining through the weave of her hat. Damp squiggles of hair were plastered to her forehead.

"You did?" Harry was uncomfortably aware of Scooter, on the deck of the *Miss Kathy,* coiling lines and getting the equipment ready for their trip to the wreck this afternoon. Despite the whine of the Jet Skis some jerk was riding not far down the beach, despite the sloshing of the waves under the dock and the faint drumming of the jukebox in the restaurant, Harry thought Scooter could probably hear at least some of what they were saying.

"The story was pretty much as I remembered it," Isabel said. "Merriam's father—my grandfather John James—gave her the bottle in 1922. It was the last time she ever saw him."

If Harry asked her to move away to somewhere Scooter couldn't hear, Scooter would want to know why. "What happened to John James?"

"I guess he drowned. There had been a bad storm, and he insisted on getting in his boat and taking off for St. Elmo the day after."

"Miss Merriam didn't say where he got the bottle?"

"I don't think she knows."

"Hmm." Harry rubbed his cheek. "There had been a storm, you said?"

"From the way she described it, it must have been close to a hurricane—big tides, trees knocked down."

"Sounds bad." Bad enough to pulverize a porcelain bottle.

She squinted up at him. "Now can I ask you a question?"

"Sure."

"Why are you so interested?"

Damn. "I don't know. The bottle sort of . . . caught my eye."

He could tell she didn't believe him, and he didn't blame her, but he wasn't going to say any more.

She didn't press. She closed her sketchbook and got to her feet. "That's it, then."

He wasn't ready for her to go yet. "Hang on a minute. How's Miss Merriam doing?"

"She's a lot better than she was. Some of her memory is coming back." She turned to go and raised a hand in farewell. The bright specks danced across her face like spangles on a fancy veil. Although he had more questions, they withered in his throat and he let her walk away.

Behind him, Scooter's feet hit the dock as he jumped from the boat. The next minute, Scooter was saying, "What bottle, Harry?"

Isabel was walking through the breezeway that separated the dock from the parking lot. "Nothing. Just a bottle I noticed at her place."

"Don't give me that shit."

Scooter's mouth was close to Harry's ear. Harry could feel Scooter's breath. It was no use. Harry said, "She's got a porcelain bottle. Blue and white, mint condition. Same pattern as those shards we've been taking from the wreck. I was trying to find out where it came from."

"You weren't going to tell me?" Scooter's tone was dead flat.

Harry let it go. "She said she would ask the old lady about it, and she did. Since you were listening so hard, I don't reckon I have to repeat what the old lady told her."

Scooter didn't answer. Harry turned and saw him looking toward the breezeway. Isabel was no longer in sight.

15

THE DIVER HOVERED IN THE GARAGE, HIS EYES ON THE house. He had been waiting for an hour or more, letting the feel of his surroundings sink in. He had walked along the alley, a rutted track bordered by unkempt bushes and an occasional sagging wire fence. A dog barked occasionally, but dogs always barked every now and then. In his progress, the diver had made no more noise than a cat.

The garage smelled musty, and the space was filled with junk—plastic-swathed furniture, sheets of plywood, an air conditioner with the front-cover panel missing. The car was parked in the driveway, convenient for the diver to use as cover when he approached the house. The right time would come. He would know when it arrived, would feel it inside him like a latch unfastening.

He flexed his fingers in the tight rubber gloves, shook his shoulders out. He emptied his mind, leaving himself open to the fugitive stirring of the air, the smell of mown grass, the gradations of shadow between his hiding place and the window that was his goal. He took a deep breath and then he was moving.

If anybody was watching, he knew he would feel their eyes. He crouched low beside the car, his steps cautious but not tentative. He lingered there only a couple of seconds, adjusting to the new angle, before crossing to the house.

The back door had an awning of white metal slats. He

stood beneath it, breathing shallowly through his mouth. Almost there.

He left the back stoop and slid along the side of the house to the windows at the corner. The sills were little more than waist-high. The closer window was half-obscured by a camellia bush. The diver stepped over the lower branches, ducked, and carefully straightened his body. Now, his face was close, almost pressed against the window screen.

A mirror above a dresser shimmered on the far wall, like the surface of moonlit water. The bedroom door was closed. The foot of the bed, an expanse of gray, was on his right. A ceiling fan circled overhead. Louder than its drone was the sound of hoarse snoring.

The window screen was fastened with a simple hook-and-eye latch. He unclasped a diving knife from a sheath snapped to his belt loop. Maneuvering as gently as he could, he worked the blade between the sill and the screen. After only a few passes, the screen was unhooked. He refastened the knife in its sheath.

He waited a minute or two. The snoring continued. He pulled the screen out just far enough to allow himself to slip under it. Easily, he hoisted himself to the windowsill and lifted one foot and then the other over into the room. Standing next to the bedside table, he could see her now, a bundle of bedclothes, a few spikes of white hair, a curved nose. He couldn't see her face.

Three steps and he was beside her. The fan stirred the air. He could smell perspiration and a medicinal odor, like mouthwash.

He allowed himself a moment to look around. There was a second pillow, lying on the floor beside the bed. He wouldn't have to use the one she was lying on.

His fingers closed on the extra pillow. Soft. Real feathers, probably. Swiftly now, no more hesitating, he bent forward and pressed it against the old woman's face.

She barely struggled. Sedated. Her arms and legs twitched in feeble protest, but there was no sound. As he pressed down, the diver got an image of a ship bucking in the waves, shuddering, foundering, succumbing to the sea at last. He removed the pillow, shook it out, then dropped it to the floor again.

Somewhere in the house, a toilet flushed.

The diver stood by the bed, rigid, listening. Within seconds, footsteps approached the door. In two steps, he was across the room, kneeling beside the dresser. He heard the knob turn, the door open. The ceiling fan whirred, drying the perspiration on his face. He heard a cough.

Another cough, another second or two, and the door closed. The footsteps receded. The diver waited several minutes before he stood. The motionless figure on the bed was in deep shadow. He strode to the window, swung his feet out, and lowered himself beside the camellia bush, pushing the unlatched screen closed behind him.

His senses were almost painfully acute. He knew how these glossy camellia leaves would taste, bitter and woody and bracing. He could feel the pressure of his feet on the ground, was aware of the hillock of fine dirt at the tree's base, the knobby surface of a fallen twig.

When he pushed his way out of the bush, the air seemed to rush and engulf him, causing an almost painful pressure in his ears, clogging his nostrils with dust and vegetable matter, coating the back of his throat with a thin layer of salt. The dark lawn billowed around him, and before he could founder, he pushed off, surging forward.

PART TWO

16

BUDDY BURKE COULDN'T SLEEP. HE TOSSED, AN ARM crooked over his eyes, nowhere near drifting off. It was the light. If it were dark, sweet black dark, Buddy could move his arm and get comfortable. He would lie back on this pillow, thin and bad-smelling as it was, and be asleep in two seconds.

Buddy didn't care what time it was. He knew it was late, and tomorrow morning, like every morning, they would get him up early. He heard late sounds around him, gargling snores, somnolent muttering, scraping footsteps, an occasional unidentifiable cry.

Buddy turned over, his back to the light, but he knew by now that didn't work, either. He stared at the pock-mark surface of the wall a foot from his nose. The wall surface reminded him of a bad case of acne. It looked like it could use a treatment with a truckload of Clearasil. Buddy had found that idea kind of amusing when it first occurred to him. He didn't find anything about this place amusing now.

His daughter, Kimmie Dee, wanted boots, had sat down and written him a letter to ask for them. *Daddy, can I have boots? Please. I don't like Mr. S.* It just about killed Buddy to think about it. What the hell was Joy doing that Kimmie Dee couldn't ask her own mother for boots? Joy hadn't written the address on the letter, either. It was in a hand Buddy didn't recognize.

Before Buddy went away, he had a clear recollection, he had told Joy to take good care of Kimmie Dee and Toby. "Take care of the young'uns, hear?" he had said.

Oh, Joy was crying, long gulps like her heart was out-and-out broken, hanging on Buddy's neck. While the boo-hooing was going on, Buddy had told her to look after the young'uns. Maybe he hadn't said it plain enough: If the child wants boots, Joy, then pretty please see about getting them for her. Okay? Okay, Joy?

Buddy sat up, swinging his bare feet to the concrete floor. He rested his elbows on his knees and hung his head. Whose fault was it all, anyway? It wasn't Joy Burke's fault. She hadn't told Buddy to haul marijuana when he already had a couple of convictions and would have to go away for sure this time. That episode had been Buddy's bright idea.

This line of work had been unlucky for Buddy. He could see that now, and he should have seen it before. The hell of it was, it was pretty easy. You could be out in a boat some. You sell to your friends and make everybody happy.

Buddy wasn't greedy, and he wasn't ambitious. For Buddy, it was a means to an end. He had a family to support, and jobs didn't appeal to him as a way to spend his time. Be a fisherman? Yeah, right. Buddy's daddy had been a fisherman, worked his ass off every day of his life until the emphysema got him. Don't come telling Buddy Burke to catch fish for a living.

In the meantime, here Buddy was. He was serving thirty months, which meant eight or nine months in real time. Joy had cried and hung on his neck like she couldn't live without him for one night, let alone eight months. Now, she wouldn't even buy their daughter a pair of boots.

Anger was working in Buddy, making his hands shake, giving him a bad, sickening taste in his mouth. Because it wasn't just the boots. The boots were number one, but Buddy hadn't forgotten item number two: *I don't like Mr. S.*

Not having that many interesting activities to take up his time, Buddy had racked his brain over Mr. S. The initial didn't fit any of the men he could think of who had a good reason to be around Kimmie Dee. It didn't fit Buddy's no-account lawyer, or Kimmie Dee's school principal, or any friends Buddy could think of. Kimmie Dee was a smart girl—Buddy was as proud of her as he could be—and she wouldn't write that for no reason. So Buddy was thinking a good deal about Mr. S.

Buddy scratched his jawline. He didn't hear much from Joy these days. She hadn't been to visit in a while. Which was probably good, because if she showed up right now, Buddy would be tempted to whip her ass.

The anger had caught hold of Buddy, pounding through him. More than anything in the world right now, he wanted to lay his hands on Joy.

To let a child go without boots. He didn't understand it. And who was Mr. S.?

After a while, Buddy lay down again. He didn't close his eyes, but stared up at the pattern the light made on the ceiling of his cell. He wouldn't, he couldn't let this pass.

17

HEART GAVE OUT. IT HAPPENS," SAID DR. MCINTOSH. OUTside, the ambulance pulled away from Bernice's front yard, taking Merriam's body to the funeral home.

"But she seemed so strong. She was getting better," Isabel protested. Yet Merriam was dead, and that was that. Unfinished business would be left unfinished; instead of a final rounding-out, there remained rough edges, forever jagged and unpolished.

"It happens," Dr. McIntosh repeated. He walked out on the front porch and lighted a cigarette. On the living room sofa, Bernice Chatham wept, her broad shoulders jiggling. Isabel was dry-eyed. To cry, to romanticize her relationship with Merriam now that Merriam was gone, would have been hypocrisy. Yet she felt breathless, caught up short, as if something of hers had been summarily snatched away.

"You have to consider her age," said Clem Davenant. Clem, looking ravaged, was wandering restlessly around Bernice's living room. He was wearing a sweatshirt and jeans. Bernice's call had come early—too early, Isabel supposed, for him to be dressed in his seersucker suit. Bernice had called the doctor and Clem; Clem had called Isabel. Clem crossed the floor once again and said, "I'm going to get myself a glass of water, Bernice."

Bernice, her face buried in a handkerchief, did not reply. Isabel followed him to the kitchen. She said, "You don't have to stay, Clem."

He filled a glass from the tap, drank, leaned on the sink. "It's all right."

"I know this is disturbing for you, and I don't—"

She saw the cords in his neck move. He said, "Isabel, if I can't perform my functions in life, I might as well go lie down and not get up, all right?"

Startled by his vehemence, she said, "I just thought—"

"She was my client, and in some ways my responsibility, and I'm here because I'm going to do my duty by her."

Isabel started back to the living room. Halfway there, she heard him call after her, "Sorry. Sorry."

Dr. McIntosh had returned, and Bernice was talking to him in a choked voice. This was at least the third time Isabel had heard her version of events. "I went to get her up for breakfast, poor soul," Bernice was saying. "I shut the door at night because I was afraid she'd wander. I knocked and poked my head in and said, 'Time for breakfast, sugar!' and then when she didn't move at all . . ." Her voice trailed off and her face went back into the handkerchief.

Isabel walked down the short hall to Merriam's bedroom. The ceiling fan whirled. The bedclothes on the narrow bed were disarranged, the pillows on the floor. On the bedside table, along with Merriam's pill bottles, were her glasses and the well-worn black Bible Isabel had memorized verses from, at Merriam's whim, as a child. One of them came back to her: "My strength is dried up like a potsherd; and my tongue cleaveth to my jaws; and thou hast brought me into the dust of death."

She should get Merriam's things together. There was no reason for them to be left here. She opened the closet and took Merriam's suitcase from the floor beneath her few hanging garments. This should take only a minute. Bernice's voice drifted from the living room: "I thought she was stirring around in there last night, but I looked in and she was quiet. I used to worry so much, because you couldn't tell what she would do, and—"

Isabel closed the closet door and leaned against it. The task of gathering Merriam's possessions seemed beyond her. She put the suitcase down and walked to the window. Beyond the burgeoning leaves of a camellia bush, the acid green lawn glistened with dew. Across the way was Bernice's open garage, too full of junk to hold the car, which had been left in the driveway.

In a minute or two, Isabel would start filling the suitcase. Clem would know what Merriam had wanted done with her effects. For the first time, it occurred to Isabel that she didn't know what would happen to the house and property. Or the trailer. She could find herself evicted shortly. "My goods and chattels are none of yours," Merriam had written.

It didn't matter. Cape Cache had not been a fortunate place for the Anders family, and as the last of the line, Isabel was not eager to be saddled with John James's folly. Somebody else could preside over its final decay.

She was going to pick up the suitcase, open it, and start folding those dresses in the closet.

The window screen was unlatched.

She felt a spurt of annoyance at Bernice. There Bernice sat in the living room bawling, and she hadn't even made sure the room was minimally secure. Merriam could have leaned against the screen and fallen out. Isabel pushed it. It opened from the top, quietly and easily.

She was closing it when she noticed a splintered place on the windowsill, a three-inch scrape in the white paint in line with the metal eye of the latch. Isabel fingered the scar. A few small splinters stuck out. It was not discolored by weathering or worn smooth by use and time. She checked the bottom of the black-painted screen frame and found a corresponding scrape, deep enough so the pale wood showed through.

"I wondered where you went," Clem said from the doorway.

She was startled. She let go of the screen, which fell closed with a gentle bump.

"I'm sorry I was rude," he went on. He joined her at the window. "What are you doing?"

"The screen was unlatched." She pushed it open again, demonstrating. "I was thinking Bernice should have been more careful."

He inspected it. "I guess she should." He looked more closely. "Miss Merriam might have done it herself, too."

"Maybe." She wiggled the hook. It slid easily in and out of the metal eye. Below the level of the sill, she saw a broken twig on the camellia bush. Several fresh green leaves lay on the carpet of pine needles on the ground around the roots. Could somebody have broken in? The idea seemed bizarre.

Clem said, "Miss Merriam had her funeral all planned, you know. She picked out the casket and paid for it, bought the cemetery plot. She even selected the hymns—'Come, Thou Fount of Every Blessing' and 'Jesus, Keep Me Near the Cross.' "

"She believed in being thorough."

His lips twitched. "Too bad she can't preach her own sermon. What do you think she'd say?"

Isabel surveyed the bedside table, the battered Bible. "If you'd asked me before I came back here, I'd have been able to answer. I would have said she'd be the image of self-righteousness. Now, I have no idea. There was more to her than I thought."

"I shouldn't have asked. It doesn't do any good to play these games." Clem moved away from the window. "I used to do it a lot after my son—after Edward died.

What would he have said? Would he have blamed me? Would he have thought Andrea—his mother—was right to leave me? You can make up answers that seem so real, and then you realize that everything you've imagined is garbage. Dead people are dead, and that means they aren't here to think or feel anything."

His voice was harsh. Isabel said, "Clem, I don't want you to—"

He held a hand up. "No. No. Bear with me. I'm shaky all right, but don't take offense. I want to do what I can to help you through this."

"All right. Thanks," she said, and some of the tension left his face.

When the doctor left not long afterward, Isabel walked with him to his car. The morning was heating up. A mockingbird warbled in the azaleas by the porch. She said, "Dr. McIntosh, are you going to do any further . . . investigation into what killed Merriam?"

He shot her a sidelong glance. "An autopsy, you mean? No need."

She was treading on delicate ground. "I wondered, with all the drugs she was taking, whether—"

"No sign of drug overdose."

"There's no reason to think it wasn't natural causes?"

The doctor stopped walking. He said, "What are you driving at, Isabel?"

All at once, she was blurting it out. "I never understood how she got that concussion. It seemed odd. And now, when she was actually getting better, to have her die like this—"

Dr. McIntosh's ruddy face got redder. "I think you've been living in New York too long," he said with acerbity. "Certainly Merriam could have been murdered, if somebody had a mind to do it. The point is, there's absolutely no reason to think that's what happened, and why would anybody have a mind to do it?"

"I don't know why."

"Indeed you don't. Merriam Anders was my patient for fifty years or more, Isabel. It strikes me that if you'd paid more attention to her when she was alive and could appreciate it, you wouldn't be making up stories about how she died."

The remark hit home. It seemed all too likely that Dr. McIntosh was right, that she was creating a bizarre scenario about Merriam's death to mask her own feelings of guilt.

Dr. Mcintosh stalked to his car without saying goodbye. The mockingbird continued to warble. Clem appeared on the porch. "Bernice is straightening the room. Let's go have coffee, all right? There are things we have to discuss."

Merriam's room looked very bare. A grim Bernice, calm now, had stripped the bed and held the linens in her arms in a crumpled bundle. Isabel said she hoped to see her at the funeral.

Bernice sniffled. "She was a handful, bless her heart."

"I know she was."

"I did my best. I'll bet she was already gone when I looked in on her during the night. I couldn't have done nothing."

Isabel was ready to get away from this room, away from Bernice Chatham.

They took Clem's car. At the highway, he turned left toward Westpoint. The bay was glassy here, less turbulent than at Cape Cache. Tiny hummocky islands, crowned with the moss-hung trunks of dead trees, reared up offshore. They discussed arrangements. Clem thought the funeral could be as soon as tomorrow. "You've got to give people time to find out about it, but news travels fast. Bernice is probably on the phone right now. I can call the minister, if you want. Set a time."

He turned in at a rundown waterfront café and they had coffee and doughnuts on a sunny deck. Pepper plants in tin cans were set out on the railings. He said, "I expect you'll get people coming by and bringing food. Make sure you've got space in the refrigerator. When Edward died—" he shook his head.

Isabel said, "Tell me about Edward."

He drew a long breath. "That's tough to do."

"I know, but he's on your mind."

He put down his mug and contemplated the bay. "Edward was my only child. He was nearly thirteen years old when he died. He was a very, very smart kid. All the tests, everything. Off the charts. But for some reason that wasn't enough for me. I wanted him to do something physical, some kind of sport, instead of sitting in a room reading all the time. Although, when I look back on it, not many kids get killed sitting in rooms reading, do they?"

"Clem—"

"Let me tell it, okay?" He was looking past her, squinting into the morning glare. "I always liked to swim. For years, I'd been a recreational scuba diver. Edward liked to swim, too, so I urged him to get certified and we'd go diving together. And he did, and we did."

Clem pushed his chair back. He stood and went to lean on a nearby railing. Far out, a brown pelican skimmed past, low over the surface of the water. He went on: "I keep telling myself Edward liked diving, that he didn't do it just for me, but the fact remains that it was my idea. The other fact remains—when the time came, I couldn't save him."

"What happened?"

"One of those things." He bit off the words. "We

were diving one day. We'd cooked up kind of a historical research project, and—"

"Historical research?"

"Underwater archaeology, you might call it." He waved it away. "It was a dumb idea. Anyway, we were diving. The water was murky. I lost sight of Edward for a minute. He'd dislodged some debris and gotten pinned down. He panicked. By the time I realized what was happening, he'd spit out his mouthpiece. I tried to get him free, but it was confusing down there, and he was scared, struggling. It was over practically before I knew it. I dragged him to the surface, got him in the boat. I radioed for help and did mouth-to-mouth, but it was too late."

He picked a red pepper off the plant beside him, inspected it, tossed it in the water. "Sometimes I dream I'm still giving him mouth-to-mouth," he said. "I wake up hyperventilating."

Isabel couldn't assure him that someday it would be all right. She didn't think it ever could be.

Echoing her thought, he said, "Eve wants me to carry on, be the way I was before. I can't."

"She wants you not to blame yourself."

"Correct. But whose fault was it, if it wasn't mine?" He straightened. "I'm sorry for talking about my troubles. You're the bereaved one now."

"I asked you."

"And I've told you." He looked around for the waiter. "We'd better get back. Can you stop by the office in the next couple of days? The will is pretty straightforward, but there are some papers to sign."

"The will?"

He gave her a quizzical look. "Miss Merriam's will."

My goods and chattels are none of yours. "Merriam disinherited me. Years ago."

He mused briefly. "Oh yeah, I guess she did, back

when my father was still handling her affairs. That didn't last more than a couple of years. No, she left everything to you. It's all yours, no strings attached."

Isabel turned in under the cabbage palms and bumped down the driveway. The house—her house—sat among the scrub and weeds, bedraggled and forlorn. She was going to have to deal with the damn place, after all.

But not right now. Right now she had a duty to perform. She parked the car and walked back to the beach. She found Kimmie Dee near the water's edge, prodding at something with a stick. When Isabel got closer, she saw that it was a beached jellyfish, a transparent blob partially covered with sand.

"I have something to tell you, Kimmie Dee," she said.

Kimmie Dee followed Isabel to a blackened driftwood log and perched next to her. Isabel said, "I have sad news. Merriam died this morning. You were her friend, and I wanted you to know."

The girl's head drooped. She said, "You mean really dead? Not just real sick?"

"No. She's dead."

Kimmie Dee scooped up handfuls of loose sand and dribbled them over her bare feet. After a while, she said, "Was she scared?"

"I don't think so."

"Miss Merriam used to tell me she wasn't scared to go. She said when the call came, she'd be ready."

That sounded like Merriam. Isabel said, "Well, the call came and she went."

Overhead, gulls wheeled and cried. Somebody's radio was playing an advertising jingle. Kimmie Dee's feet were nearly covered with sand. "You're sure she wasn't scared?" The point seemed to bother her.

"There's no reason to think so. Really."

Kimmie Dee wiggled her toes and most of the sand slid away. "I guess he didn't get her, then, because she was sure scared of him," she said.

Isabel wasn't sure she'd understood. "Who didn't get her?"

"The man in the hood didn't get Miss Merriam."

Isabel had been picking at the crumbling wood of the log. Her fingers stopped moving. *Make sure you understand,* she cautioned herself. "What are you talking about, Kimmie Dee?"

"That day. She was scared of the man in the hood. She told me to watch out."

"You mean the day you found her on the beach? The day she got sick?"

"Yes."

The surface of the log was spongy, dry wood flaking off in her hand. "Why didn't you mention the man in the hood before?"

"Because I'm scared of him, too." Kimmie Dee stretched toward Isabel's ear and whispered, "I've got his picture."

Isabel waited until she thought she could sound casual. "You have a picture of the man in the hood?"

"Yes. In my room."

"Do you think—would you mind getting it, so I can see?"

"Okay." She jumped up and ran, sand spurting out behind her. Isabel kept her eyes on the diminishing figure with its flying hair. Something had happened to Merriam, something real. The event was hidden, its outlines obscured, but it was there. She very much wanted to see Kimmie Dee's picture of the man in the hood.

When the girl came back, she was carrying a large floppy book. "Here it is," she said.

Isabel took the book. It was a Halloween coloring book with a lurid cover depicting a monster emerging from a crypt. The title was *Ghouls, Goblins, 'n' Ghosts.* She leafed through it. A halfhearted attempt had been made to color some of the monsters and haunted houses, but most of the pages were untouched. "Here it is," said Kimmie Dee. She pointed to a picture of a skeleton wearing a hooded robe and carrying a lantern, standing among tombstones in an overgrown graveyard. "That's him," Kimmie Dee said. "The man in the hood. That's the one she was scared of, isn't it?"

So much for easy answers. A hearty voice behind them said, "What are you two doing? Having a coloring party?"

Isabel felt Kimmie Dee, sitting beside her, stiffen. She turned and saw Ted Stiles standing over them, looking with interest at the coloring book open on Isabel's knees. He was wearing his usual black slacks and white shirt, with the large many-dialed black watch on his wrist and a package of Marlboros showing through his breast pocket. His black leather shoes were hardly appropriate for a stroll on the beach, and Isabel assumed he had followed Kimmie Dee from the house.

With frost in her tone, Isabel said, "I was telling Kimmie Dee that my aunt died last night."

His face fell. "She did? Now, that's a shame. I'm so sorry." He settled into a relaxed stance and began digging in his shirt pocket for a cigarette. "Did she ever remember what happened to her?" he asked.

"Not really."

He bent and studied the picture of the hooded skeleton. "Oo! That's ugly! Are you going to color that picture, Kimmie Dee?"

Kimmie Dee's face was turned away from him. She said faintly, "No."

In an even more ingratiating tone, he said, "What is that a picture of, anyway?"

"Man in a hood." Kimmie Dee snatched the book from Isabel, said, "Bye," and ran toward her house.

Ted Stiles, watching her go, seemed unperturbed. "The ideas young'uns get are amazing, aren't they?" he said. He lit a cigarette, threw the burned match at Isabel's feet, and strolled away, his black-shod feet making hollows in the sand.

18

WIND CAUGHT THE BILL OF THE YELLOW PAINTER'S CAP Buddy Burke was wearing and nearly took it off, but Buddy caught it in time and pulled it lower on his brow. He had found the cap beside the road. Luck.

The truck he was riding in the back of hit a bump and sent him up in the air, to crash down on his butt. Tough on the sacroiliac. He settled against the cab and looked around for something to hold on to. There wasn't anything but the side of the truck, so he latched onto that.

Buddy had companions here, a couple of liver-mottled bird dogs. Vaccination tags clinking with every bounce, they lay calmly on their filthy blanket and eyed Buddy with expressions that said, We've seen a lot, and you're the least of it. That was all right. If the old dude who'd stopped and picked him up didn't want Buddy next to him, Buddy would ride with the dogs. He was happy to be here. He was willing to kiss the old man's busted-up work boots for giving him this ride.

Everything had gone so well, Buddy thought maybe God Himself wanted him out of the Correctional Facility. Buddy had walked off his work-release job so easily, it amazed him. He put up his hoe and shovel, neat, like he was supposed to, and said to himself, "I done the work. Now it's time for the release." While everybody was milling around, he walked back to the dirt road, found the painter's cap in a patch of briars, and hitched a ride with the old man and his dogs. He might not have been missed yet.

"Where you going to, son?" the old man had asked.

Buddy scratched under his new cap. "Sawmill Branch. Visit my mama." He knew it was going overboard to say "Visit my mama," but he was excited. At night in his cell, he had thought about where to claim he was going. He wouldn't say he was going to St. Elmo, because when they realized he was out, they'd be looking for somebody heading for St. Elmo. Sawmill wasn't far outside Tallahassee. Once he got past Sawmill, he'd say he was going to Alma. Once past Alma, he'd say Westpoint. Once past Westpoint—

"I can get you up to the highway, anyway," the old man had said. He jerked his thumb toward the back. "Jump on in. They won't bite."

The truck hit another pothole and sent Buddy sky-high. Maybe the old fellow's eyesight was bad and he couldn't see the holes. Maybe he was just a straight-ahead daredevil, willing to ruin his suspension for a few thrills. Buddy dug his heels against the rust spots on the truck bed and clenched his teeth, waiting for the next jolt.

He was out of jail. He had walked off work release. The truth of it started to hit him.

Buddy Burke had never, not ever, figured himself to want to escape, which is probably why he got on work release in the first place. What he had intended to do was serve his time and get out.

Until he got that pitiful letter from Kimmie Dee. *Daddy, can I have boots? Please. I don't like Mr. S.*

Lying in his bunk, Buddy had gone over ways and ways of handling the situation. He thought of writing to tell Joy to buy the boots, or asking who the hell this Mr. S. was, or combinations of those possibilities. What came clear was, at any point Joy could flimflam him. Buddy wanted to see what was going on for himself. If he didn't like what he saw, he wanted to whip Joy Burke's tail.

The old man swerved to the edge of the road for some reason, raking the side of the truck, and the side of Buddy Burke, with sharp branches from an overgrown bush. "Get over!" Buddy yelled, but he doubted the man could hear him because of the gospel music on the radio. "Just to the highway," Buddy muttered to the dogs.

If Joy was messing with him, Buddy wanted to whip her tail. It had gotten to be a need.

Up to now, the only person in the world Buddy had wanted to hurt was the Marine Patrolman who had stopped his boat and arrested him, a smartass yelling at Buddy through a megaphone. Buddy had definitely wanted to hurt that boy, but then he got over it. In truth, it had made him feel odd when he read about the death of the patrolman, Darryl Kelly, in the papers after he was already inside. He had read how they found Darryl Kelly's arm in the shark's stomach, and it gave him the heebie-jeebies. He wondered whether the arm they found was the same arm Kelly was holding the megaphone with when he was hollering at Buddy.

Anyway, most of his life Buddy's motto had been "I'm a lover, not a fighter." He once had a T-shirt with that saying printed on it. So it was hard to explain, even to himself, why he wanted to hurt Joy. He did, though. He wanted to so badly, he had walked right away from his work release and built up real trouble for himself, and the only explanation he could make was that it would be worth it.

Buddy had a little money with him, but he knew it wasn't going to be enough. He had to cover a hundred miles between here and St. Elmo, and he'd have to stop hitching rides when word of his escape got out. He might have to steal. He had never stolen anything in his life, not so much as a stick of gum, but if he had to steal, he would. He had come to terms with it those nights he lay thinking.

He wouldn't start stealing today. Escaping from jail was enough for today. If he got hungry, and as a matter of fact he was hungry already, he'd buy a candy bar or something.

They had turned onto a paved road, compressed gravel hissing beneath the tires of the truck. The dogs were stretched out, sound asleep. The paws of one of them jerked and quivered as he pursued something in a dream. The truck stopped at a red light and the old man stuck his head out the window and yelled at Buddy, "Highway up yonder! Next stop!"

"All right," Buddy yelled back, and stretched his legs. His back hurt and his butt had gone to sleep. Now that he was leaving, he wished he could stay with the old man and the dogs, go home with them and spend the night. Maybe the old man had a wife who was a good cook. They'd have chicken-fried steak and gravy, and biscuits and sweet corn and collard greens. Sara Lee banana cake for dessert. The dogs would lie under the table, their tails thumping, and after supper they'd all watch TV and eat some vanilla ice cream before going to bed.

The old man pulled up at the intersection. "Here we are!" he yelled. Buddy looked around: auto dealerships, fast-food restaurants, gas stations on all four corners.

He vaulted over the side of the truck, nearly losing his cap, his feeble disguise, again. "I thank you," he called to the old man as he sprinted to get out of the traffic. The old man didn't even look at him, just lifted his horny hand in farewell.

Buddy stood on the traffic island, cars whizzing around him and creating a hot wind that tore at his shirt. He should cross to the roadside, get over there and hitch, but suddenly he was afraid. Word might be out already. Had he been in the old man's truck thirty minutes? Longer? His hands clenched and unclenched in his pockets. He looked around. In back of the gas station catty-corner across the intersection was a stand of pine woods. He had to get over there, get under cover, so he could think.

The lights seemed to take a long time to change. Buddy shifted his weight and ran when he had the chance. He forgot to worry about how he was acting or whether anybody was looking. He kept his eyes on those trees. He was naked out here.

He made it. Sweating, he strode by the gas station bathrooms, across a strip of ground strewn with plastic bags and empty motor-oil cans, and into the shadow of the pines. It was late afternoon. He had forgotten about his candy bar. He felt the woods close around him.

19

In the cross, in the cross,
Be my glory ever
Till my raptured soul shall find
Rest beyond the river.

The last note of the organ faded. In the front pew, Isabel closed her hymnal and bowed her head for the benediction. The scent of carnations was heavy in the unmoving air, the light in the sanctuary subdued. The amen was pronounced, a nose was blown, and behind Isabel the men from Merriam's Sunday school class, her pallbearers, shuffled in preparation for their march out. Eve Davenant, on Isabel's left, settled her pocketbook strap on her shoulder. Clem stood at the end of the pew, offering Isabel his arm.

There was a decent, if not huge, crowd. Isabel was conscious of solemn and interested faces turned toward her as she and Clem walked up the aisle. The carpet seemed to stretch out forever, and then they were through the doorway and in the vestibule, and Clem was murmuring, "Nice service, wasn't it?"

It had been. The minister obviously had known Merriam well and had given her a good send-off. Now the car was waiting to take them to the cemetery.

They crossed the broad porch of the church. The air was bathwater temperature. Behind them, a discreet buzz of conversation started as people straggled out. "Lovely service," said Eve, and then, "Are you riding out there with me, Clem?"

"I thought maybe I'd go with Isabel." He hesitated. "If Isabel would like me to."

Isabel had begun to think Clem was pushing duty too far. There was no need for him to reawaken painful memories of his son's death by going to the cemetery at all, and to go in the funeral director's limousine seemed masochistic. On the other hand, he could be treating the occasion as a private rite of passage. She had protested enough. "I'd appreciate it."

"I'll see you out there, then," Eve said. She parted from them, and the driver ushered Isabel and Clem into the backseat of the limousine.

Isabel leaned against the soft gray upholstery. The air conditioner had kept the interior almost too cool. The driver stood outside, waiting for the coffin to be loaded into the hearse.

Clem touched her sleeve. "Hang in there," he said.

"I'm all right." Through the tinted glass, she watched the dispersing crowd. Some of them had come out to the trailer earlier and left food—baked ham and fried chicken, potato salad, mandarin orange and marshmallow salad, turnip greens, lemon meringue pie. There was no way Isabel could eat it all, but that wasn't the point. They had brought it because that was part of what you did when somebody died.

"Are you really all right?" Clem asked.

She turned to look at him. His dark navy suit and tie accentuated his pallor. "What do you mean?"

"I get the feeling something is bothering you. Maybe I'm wrong."

Isabel studied her folded hands in her lap, the weave of her skirt. "No. You're not wrong."

"Can you tell me what the problem is?"

Could she? Maybe it was time for a reality check. "I think there was something strange about Merriam's . . .

accident, or whatever it was. And her death." She said it with more defiance than she'd intended.

A crease appeared between his eyes and disappeared a second later. "Strange?"

"To be blunt about it, I think it's possible somebody attacked her—and maybe even killed her." Launched, she pressed on. The mysterious concussion, the man in the hood, the unlatched window screen. There was so little to tell, she was finished by the time the driver got in and eased the limousine into the street behind the hearse.

Clem listened without changing expression. When she stopped talking, he nodded gravely. "Isabel, everything you've said is logical, except for one thing—your opening premise. You're saying somebody would want to kill Miss Merriam."

"I know. I know." Was Isabel the only person in the world who could imagine wanting to kill Merriam?

"I mean, people do atrocious things, and attacking a woman eighty-plus years old isn't unheard-of, but she wasn't robbed. Robbery's the only motive I can think of."

Isabel had been through this on her own already. "It could have been bad luck. Bad timing."

"What do you mean?"

"She could've seen something she wasn't supposed to. Blundered into something." Faced with his opposition, she felt herself digging in her heels.

A flush had colored his cheekbones. "Something criminal, you mean? Keep in mind that this isn't New York."

"I'm not likely to forget it," she snapped. "If you'll do me a favor and consider the possibility that I could be right—"

"I *said* it was logical—"

"—then you'll see it's entirely possible Merriam

found out something she wasn't supposed to know and that she could have been in danger because of it."

They glowered at one another. Clem said, "I'll be happy to concede your point if you can tell me what you think she found out."

"I don't know, Clem."

"Right."

A few minutes later they passed under the wrought-iron entrance arch at the St. Elmo municipal cemetery. Across the expanse of tombstones, pine trees, and patchy grass, a green canopy marked the grave site. Clem was looking out the opposite window. When they got out of the limousine and walked across to the canopy, she didn't take his arm.

The crowd at the cemetery was reduced in numbers from the church, the ceremony brief. Heat gathered under the canopy. Gnats danced in Isabel's face and she was dazzled by the sunlight on the polished headstones.

Afterward, she was surrounded by people offering condolences. Bernice Chatham, in a black straw hat, pressed her hand and whispered, "I did my best. I couldn't have done no more."

As Isabel chatted with the mourners, she caught sight of Clem standing immobile at a grave not far away. She saw Eve come up to him and speak. Clem gave no indication of having heard. Eve put her hand on his arm. He jerked it out of her grasp, turned, and walked rapidly away from her toward the parked cars.

In a moment, Eve materialized at Isabel's elbow. "Clem has to get to the office. He's going back to town with me," she said.

"All right." Many people were leaving. When Isabel had a moment, she walked to the grave where Clem had been standing. The tombstone read, EDWARD CLEMONS DAVENANT III, and gave the boy's birth and death dates.

Underneath was carved, *"He cometh forth like a flower, and is cut down."*

People stopped by the trailer all afternoon to pay their respects, and by the time the last visitor left it was late. Isabel kicked off her shoes, removed the suit jacket that had been roasting her all day, stepped out of her skirt, and peeled off her panty hose.

Someone knocked at the door.

Cursing, she pulled on shorts and a shirt and yanked the door open, to find a short, sturdily built young man in a uniform standing by the step. He had a brush haircut, pimples dotting his chin, and a gun on his hip. He said, "Deputy Jones, Sheriff's Department. I'm speaking to the residents in this immediate area about Buddy Burke. Do you know Buddy Burke at all?"

Buddy Burke. Kimmie Dee's father, who was in jail. Kimmie Dee had written to him about boots. "I've never met him. I know his daughter."

"He was incarcerated up in Tallahassee and walked off from his work-release program," the deputy said. "We're asking folks around here to keep an eye out for him, since his family lives right over yonder."

How terrible for Kimmie Dee. Isabel said, "Is he dangerous?"

"No, ma'am, we don't think so." The deputy seemed almost apologetic. "Matter of fact, they figure he'll turn himself back in. Either that or show up here to see his family. It's the first time he's been sent away, and they reckon he got a little homesick."

Isabel tried to remember what Kimmie Dee had said about her father's crime. "He sold marijuana, is that right?"

The deputy nodded and shifted his weight so the gun on his hip jutted out. "That's right. We got him for selling a couple of times, and then the Marine Patrol caught him hauling some in his boat. That's when he had to go off for a while."

The deputy turned to go. "You happen to see him, ma'am, you give us a call. All right?" With a bowlegged stride, he walked away up the drive.

Isabel closed the door. Everything seemed burdensome—the plates of food everywhere, her shoes in the middle of the floor, John James's photograph and the bottle on the table beneath it, the grumbling air conditioner. And now, Buddy Burke. She went into the bathroom, wet a washcloth, and pressed it against her face. When it was warm, she squeezed it out, wet it again, and went into the bedroom to lie down with the cloth draped over her eyes.

The trailer smelled like cigarette smoke, perspiring bodies, turnip greens. She thought of her apartment in New York, her cool, quaint aerie overlooking the leafy garden. She thought about Zan, her lost job, Chinese food. All of it seemed as insubstantial as a dream, and it modulated into one as she dozed off.

She woke half an hour later, only slightly refreshed.

She was standing in the kitchen, contemplating which of her many home-cooked donations to choose for supper, when there was another knock at the door.

She answered. It was Harry Mercer.

To her great surprise, a tremor she could almost call happiness went through her. Harry was a person she had known a long time, a person who knew her. She said, "Harry, thank God it's you."

She couldn't tell whether he was surprised at the warmth of her greeting. He said, "I had to stop by. I heard about Miss Merriam."

She stood back. "Come in."

Inside, he surveyed the array of covered dishes. "You think you got enough food here?"

She chuckled. "Do you want something? I've got everything you can imagine."

"You got Jell-O mold?"

"Yep."

"Baked ham?"

"Right."

"Bean salad?"

"Absolutely."

He gave her a shrewd look. "How about tuna casserole?"

"Oh damn." She picked up several lids and foil coverings. "No tuna casserole."

"Then I'm not going to stay."

"Come on, Harry. I've got fried chicken. And molasses-baked beans."

"Well . . ."

She got out plates and cutlery and a couple of beers, and they served themselves and ate in the living room because there was no room on the table. Harry did not, she noted, pay special attention to the porcelain bottle. They talked about who had been at the funeral, and Isabel found herself musing aloud about Merriam.

"One of the hardest things is to realize that it's over," she said. "I won't have any more chances to understand her, or to make her understand me."

Harry's reply was vehement. "Don't go feeling too sorry about it. She gave you a real bad time. Gave *us* a bad time."

Surprised at his bitterness, Isabel said, "Yes, she did."

"She used to make you cry, Isabel. She put bruises on your arms where she grabbed you. She locked you in your room. Do you remember all that?"

"Yes." Isabel put her plate aside. "I remember." It was coming back. The way she had cried in Harry's arms. She had never cried like that since. She did have bruises sometimes, small greenish fingerprints on the insides of her arms, and she remembered Harry kissing them, his mouth warm against her flesh, and Harry whispering, "I hate her. I *hate* her."

Harry stood and took his half-finished plate to the kitchen. When he returned, he said, "I have to ask you, Isabel. I have to know why you ran off back then. Left the way you did."

She had wondered what she might say. Clarity descended. "Ben Raboski was ready to take me away," she said. "You weren't."

Isabel had met the man she ran away with, Airman First Class Ben Raboski, on a night when Harry came down with the flu and didn't show up for choir practice, and therefore couldn't be with Isabel afterward.

Isabel couldn't go home early because any change in routine made Merriam suspicious. Instead, with a group of other choristers, Isabel had done yet another forbidden thing. She had ridden out to a teenage beach hangout called The Dunes, which had an open-air patio with a jukebox and a Coke machine. Several young men from the base, including Ben Raboski, were there, sitting at a broken-down picnic table at the edge of the pool of yellow light.

Ben was sharp-faced, reckless, northern. He had regulation-short black hair and brilliant blue eyes with curly lashes. When he sought Isabel out at the Coke machine and asked her to dance, his voice had an exotic Yankee twang. Boys from the air base were dangerous, but Isabel said yes. It was a slow number, and as they danced, Isabel rigid in his arms, Ben said, "Relax. We're only dancing."

We're only dancing. Ben always claimed he had known from their first dance that Isabel wasn't a virgin.

After that, she deceived both Merriam and Harry.

Harry was faithful, familiar. She knew Harry's body as well as she knew her own.

Ben was the opposite, moody and unpredictable. He had many claims on his time and attention. He raced motorcycles, went to movies, hung out with his buddies. Isabel wasn't sure he ever thought about her when they weren't together, so it came as a shock when he told her he was being transferred and suggested she go with him.

They were sitting at the drive-in, drinking vanilla milk shakes. "What do you mean?" Isabel had said. She had the impression the ice cream had frozen her lips, making it hard to form words.

Ben whooped with laughter at the sight of her face, and it was a few minutes before he could repeat his offer. He amplified. "You're always complaining how your aunt rides you. Why not cut loose?"

"I can't do that."

He leaned back and took a long slurp of his shake. "That's what I thought you'd say."

Isabel was insulted. "Why?"

He patted her knee. "Because you're a good girl."

His words filled her with rage and gloom. She hadn't been a good girl in a long time, not since she'd started having sex with Harry. The question entered her head: Why pretend?

Why pretend? Why not cut loose?

It had come clear, later, that Ben had imagined himself to be doing her a favor out of the goodness of his heart. Considering consequences was not something Ben ever did. Ben loved excitement. He would liberate Isabel from her oppression with a fine, gentlemanly nonchalance. Ben did not love responsibility, but at that point responsibility was the last thing on anybody's mind.

When she told Ben she would go with him, they had known each other a month at most.

Ben Raboski was handsome. He was full of energy, and he loved to have fun. Isabel couldn't have known, although a woman older than sixteen might have guessed, that once the initial tumult subsided, Ben's enthusiasm would give way to black, immovable gloom. He would sprawl unspeaking, watching television, smoking Camels down to the tiniest nub, refusing to acknowledge her presence, her existence. This went on until the next thing caught his attention and revitalized him. Isabel learned the magnitude of her mistake, but she had the Anders stubbornness. She was gone, and she didn't imagine herself ever coming back.

"You should have asked me. I would've taken you away," Harry said. During her story, his eyes hadn't moved from her face. Now he walked to the window and pushed the curtain back, staring out toward the house.

"I'm not sure you would've."

He turned. "Why not?"

"Well—" She shrugged. "You're still here, aren't you?"

"Yeah," Harry said heavily. "Yeah. I'm still here."

He came and sat beside her. "I'm still here," he repeated. He slid his hand beneath her hair, caressing her neck.

She remembered the smell of his body, its contours beneath her hands. She remembered the silky, cushiony feel of his hair. His kisses were familiar, too—consoling, but with a driving undercurrent. Ever since she had seen him at the Beachcomber, she realized, she had felt its pull, as strong as ever.

20

I'M SORRY, MA'AM," THE DISPATCHER SAID. "THAT CASE IS still open and I'm not supposed to discuss it." The dispatcher, a middle-aged woman with a pair of glasses hanging around her neck on a chain, did sound, and look, regretful. The Marine Patrol substation in Westpoint consisted of one small room containing the switchboard, and a couple of small offices whose open doors revealed them to be empty. Back windows overlooked a dock. There was no higher authority on the premises to appeal to, and Isabel wouldn't have known what appeal to make.

"Thanks anyway," Isabel said. It had been a quixotic idea. She walked out to the waterfront lane that was the major thoroughfare of Westpoint.

The street was empty. She strolled back to the car, the morning sun warming her back. She had hoped the drive would give her some perspective—if not about what had happened to Merriam, then about what had happened with Harry.

Making love with Harry again was like being rocked by an explosion. Afterward, she had been wrung out and disoriented, but with a firm grasp of one crucial idea: This could not go on.

Harry was married. Isabel had gone that route with Zan and did not intend to travel it again. She had told Harry so before they got out of bed, but he hadn't seemed to take her seriously. Since she had so obviously enjoyed being with him, she could understand his attitude.

"You're not going to dump me again. I won't let you," he had said.

"Harry, I'm telling you—" He reached for her, and she lost the drift of the argument.

Eventually, though, the moment arrived when they had to extricate themselves from the wreckage of tangled sheets and discarded clothing, and Harry had to dress and go home. Clothed, she had been able to make her point more strongly. "I can't let this happen."

"It did happen."

"All right, it did, but I have to live with myself. Not again."

He rested his hand against her cheek. "We'll see," he said, and that was as close as they had gotten to agreement.

After Harry left, in the aftermath of washing dishes, straightening the bed, trying to restore order to a scene of abandonment, Isabel had remembered the Marine Patrol. Eve Davenant had told her a Marine Patrolman had disappeared around the time Merriam was injured. It was a stretch to imagine the two events were connected, but looking into it would give her an excuse to take time out, drive to Westpoint, get some perspective.

Even if her purpose hadn't been accomplished, the drive was pleasant. The road back to St. Elmo hugged the coast. On the placid bay, oyster fishermen were out in flat-bottomed skiffs, prodding with long-handled tongs. Seafood houses on stilts lined the roadside and piles of oyster shells sloped down to the water's edge.

She hadn't learned anything from the Marine Patrol, but she didn't have to get her information from the Marine Patrol. Any resident of Westpoint or St. Elmo could probably tell her everything she wanted to know about the case. In the interest of accuracy, she would try the newspaper. There must have been a story about the patrolman's disappearance in the *St. Elmo Dispatch.*

In another ten minutes, she was driving through downtown St. Elmo. The *Dispatch* office had been, she recalled, at the end of the main street, Harbor Street, next to the hardware store. That cramped frame building, she discovered, now housed a marginal-looking upholstery shop. One of several men sitting on a sidewalk bench by the door told her the *Dispatch* was now located in a new building over behind the courthouse.

She found it without much trouble—a flat-roofed structure of pink brick and plate glass, the facade embellished with undersized Doric columns, ST. ELMO DISPATCH AND COASTAL ADVERTISER painted on the front window in gold Gothic letters. She walked into a carpeted large room where a young man who looked about sixteen sat at a desk tapping at a computer. He wore tortoiseshell glasses, Bermuda shorts, loafers with no socks, a T-shirt with *London—Paris—Rome—St. Elmo* printed on it, and yellow suspenders. A bell jangled when she walked in. He looked up and said, "Hi. Help you?"

"My name is Isabel Anders," Isabel began.

The young man said, "Oh, right," and got to his feet. He stuck out a hand and said, "Dustin Timberlake. I'm really sorry about your aunt. We'll have an obituary in the next issue. The spelling is M-E-R-R-I-A-M, correct?"

"Yes. I didn't—"

"I'm glad you came in. Saves me the phone call. Would you like to proof the copy? Cuts down on stupid mistakes." He dug through an overflowing basket on the desk, pulled out a sheet of paper, and proffered it to her. "Here it is."

The obituary was brief but accurate. Merriam was described as "the daughter of John James Anders, a pioneer settler of Cape Cache." Her only survivor was "a niece, Isabel Anders, of New York City."

Hovering, Dustin Timberlake said, "I got the information from Clem Davenant. Is it all right? I can still make changes."

"It's fine."

"Good. Thanks." He took the article back, dropped it in the basket, sat down at the computer, and began tapping again.

Isabel said, "Actually, I'd like to get some other information."

He turned from the screen and cocked his head. "Information is our business. We cover St. Elmo like cooties can cover your backside. Notice I'm using the editorial *we,* to make the operation sound more impressive."

Isabel had imagined she was talking to the office boy. Maybe he was older than sixteen. "You're the editor?"

"And publisher." He swept his hand at the metal filing cabinets, stacks of newspapers against the wall, and metal utility shelves. "What can I fill you in on?"

She leaned on the counter next to a stack of blank forms headed "Wedding Announcement." "A few weeks ago, a Marine Patrolman disappeared. I want to know the details."

Dustin gave her a calculating look. "You don't happen to have anything new on it, do you? If you do, come right in and sit down."

"I don't have anything. I just want to know what happened."

He stood. "We covered it, naturally. I'll find you a back issue. It was the biggest story around here so far this year. A definite for the New Year's roundup." He went to the stack of papers by the wall. "Let's see. That would be along about—" He poked around, said, "Nope," then tried another stack.

Continuing to search, he said, "The patrolman's name was Darryl Kelly. Disappeared into thin air, it seemed, and then part of his arm was found in a shark caught by a fisherman over in Westpoint. Apparently, it was an accident, but as you might expect, one school of thought claims there was something funny about it. Ha! Here it is." He pulled out a paper and waved it at her. "I'll get you the next week's, too. That covers finding the remains."

"Thanks." Isabel took the paper from him. The date was late May.

"You know, speaking of poor Darryl Kelly," said Dustin, digging, "there's a Darryl Kelly angle in this week's top story."

"What's this week's top story?"

"Jailbreak. A local marijuana dealer named Buddy Burke walked off his work-release job in Tallahassee."

"I heard about it. What's the Darryl Kelly angle?"

"The Darryl Kelly angle—here it is!" He retrieved another paper and handed it to her. "The Darryl Kelly angle is that a couple of months before he died, Darryl Kelly arrested Buddy Burke. He's the one who sent Buddy to jail."

She thought about it. "Have the people investigating Darryl Kelly's death thought of talking to Buddy Burke?"

"I hear that they have. There seems to be less to the connection than meets the eye. In the first place, Buddy himself was in jail when Kelly died."

"But what about his associates?"

Ruminatively, Dustin slid his thumbs beneath his suspenders. "Buddy did have a couple of associates—the guy who was growing the stuff over in the woods near Westpoint and the guy's cousin, who was helping him. That's about it. The cops got them, too. What I'm saying is, this wasn't the Medellin cartel. These are local boys without fancy connections. It's hard to imagine them going after Darryl Kelly for revenge or something dramatic like that."

Isabel was relieved. She was not eager to think of Kimmie Dee's father as a potential killer. Still, Darryl Kelly's involvement in Buddy Burke's arrest seemed a strange coincidence. She waved the newspapers and said, "Thanks again."

"No problem. If you spot Buddy, give me a call. My deadline's tomorrow afternoon." When she left, he was gazing raptly at the computer screen.

She glanced through the papers, sitting in the car with the door open to promote air circulation. Darryl Kelly had disappeared on May twentieth. Nobody knew exactly where he had been when fate overtook him. He had driven to the Westpoint Marine Patrol substation early in the morning, before his shift started, and taken out a boat. He had not said where he was going. When his shift began and he hadn't radioed in, the dispatcher tried to raise him. He never answered, never turned up, was, in fact, never seen again. His arm was found in the shark three days later and was identified by a plaid fragment of a jacket sleeve.

May twentieth. Isabel dropped the papers on the seat and drove around the corner to Harbor Street. She parked in front of Clem Davenant's office and went inside.

The office was modest but comfortable, with polished wooden chairs in the waiting room, as well as old maps of St. Elmo and Cape Cache and historic photos on the wall. There was a bowl of peppermint candies in a cut-glass dish, and the place smelled of lemon oil. Clem's secretary, a young blond woman wearing a pink sundress, buzzed Clem, and soon the door of his office opened and he stuck his head out. "Come on in, Isabel."

Clem's office was dominated by an antique rolltop

desk with many cubbyholes, all of them tidy. The dark green walls were hung with nautical charts. Clem seemed cordial but remote. After she sat down, he opened a folder on his desk and launched into a discussion of the value of Merriam's property (not great, because it wasn't beachfront); the taxes (considerable); the condition of the house (terrible). "After her expenses are paid, there'll be a little cash left over," he said. "I'm not sure exactly how much. Maybe ten thousand." He closed the folder and sat back.

Isabel tented her fingers and pressed them against her lips. "I'll have to sell it. What else can I do?" she said at last.

He tapped his gold pen on the blotter. "The house is a local landmark. It ought to be preserved."

"Yes, but you're talking about a lot of money, and I don't have it. I can't look after the place any better than Merriam could." She had never liked the damned house, never been happy there. Why should the thought of selling it be so painful?

"You don't have to decide right now. Give it some thought." He opened his desk drawer. "Here are the keys." He pulled out a small stainless-steel ring and handed it to her.

She dropped them in her bag, started to stand, and said, "One other thing. What day was it that Merriam had her accident?"

"What day?"

"The date. Do you remember?"

He leafed through a leather-bound calendar on his desk, ran his finger across it, and said, "I have a notation here that she was taken to the hospital on May twentieth."

"Thanks."

"Isabel—" He played with the pen again, let it go.

"I'm disturbed by what you said about Merriam yesterday. About your suspicions."

"Oh, well—" She shrugged. She didn't want a replay of their disagreement.

"I hope you'll let me know if you discover anything."

"All right." Maybe she would. More probably, she wouldn't.

The drive to the Cape gave her a chance to muse about her research. Both Merriam and Darryl Kelly had been extremely unfortunate on May twentieth. Darryl Kelly could have been at Cape Cache that morning, although nobody had seen him.

Unless Merriam had.

Preoccupied, Isabel walked into the trailer. She was standing on a white envelope—a blank envelope. She had not put the weather stripping along the bottom of the door, damn it. She picked the envelope up. Sealed, like the one before.

She tore it open wearily. The printed message, in red felt-tip pen, was similar to the first: NOW YOU CAN GO BACK WHERE YOU CAME FROM, YOU WHORE. She closed her eyes and leaned against the wall.

21

THE BLOWER HAD UNCOVERED A LINE OF BLACK SAND. Harry stared at it through the shifting green haze, then looked around for Scooter. Black sand meant silver.

He gave Scooter the high sign and watched him drift over. The black line, about three feet long, was getting darker, more distinct. Scooter nodded and gave Harry a thumbs-up, and Harry reached forward, scraping gently at the line with his gloved hands. He would never get tired of this feeling, never get tired of knowing something was there, lying there waiting, and in a minute it would show itself to him. There was nothing on earth like this coursing excitement.

An image of making love to Isabel last night came into his mind. That was different, not like this. Although he had to admit there were similarities.

Harry had not gone to Isabel's last night with the intention of making love to her. The intensity of what had happened scared him a little. He couldn't afford that right now, could not afford to be knocked off balance.

Carefully, carefully, he brushed at the line. His fingers were passing over something hard now, hard and rough with corrosion. It could be silver *reales,* a pile of coins fused together into conglomerate. It could be—

The object dislodged and he freed it. He was holding a Spanish sword, all in one piece. They had found only a hilt before, so disfigured with limestone accretion, it was almost impossible to tell what it was. This one was encrusted, too, but you could see the shape of the whole thing—fancy curved hilt, long blade. Harry's heart was pumping. Nobody had touched this sword since the ship went down. He was the first in centuries.

Scooter was already on his way back to his workplace. He wanted coins. A sword wasn't a big deal to him.

Holding his find reverently, Harry kicked upward. To hell with Scooter.

He broke the surface, spit out his mouthpiece, and paddled to the back of the boat where the ladder was, cradling his sword. He would put it in the tank, keep it covered with water until they could chip the corrosion off and treat it chemically. Making sure he didn't bang it into anything, he climbed up the ladder.

The sword safely stowed, Harry leaned on the side of the boat to catch his breath. The afternoon was waning, the sky slightly overcast. The orange anchor buoy was vivid against the gunmetal-colored swells. When Isabel said this couldn't go on, Harry shouldn't have argued. He wasn't sure why he had. Just a dumb knee-jerk reaction to having sex with her again.

The bottle had been there last night, on its table under the photograph of Isabel's grandfather, but he had been careful not to pay attention to it. He had actually forgotten about it for a good while, but when he started to leave, he noticed it again, shining at him from across the room

He watched the seesawing horizon for a minute longer, took a deep breath, then pulled his mask down over his eyes. He'd better go see what Scooter was up to.

They got in late and he really didn't have time to stop by Isabel's. But when he got in his truck to go home, without quite deciding to he turned toward the Anders place instead.

Isabel must have heard him, because she was looking out the window. By the time he had gotten out of the truck, she was standing in the doorway.

Harry stood by the step. He said, "I came to see how things went today."

"Not too well."

Harry didn't know whether her bad mood had to do with him or something else. "What's the matter?"

"Oh"—she pushed hair off her forehead with a worn-out air—"I talked to Clem Davenant about Merriam's estate, and I think I'm going to have to sell the house. There isn't enough money to keep it up."

"Did you want to hold on to it?"

She looked toward the old building. "Why should I? To hell with it." The corner of her eye jumped, the way it used to when she got jittery.

He said, "Something else is wrong. What is it?"

He wasn't sure she was going to answer. Finally, she said, "I'm getting anonymous notes."

The mosquitoes were descending. A cloud of them had congregated around the lamp by the door. "What do you mean?"

"Somebody is writing notes calling me a whore and saying I should go back where I came from. I found the second one when I got home this afternoon."

"Can I see them?"

She let him in. A piece of paper and a torn envelope were lying on the table. She handed the paper to him.

Harry studied it. NOW YOU CAN GO BACK WHERE YOU CAME FROM, YOU WHORE. Written in red felt-tip marker. He shook his head the way he did when water clogged his ears. Isabel handed him another paper. Same general message.

A drumming had started up inside Harry's head. "I can take care of this for you," he said.

"What do you mean?"

"It won't happen again." He dropped the notes on the table. He had to get out of here.

"Wait a minute, Harry. I want to know if you—"

He didn't wait. He remembered the door slamming, but he didn't remember getting in the truck. The first thing he knew he was on the road, heading for home.

"I wrote them because I wanted her to go away and leave us alone, Harry," said Kathy Mercer.

Harry tried to feel something for her besides revulsion. "You're damn lucky she didn't tell the cops," he said. He was overcome with disgust.

Harry and Kathy were in their kitchen breakfast nook. An uncut meat loaf and cool baked potatoes with puckering skins sat in congealing grease on a platter between them. Limp green beans swam in a bowl. In the tea glasses, ice cubes had dissolved to slivers.

"You used to be in love with her," Kathy said. She pressed her hands to her face. Her body shuddered.

Harry had an impression of watching this scene from a long distance away. Kathy's distress couldn't touch him.

Harry had not confessed to sleeping with Isabel. He had stormed in to confront Kathy, and he had told her he happened to run into Isabel and she happened to complain about getting anonymous notes. He had taken the high ground, gone on the offensive before Kathy could start asking questions.

Blindly, Kathy reached across the table toward him. Her arm hit a tea glass, knocking it off balance. He caught it before it tipped over and said, "Watch out, for Christ's sake."

Kathy quailed. "Don't you love me at all?" she whispered.

Harry couldn't answer. He could not say a word. To put everything back like it used to be, all he had to do was say yes, he loved her, but his jaws might as well have been welded shut.

He didn't even have to conceal what had happened

with Isabel. He could speak up and tell Kathy everything. Kathy wouldn't like it, but she would forgive him.

Or, if he could force himself to speak, he could gloss over the whole thing with lies. Kathy would jump at any flimsy, farfetched excuse. Everything could be exactly the same.

Harry closed his eyes and willed himself down into the cool underwater world of the Cape Cache shoals. He felt himself becoming weightless, unencumbered. All he could hear was his own breath, in and out. The surface shimmered above him, silvery and remote.

"Harry?" Kathy's voice sounded gargly, like she was choking.

He opened his eyes "What?" His own tone was dry and brittle.

"Don't you have anything to say?"

The time had come. He had to speak his piece now, make everything all right. He wet his lips. "Maybe I should move out," he said.

Kathy recoiled as if he'd hit her. "No!"

"Yeah. I think I better."

Kathy scrambled around the table and threw herself against him. He could feel her heaving as he rocked backward. Woodenly, he put his arms around her and patted her back. He was going. It was so simple and obvious. It occurred to him that he had been planning to go all along.

"I hate her!" Kathy screamed, her voice reverberating in his ear.

Harry winced. "It doesn't have anything to do with Isabel," he said. He thought maybe it was the truth.

"I don't believe you!" She pulled back to look at him, her face smeared and damp. "I don't!" She pounded his chest with her fists.

Breath jerked out of him. He fought her, caught her

wrists in his hands. He was calm but sensed the beginnings of a yawning sadness.

She struggled briefly before pulling away. She stood up. "All right, go, you bastard."

Jerkily, as if his legs were likely to give way, he walked down the hall to their bedroom and got his duffel bag from the top of the closet. He stared at his clothes hanging on the pole: his one good suit; a metal hanger contraption holding the Christmas-gift ties he never wore; his down jacket, chinos, sport shirts. He couldn't imagine what to take.

He went to his dresser and started unloading his underwear drawer, stuffing jockey shorts into the duffel bag. He would need underwear. Somehow, it seemed as if he could do without most of the rest.

He was in the bathroom getting his toothbrush and razor when Kathy came to the doorway. She wasn't hysterical now or even crying. Her face was yellow-white, her eyes behind the lenses of her glasses big and shocked. "You aren't really leaving, Harry?" she said.

Of course he wasn't really leaving. This was his house. Kathy was his wife. He had two daughters who would be coming home from camp next week. This was his life, a bedroom with a satin spread on the bed and a big TV and meat loaf on the table and a truck in the driveway and a boat berthed out at Cape Cache.

"I better go on," he said. He saw himself in the bathroom mirror. His own eyes looked big and shocked, too.

"Don't," she said, but now it was clear in his mind.

"I'll be at the Beachcomber," he said. Less than five minutes later, he was on his way.

22

BUDDY BURKE STOOD IN THE DANK MUD AT THE RIVER'S edge and listened to cars whizzing by on the bridge over his head. In the near cool of morning, the concrete pillars around him emitted a clammy chill. There was a smell down here of muddy water and rotting vegetation. Part of a Styrofoam chest, lost off somebody's boat, lay half-buried in ooze.

Buddy could feel his heart beating. He could smell his own rank smell mingling with the other odors around him.

If Buddy had been smart, which he would be the first to admit was questionable, he would have gotten here to cross the bridge early, when the traffic was light and the chances of being seen slim. He hadn't done that. Hell, he hadn't thought about the river at all until fifteen minutes ago, when he was in the woods pissing by a tree and caught a glimpse of it in the distance. After he arrived and assessed the situation, he had scrambled down the bank with the thought, humorous as it was, that he might find a skiff here, or even swim across. He took three seconds to discover that his fairy godmother had not left any skiff for him, and two more seconds to decide he wasn't about to swim. Get into that water? No way. So here he was, listening to the cars go by.

Buddy's jailbreak was turning out to be a bigger pain than he'd anticipated. Mainly, he was a lot more scared than he had imagined he'd be. The idea of standing out and hitching a ride, which had seemed perfectly reasonable back at the Correctional Facility, struck him as suicidal craziness now. With the fear in him, he believed anybody who stopped to pick him up would know right away he was Buddy Burke, escaped convict, armed and dangerous. Except Buddy wasn't armed and dangerous. He only wished he was.

When he thought about Joy, some of his zip came back. He would get the story, the full story, on Mr. S. He would, God help him, buy his daughter, Kimmie Dee, a pair of boots.

Overhead, the car sounds stopped. Buddy stepped back to look. Nothing. He scrambled up the bank and had almost made it to the roadbed when a semi rounded the curve and roared past him, nearly blowing him off his feet with the gust of hot air and gravel it created going by. Buddy lost his purchase and slipped a ways, and then the cars started again. He returned to his shelter under the bridge.

Buddy had tromped through the woods until late the night before, unsure where he was heading until by sheer luck he found himself at Sawmill. The gas station and the convenience store attached to it were about to close. It must have been eleven o'clock or thereabouts when he went in to buy himself a Coke and some beef jerky sticks. The clerk was more interested in closing up than he was in watching Buddy, so after Buddy paid, he stole a Reese's peanut butter cup, slipping it in his pocket on the way out the door, sweating like a pig the whole time. He hadn't even eaten the damn thing. It was still in his pocket, probably smushed by now.

Buddy had slept last night, what sleep he got, in a spider-filled woodshed behind a brick ranch house in the middle of nowhere. The house was dark, no car in the drive, no dogs in the wire pen out back, a satellite dish near the shed like a big white moon.

Buddy was pretty sure nobody was home. He thought about breaking in and watching some TV but was afraid somebody might be there, after all. He dozed barely two hours in the woodshed before the sky started to brighten and he went on his way and got stuck here at the river.

The sun was up good and proper now. A yellow jacket buzzed past and the mosquitoes were getting bothersome. Water sloshed at the toes of Buddy's boots. Across the river, next to the bridge, was a low wooden structure with a painted sign: RIVERSIDE TAVERN. It put Buddy in mind of the song: "Gonna lay down my burden, down by the riverside, down by the riverside—"

No cars were coming. He'd make it this time. He galloped up the bank and onto the bridge. There was no walkway on either side. Feet pounding, hugging the railing, he sprinted forward. His boots were so heavy, he could barely lift his legs. If a car came, he would slow down but keep walking. He didn't want to look scared or like it wasn't perfectly natural to cross this bridge on foot.

He heard a car behind him. His backbone prickling, he slowed to a fast walk and didn't turn around. The car swooshed past, horn blaring. Buddy didn't give him the finger or even look up. He was halfway, more than halfway, across.

He picked up to a trot, and first thing you know he had made it, was standing in the packed-clay parking lot of the Riverside Tavern, bending and heaving to catch his breath. His sense of triumph was so keen that he thought he'd go in the tavern and have a beer, early as it was, to celebrate, but of course when he looked closer, he saw the place was locked up tighter than a drum. He was propped against the building, still breathing hard, when he saw the back wheel of the motorcycle.

There was a motorcycle behind the tavern, half-covered with a tarpaulin.

Buddy moseyed back there, took off the tarp, and inspected the machine. A Yamaha. Some trusting soul had even left a helmet hanging from the handlebars. Buddy loved motorcycles. He'd had several. Joy had made him sell the last one when Toby was born.

In a lean-to in back of the Riverside Tavern, Buddy found paint cans, brushes with their bristles stuck together, a quantity of rags, a tackle box filled with rusty fishhooks and moldering lures, and several kinds of wire. He found enough makeshift equipment so he could easily crank the motorcycle. Without letting himself think about it too much, that's what he proceeded to do. The engine spit and roared into life. "Aw, baby," Buddy said.

Nobody came rushing out of the Riverside Tavern to demand an explanation. "Let's go, baby," Buddy said. He stuffed his cap in his pocket and put the helmet on. He didn't even have to adjust the strap.

He wheeled around and putted down to the road. He loved this machine. Loved it. Next break in the traffic, he was on his way. The sun was strong now, warming his forearms, and the wind was full in his face. In a short while, he passed a sign that told him he was only five miles from Alma.

23

I RECKON HE ESCAPED SO HE COULD BRING ME SOME boots," said Kimmie Dee Burke. She pronounced it *ex-scaped.*

"Maybe," said Isabel. "Be still for a second more, all right?"

Kimmie Dee was sitting on an upturned bucket by the trailer door, a crocheted shawl of Merriam's draped around her head and shoulders. She looked more striking than Isabel had anticipated. In repose, her face had a pensive sweetness that was almost too appealing for the villainous Marotte. Isabel was working as swiftly as she could, since Kimmie Dee was not the most patient sitter in the world.

"I'm hot with this thing on," the girl complained.

"Just half a second, all right? Look the other way, like you were doing before."

Kimmie Dee sighed but resumed the pose. Great. Isabel made a few modifications. "Okay. All done."

Kimmie Dee took off the shawl and dropped it on the step. She said, "Don't you think that's right? He's coming to bring me the boots?"

Isabel wasn't sure what to say. "Maybe so, Kimmie Dee."

"If he does bring them, I'll have two pairs."

Kimmie Dee was wearing new white majorette boots, boots Isabel had bought for her in town that morning. According to Kimmie Dee, her mother knew about their outing and its purpose. "I told her. I sure did," she had declared.

"What did she say?"

"She said okay."

"Just okay? That's all?"

"That's all. She wasn't paying much attention, because she's worried about my daddy."

Kimmie Dee studied her feet for the hundredth time. "These are just right," she pronounced. Then she said, "Isabel, I'm kind of worried."

"About what?"

"My daddy."

Why shouldn't she be worried? Still, Isabel asked. "Why?"

"I'm afraid Mr. Stiles will shoot him."

Isabel had been studying her drawings. She closed the sketchbook. "Why should Mr. Stiles do that?"

"I don't know. But he's got a gun. I saw it."

This was not good news. "Are you sure?"

Kimmie Dee nodded. "I *saw* it. It's under his jacket." Her face clouded. "I wish I could tell my daddy to stay away."

Guns were common around here. It wasn't terribly surprising that Ted Stiles would have one. "Just because Mr. Stiles has a gun, it doesn't mean he'd shoot at your father."

"I bet he would, though."

Isabel began to comprehend how upset the girl was behind her matter-of-fact facade. "Kimmie Dee, don't you think your father will turn himself in? That's what the police are hoping."

Kimmie Dee shook her head. "He's coming. He got my letter, and he's coming."

Isabel had no counterargument to make. She gave Kimmie Dee a peanut-butter-and-jelly sandwich and a glass of lemonade. Just before Kimmie Dee left, she took off her boots, dusted them with a tissue, and replaced them in their square white box. She offered the box to Isabel. "You keep them for me. Keep them here."

"Don't you want to show them to your mother?"

"No. Not right now."

Isabel hesitated. Kimmie Dee held out the box again. "All right?"

"All right."

Isabel walked Kimmie Dee to the road, watched her cross it and run to her back door, and came back down the drive. A bright green lizard on the path puffed out his chest.

Instead of turning toward the trailer, Isabel stopped to look at the house. There was her inheritance, the local landmark that should be preserved, John James's folly. Legs apart and hands clasped behind her, feeling like David confronting Goliath, she contemplated it.

Maybe she should go inside.

The thought felt as if it had been in her head for a while. She was planning to go in, of course. She had the keys in her handbag. She was planning to go in when she was ready, when the time was right.

The house stood before her, indifferent.

Isabel had first entered that house as a cowed nine-year-old, her parents recently dead. Because her father and Merriam had been estranged, she had never been inside it before. She still remembered dust motes whirling in a beam of sunshine in the wide central hallway, the hall coat tree with its threatening curved hooks, the shadows at the top of the staircase. She had followed Merriam through the door and been engulfed.

She massaged her forehead. She remembered the texture of the green velvet curtains in the parlor, the cool marble mantelpiece, the scuffed flowers on the linoleum of the kitchen floor. The front porch swing had creaked when it was pushed too far. The glass in her bedroom windows was old and distorted the light. She had no need to go in to be reminded of any of this.

A crowbar. She would need a crowbar or something to pry the boards away. A crowbar, and the keys. There was a crowbar in the trailer, in the cabinet under the sink. She went to get it.

It seemed fitting to go in the back door, since, years ago, she had left by it. Then, she had tiptoed downstairs and through the kitchen, let herself out and crossed the creaking porch. Ben was up on the road, waiting in his car. When she saw him, saw that he had really come, she had been filled with the most exquisite delight.

Crowbar and keys in hand, she rounded the back corner of the house. The back porch was sagging badly. The wooden lattice surrounding the base of the house to keep animals out had fallen down. The rusting screen was bowed, split, and curling. A cane-bottomed rocking chair lay tipped over, its rockers pointing upward. The screen door to the porch hung open.

The slats that crisscrossed the kitchen door were half-rotten, the nails rusty. She used the crowbar to loosen them, but she could almost have pulled them off by hand. She dropped the boards and searched for the right key. She found it and eased it in the lock. You have to jiggle this one a little, she suddenly remembered, and then she had turned it. The door opened.

There was a faint scurrying sound when she stepped in. Mice or rats, probably. She set her teeth. The air was baking hot, with an overpowering smell of dust and mildew. The empty kitchen cabinets stood open, and the deep sink was badly rust-stained. A shiny brown palmetto beetle, two inches long at least, scuttled across the counter, sunlight glinting on its back.

She walked into the dining room. The table and chairs were gone, the built-in sideboard empty except for a tarnished silver ladle lying on its side. She didn't remember the ladle. Had there been a punch bowl? She couldn't imagine anything she and Merriam would have had less use for.

A feather, a small curl of down, floated past her face. This room was slightly less hot. Air was coming in from somewhere. The floor in front of one of the tall windows was spotted with bird droppings. She crossed to the windows, which were nearly blocked by intruding undergrowth. Yes, one of them was open a crack. At some point, it must have been open wider, if birds had gotten in.

She continued through the downstairs rooms—the front parlor, where furniture still huddled under dust sheets in the middle of the floor; the back parlor, with an abandoned wasp's nest in a corner and a carpet rolled up against the wall; the entrance hall. The hall coat tree still stood by the door, a red baseball cap hanging on one of its hooks. Isabel picked up the cap. *Beachcomber Boatel* was embroidered on the crown in flowing white script. She hung the cap up again.

She was standing at the foot of the staircase. When she had come here with Merriam, she had never lived in a place with stairs before. They had added to her feeling that the distances in this house were enormous.

Having come this far, she wouldn't leave without looking at her former bedroom. She started up.

She was only halfway to the top when she knew something was not right. The air had a different feel up here. Instead of the deadness of neglect, it had smells, a quality of disturbance and habitation. She stood still, her head raised, her hand on the banister rail.

She heard nothing except sounds she was now accustomed to, the creakings and scrabblings that accompanied emptiness. She thought about the red gasoline can she had seen on the front steps, the open window, the cap hanging on the hall tree.

Everything was quiet. She took another step, two more. Her head was even with the landing now. The landing was ringed with doors, all but one of them closed. The door to the corner back bedroom, the room that had been hers, stood ajar. A beam of light sifted out and made a dim gold track across the floorboards.

She had reached the top of the stairs. She called out, "Hello? Is anybody here?"

Silence. An insect whined. She crossed the landing and pushed the open door.

It swung inward silently and she stood on the threshold. Nobody was in the room, but it was neither empty nor uninhabited. Sunlight, coming in through torn places in the disintegrating window shades, illuminated a roomful of clutter: a sleeping bag, a tangle of snorkels and masks, an ice chest, a wadded T-shirt. In the middle of the floor lay three medium-sized iron balls, their surfaces flaking with rust. In the corner where her bed used to be were shelves holding a battered-looking pewter pitcher, an enamel dishpan, various distorted-looking pieces of metal, bottles of chemicals.

"Anybody here?" she said again, with less trepidation. She stepped into the room. Somebody had been staying here in reasonable comfort, it seemed. She looked in the ice chest. Half-submerged in a sloshy combination of water and ice were cartons of yogurt, a package of cheese, a jar of peanut butter, a couple of bottles of club soda, and a tomato.

She checked the closet. It was empty except for a pile of burlap sacks in the darkest corner. She started to close the door again, then reached in and looked underneath the pile. Concealed there was a beige plastic tackle box closed with a combination lock. She pulled at the lock, but it didn't give. After a minute or two, she rearranged the burlap over it. Why padlock a tackle box?

Someone had been here all this time, living in her old room, hiding.

She knelt to examine the iron balls. She poked at one, then picked it up. It was about the size to fit in her two cupped hands, heavy, rusty enough so the surface crumbled against her fingers. She wondered for a moment whether these could be old-fashioned bowling balls, then shook her head. Surely they were cannonballs. She put down the one she was holding, wiped her hands against the legs of her shorts, and moved on to the objects on the shelves. There was the pewter pitcher, as well as bottles of chemicals, a coffee can containing square-headed nails, several misshapen pieces of corroded metal. And an enamel dishpan half full of pieces of broken porcelain.

Blue-and-white porcelain.

She sorted through the dishpan, picked out a large piece, and took it nearer the window. Flowering branches and flying birds: The pattern was identical to the pattern of the bottle in the trailer, the bottle John James had given Merriam.

Isabel stood by the window, rubbing her thumb over the porcelain surface. She was thinking hard about Harry Mercer.

After a while, she put the fragment in her pocket. When she left, she closed the door of the room until it stood as it had been. She descended the stairs noiselessly and let herself out the back door.

The boards that had been nailed across the door lay with rusty nails protruding. She replaced them as best she could, pushing the nails back into their former holes. It didn't look exactly as it had before, but it didn't look too different.

The air seemed almost cool after the close atmosphere of the house. Isabel pulled her damp shirt away from her body. Crowbar in hand, she returned to the trailer.

The patterns were exactly the same. She held the bottle and the shard under a table lamp. Not only were the patterns identical but the thickness and weight of the glass seemed similar to her untrained eye. There were probably tests that could determine the truth once and for all, but for now she would assume they had come from the same place.

Which meant—what?

For one thing, it meant Harry Mercer was involved in whatever was going on in the house. His puzzling reaction to the porcelain bottle was not so puzzling now. Harry, she was sure, had known about these broken pieces.

Isabel was stung. She had responded to Harry, made love with him. The encounter had been ill-considered but full of tenderness. Or so she had thought. Now, she had to ask herself what his underlying motives were.

She snapped off the lamp. What was going on here? Cannonballs, a pewter pitcher—these objects seemed to be historical artifacts, presumably taken from a shipwreck. Harry, and whoever else was involved, wanted to keep their activities secret. That's why they had commandeered the broken-down, deserted Anders place, the old house nobody cared about.

This must have been going on while Merriam was here, too. Merriam, her eyesight and hearing not as sharp as they used to be, would have been fairly easy to fool.

Or would she? Merriam's "accident," the "fall" Isabel had found so hard to credit, began to seem even more sinister. The idea that Harry might have been involved made her sick.

The anonymous letters. Isabel had suspected Harry

of sending them. She could understand now why he would want her to go away, leave him to whatever secret operation he had going. *Now you can go back where you came from, you whore.* She thought of his promise to put a stop to the letters. What could be easier, if he was writing them himself?

All right, she had been stupid. She admitted it. She waited for the flood of heat to subside from her face.

It must be against the law to take objects from shipwrecks without permission. Surely there were regulations governing it. Shipwrecks would have historical value, archaeological importance.

Underwater archeology, you might call it.

Clem Davenant had said that, talking about his son's diving accident. Was Clem involved, too?

The thought of something more valuable than cannonballs came into her mind.

Sunken treasure? Oh please. That was a topic out of kids' adventure stories. Chests spilling over with coins, bars of gold, ropes of pearls, surrounded by cartoon fish blowing cartoon bubbles.

There had been cases in recent years, though. She reached into a hazy memory of newspaper articles skimmed on the subway. Sunken treasure, from Spanish galleons and other ships, had been found from time to time—down in the Keys, off South Carolina, in Bermuda, the Bahamas, or somewhere. Gold was recovered, millions of dollars' worth.

What she remembered best, better than she remembered anything else, was that treasure hunting was a business these days. It was carried on by well-financed consortiums with high-tech equipment and legions of experts. She had trouble squaring this with rusting cannonballs and a locked tackle box—she had just thought of the tackle box—in a bedroom in a derelict house.

She moved to the window. The house looked, as

always, deserted. The dining room window had been open a crack. That would be how he got in and out—on the other side, where she wouldn't see. She was ashamed that she'd been so easy to fool. She left the window, pacing.

The other question was the porcelain bottle. John James had given that bottle to Merriam in 1922. How did it connect with the broken pieces of porcelain in the enamel dishpan? John James Anders had not been a scuba diver, or any sort of diver. The bottle could have washed up in the storm, she supposed, although it seemed too fragile to have stayed in one piece.

She wished she could stop thinking about Harry.

Her thoughts had begun to curl in on themselves, in tighter and tighter circles. In an effort to clear her mind, she tried to work on *The Children from the Sea.* The sketches she had done of Kimmie Dee were full of verve, but right now she couldn't connect to them. She was sitting with her chin in her hands, staring at the ugly beige Formica of the tabletop, when the telephone rang.

It was Clem Davenant. "I got a call this afternoon, out of the blue. I may have a buyer for your property," he said.

"A buyer?" She could hear how vacant she sounded.

"Remember you said you'd probably have to sell?"

Sure, she'd said she'd have to sell. Of course she remembered. But that would be sometime in the future, not a mere day after she'd said it. "I didn't know you thought selling was such a good idea."

"I don't, particularly. Am I dreaming? I was sure you said—"

"You're right. I did say it. What's the story?"

There wasn't much of a story so far. Clem had gotten a call from a developer in Bay City, strictly exploratory. Clem had put the man off until he could talk to Isabel.

"I thought you might like to come over to dinner and discuss it."

"I can't keep coming to your place for dinner. Eve is going to think I'm a terrible freeloader."

"Actually, Eve will be at choir practice." While Isabel took this in, he went on. "I was going to bake a red snapper. It's my specialty. I haven't made one in a long time."

She could ask him about the underwater archaeology project. She was sick of the trailer and her thoughts. She said she'd be delighted.

When she arrived, Clem, his face flushed from the kitchen heat, was wearing a terry-cloth apron over Bermuda shorts. He said, "I'll get you a drink and put you on the porch for a few minutes, all right? Do you like garlic?"

"I love garlic." Within minutes, she was settled on the back porch with a gin and tonic, while he rattled around in the kitchen. The lawn under the moss-hung trees was dappled with the last rays of the sun, a breeze was stirring, and she felt better than she had all day.

After a short while, he joined her. As they sipped their drinks, the smell of garlic and Parmesan cheese began to fill the air. He chatted about the Bay City developer. The man wanted to build a subdivision of town houses. He had actually had his eye on the Anders property for a while. "He told me he had contacted Miss Merriam about buying it once, and she didn't even want to talk about it. He heard she'd passed on, and he didn't waste any time getting back in touch."

"He certainly didn't." Isabel wondered whether her irritation was because of the developer's indelicacy or her own ambivalence. She pictured rows of identical town houses, streets with names like Seashore Drive. What would the subdivision be called? Cape Estates?

Sunny Shores? "If Merriam didn't want to sell, it seems crummy to start doing deals before she's been dead a week."

He looked annoyed. "If I'd known you felt this way, I would have told him to back off."

"I'm sorry. I'm confused. I'm not sure what I want to do."

She gave his shoulder a conciliatory pat and was surprised when he caught her hand and squeezed her fingers briefly. He got up and said, "Better check on the snapper. It can get overdone if it's in a minute too long."

The snapper was delicious. The developer wasn't mentioned again, and Isabel couldn't quite shake the idea that he had been an excuse for the occasion. Clem, bright-eyed, talked freely, solicited her opinions, listened to them intently. There was no opportunity to bring up underwater archaeology. She noticed that he made excuses to touch her, brushing against her when he refilled her wineglass, ushering her into the living room for coffee with his hand on the small of her back.

She sat on the sofa. He poured the coffee, handed her a cup, and took a chair nearby. He said, "I'm glad you were willing to come tonight, Isabel."

"I've enjoyed it."

"This is the first time since Andrea left that I've wanted to be with somebody."

"I'm flattered."

Yet she was uncertain about Clem. She wasn't sure anyone could overmatch the darkness that had him in its grip.

He put his cup aside and moved to sit by her, taking her saucer out of her hand and putting it on a side table. When he kissed her, his ferocity was startling. He was very strong, his grip painful. His mouth ground against hers until she could hardly breathe. There was no tenderness here, no companionability, no mutuality—only his raw, desperate need.

At last, she managed to pull her head away. "Don't, Clem."

He wound his arms tightly around her, straining against her. His breath rushed, hoarse and ragged, next to her ear. He said, groaned, a word that might have been her name. She thought, *Eve—choir practice—neighbors,* and prepared herself to fight. "Stop it!" she gasped.

He shivered, pulled back, and said, "Oh God. Oh no." He let her go and sat forward, his face in his hands.

Isabel cooled her lips with cold fingertips. Her face prickled from being raked by his beard. It had happened so fast. She could still taste her last swallow of coffee.

"Sorry," Clem said, his voice tight.

Isabel was still too astonished to speak. All right, she had seen it coming, but—Clem Davenant? He was so proper, so buttoned-down.

"Don't walk out. Don't leave," he said. "Wait a while, all right? Eve will be back pretty soon."

Warily, Isabel began, "Clem, I can't—"

"Just stay, don't walk out. Here. Your coffee's still warm." He handed it to her, the cup clattering against the saucer.

She took it and drank. It was only lukewarm.

He retrieved his own cup and returned to sit beside her. After a few minutes, he said, "I haven't been functioning. As a man, I mean. For a while it didn't matter, but now I'm getting—desperate."

"I understand."

"It doesn't give me the right to prey on you."

"No."

He said, "Don't worry. I'm not going to bend your ear about Edward again."

She had wanted to talk about Edward, hadn't she? "I don't mind."

"No. It's time to stop imposing, on you and everybody."

"Actually, I was wondering about something. The underwater archaeology project you mentioned."

"The *Esperanza?* It was stupid."

"What was the *Esperanza?*"

He grimaced. "The Spanish ship Edward and I were diving for. At least, it was the excuse."

Rusting cannonballs, square-headed nails, a pewter pitcher. "That was your project?"

"Right. Come and look." He seemed relieved to have something to talk about.

She followed him down the hall to the room where, on her first visit, she had found him looking at his shell collection. He flicked on the light. The shells were still there, delicate and beautiful in their glass case. A desk stood under the windows. The walls were lined with bookcases overflowing with books and documents. "I hate this stuff. I want to get rid of it all," Clem said. "It's just that I can't. I try, and I can't."

He opened a drawer, brought out a fat accordion file, and tossed it on the desk.

Isabel picked up the file and glanced through it. Pages of calculations, notes, a rough map.

"The search for the *Esperanza,*" said Clem with sarcastic solemnity. "The last great father-son adventure of Clem and Edward Davenant."

This was not a coincidence. There had to be a connection between Clem's project and the artifacts she had found in the house. Isabel said, "The *Esperanza* was a Spanish ship?"

Clem shoved his hands in the pockets of his shorts and looked out at the night. "Yes, she was Spanish. The *Esperanza* was what they called a *patache,* an all-purpose packet boat. A *patache* wasn't a prestige vessel—more of a scout or an escort to an armada. Some *pataches* did carry treasure, though. The *Esperanza* did. Edward and I looked into this, you see. Read up on it. That was part of my plan."

"Your plan?"

"To get him interested in scuba diving. So he could get some healthy outdoor exercise. I thought, What could appeal to a twelve-year-old kid more than a treasure hunt?"

Clem continued to look out into the darkness. "It was an excuse, that's all," he said. "If we'd been serious, we'd have had to follow a lot of regulations, get permits from the state. It was a fantasy."

"How did you learn about the *Esperanza?*"

"The *Esperanza* is no secret. There are plenty of books about treasure hunting and Spanish wrecks. The *Esperanza* gets mentioned sometimes, along with a lot of other ships that are out there somewhere."

He turned to face her. "You know, Spain shipped gold and silver and other stuff over from the New World for several centuries. When a ship sank, the Spaniards hated to let it go. They put a lot of effort into salvaging it themselves, but that wasn't always possible. A lot of treasure was left down there. You don't hear much about treasure wrecks in these waters, but the ships used to leave Veracruz, in Mexico, and sail along the Gulf Coast to Havana, so it isn't inconceivable. Or at least, that's what Edward and I figured."

He took the file from her and shuffled through it with trembling fingers. "Edward got interested. He liked it. I didn't force it on him. That's what I have to remember."

"What happened to the *Esperanza?*"

He put the file down. "The *Esperanza* left Veracruz as part of an armada in 1725, heading for Havana. They ran into bad weather and the other ships lost sight of her. She was never seen again. They kept close track of these things in Spain, and in the archives it was noted that her cargo included gold, silver, and Chinese porcelain. That's most of what I know about the *Esperanza*. The rest is conjecture."

Chinese porcelain. Gold, silver. "What did you conjecture?"

"I challenged Edward to figure out whether the ship could have ended up near Cape Cache. I mean, this was a project with everything—history, geography, meteorology, astronomy. You have to figure currents and weather, know latitude and longitude. I told him if he pinpointed some possible locations, we'd go diving and search for it. I told you he was smart. He ate it up. He was so caught up in the *Esperanza* project, we had to make a rule that he couldn't work on it until he'd done his homework."

"And did you—" Isabel cleared her throat. "Did you find it?"

"Oh, hell no," he said dismissively. "I don't think either of us really expected to. Edward did a lot of calculations and figured out several general areas where he thought it could be. I mean, all of this is such a long shot. People don't realize how big the ocean is, how hard it is to locate anything. We knew that. We weren't serious." His face grew more solemn. "Not serious," he repeated.

"And you were searching one of Edward's locations when—"

"When he died, yeah," he said, almost angrily. "We'd just started. There were some beams down there, loose lumber, and he got pinned. He was panicking; his mouthpiece came out. I couldn't get to him—" He closed his eyes for a moment, swallowing. "I got his weight belt unhooked and dragged him to the surface. I don't know how I got him on the boat. He was limp. He was—he was dead, but I didn't know. I radioed for help, tried to resuscitate him. Another boat came up soon, then several more, but it was too late."

The silence stretched out. Isabel said, "The people who came to help—were they people you knew?"

He thought. "A couple were tourists. The first boat to get there was a scuba party coming in from diving nearby. A local captain, Harry Mercer."

Yes, Harry Mercer. She said, "Harry Mercer and I were in high school together."

"He tried to help. His deckhand made several dives to retrieve our equipment. But there was nothing anybody could do for Edward."

Headlights shone through the window, and in a minute Isabel heard the front door open. Eve's voice called, "Clem? I'm home."

"We're back here."

Footsteps sounded in the hall. Eve stuck her head in the door. "Hello, Isabel. What are you doing in here, Clem?"

"Just—talking."

"Talking?" She clasped her hands nervously. "Isabel, I hope he hasn't been depressing you. It would be so much better if he'd—"

Clem turned on her. "For God's sake, Eve! Leave me alone!"

Her face flushed. "Sorry." She stepped back. "Excuse me."

As her footsteps receded, Isabel said, "I'd better go."

He gestured at the file. "I'm going to throw all of it away. That'll make Eve happy."

He walked her to the door and she said good night. When she pulled out of the driveway, she could see him through the windows. He was back in the study, sitting at the desk, his head in his hands.

24

AT 7:15 A.M., WHEN HARRY WALKED OUT OF HIS BEDROOM at the Beachcomber, Scooter was already on the dock, leaning against a post and eating one of his yogurts with a plastic spoon. They were scheduled to take out a dive party. Harry had not mentioned to Scooter that he and Kathy were separated, and he could see by the set of Scooter's body that Scooter was wondering what he had been doing in the room.

Their party was nowhere in sight. Harry waved at Scooter and veered off toward the restaurant to get some coffee. He was a little hung over from spending the evening at the bar, and the sun on the water wasn't helping.

Harry had moved out on Kathy. The thought was still strange to him. He was living in a room with twin beds, dingy orange curtains, a braided rug on the floor that looked like the potholders his daughters used to make at camp, a toilet that gurgled all night, and a television that showed more static than picture.

But he was glad. It had been coming a long time; he saw that now. He got his coffee and, carrying the giant-sized Styrofoam tumbler, left the restaurant and walked along the dock toward the *Miss Kathy* and Scooter.

The air was still and moist, full of the scent of the many fish that had been cleaned in the neighborhood. Ripples washed against the barnacle-encrusted pilings. Scooter had gone back to his yogurt, and the sight of the spoonfuls of pink stuff going into Scooter's mouth made Harry's stomach more sour. He blotted his face with his napkin and hardened himself to face Scooter's level gaze, which didn't exactly inquire why Harry was sleeping here but made Harry feel he had to say something. He delayed for a minute by asking, "The boat gassed up?"

Scooter nodded.

"Everything on board?"

Another nod.

Harry waved toward number twenty-one, the room he was occupying. "I've moved out here for a while," he said. He tried to sound as if it didn't much matter, and basically he thought he succeeded.

Scooter had gotten still. He looked as if he was listening to something besides what Harry had told him. "Yeah? Why?" he asked.

"Well . . ." Harry took a swallow of scalding coffee and choked it down. "Kathy and I haven't been getting along too good."

Scooter walked to the garbage can next to the bait tanks and dropped in his cup and spoon. When he returned, he braced himself against the post and started stretching out his hamstrings. He was wearing his usual ragged cutoffs and sneakers without socks. His hair was skinned back in the ponytail he wore diving. Harry watched him press down one heel and then the other. His head lowered, Scooter said, "This is because of Isabel."

"Isabel? What? No it isn't."

The sinews in Scooter's bare arms stood out as he gripped the post. "Don't bullshit me, Harry."

Harry was getting a crick in his neck. He eased his head around, trying to work it out. "Answer me one thing," he said.

No response.

"What the hell is it to you?"

Scooter didn't reply right away. His head still bent, he continued to press his heels down. Finally, he stood upright and looked at Harry. "She went into the house," he said.

A goose walked over Harry's grave. "Why do you say that?"

"Because somebody was in there. She was in there."

Scooter began doing deep knee bends. Why he didn't barf that yogurt, Harry did not understand. "How do you know?"

"I felt it."

"You— Was anything moved? Was anything missing?"

"No."

"Then what in the hell did you feel?"

"I felt a presence."

Scooter moved smoothly, effortlessly, up and down. He could keep going for a long time, Harry knew, up and down and up and down until a sheen broke out on his shoulders and upper lip, but still he wouldn't be breathing hard. "It's time to put a stop to it, Harry," Scooter said.

Harry shaded his eyes and looked toward the parking lot. "Where in the hell are those folks? We're losing time."

Scooter's tanned back moved up and down. "I don't care what you've got going with her, Harry. It's time."

Harry thought about Isabel going into the house. Goddamn. He wanted to punch something.

A couple of minutes later, the people in the morning dive party came trailing up, full of excuses, and they were ready to leave at last.

25

ISABEL HUNCHED FORWARD, STARING AT THE BLUE-AND-white bottle. She had been trying to draw the bottle all morning.

It should have been easy, a beginner's exercise. The bottle was square. At the top, the corners modulated into rounded, sloping shoulders culminating in a short neck. It was a simple, unpretentious shape, yet she had been unable to capture it. Her attempts were so awkward, they would have been an embarrassment in a mail-order art course.

Isabel wanted to believe that if she could produce a clean sketch of the bottle, it would help her figure out what was going on. If she could see it clearly—but she couldn't. Images arose, clouding her vision: Clem Davenant with his face in his hands, cannonballs on the floor of her bedroom, Harry Mercer's face when he said, "I'm still here."

Clem and Edward must have located the shipwreck without knowing it. Harry and his deckhand came to Clem's rescue, and the deckhand dove to retrieve their equipment. He must have found something then, enough to interest them in exploring further. By that time, Clem had other problems. He wasn't likely to lay claim to the *Esperanza.*

Isabel might as well give up on drawing the bottle.

Her eyes moved to the photograph above it, the sepia-toned portrait of her grandfather—John James. He gazed into the distance with bulbous, unseeing eyes, a man whose essence was mystery, a man who had handed his daughter a Chinese porcelain bottle and was claimed by the sea he had foolishly defied.

Isabel began to see John James's disappearance as the force that had driven them all these years. The extravagant, burdensome house stood as his monument. He was the deity Merriam had set up her altar to. John James was a myth.

Or was he? Isabel put the pencil behind her ear and told herself to get real. John James Anders was not a myth. His disappearance had not taken place in a misty ancient age, but in 1922. Even if you saw it as symbolic, there were facts involved.

She considered those facts: There was a terrible storm. A tramp called River Pete took shelter with the family. The baby had colic. John James and River Pete cleared out fallen trees. John James checked the foundation of the house. Over his wife's protestations, he decided to take his boat to St. Elmo. Merriam walked him to the landing and he gave her the porcelain bottle and a letter for her mother. Merriam lost the letter on the way home. John James never came back.

The story was as smooth and self-contained as an egg—no handles, no rough corners.

Isabel tossed her sketchbook aside, went to the refrigerator, and poured herself a glass of iced tea. She had started keeping a pitcher made, the way Merriam used to. If she kept her mind on John James, she wouldn't have to think about Harry. She wouldn't have to wonder whether Merriam had discovered what Harry was up to.

Divers wore hoods sometimes with their wet suits. Harry was a diver. She didn't want to go on from there and ask herself whether Harry was the man in the hood, the figure who had terrified Merriam.

John James's story was complete. Isabel had had the images in her head since she was a girl, and Merriam had stood her in front of John James's picture and told her the story for the first time.

She finished her tea and put her glass down, mulling over each element of the tale. River Pete, the tramp. She had never thought much about him, but now she found herself wondering what had happened to River Pete.

Isabel supposed River Pete had gone on about his business. He had lived on the beach in a driftwood shack that blew away in the storm. He did odd jobs at a store, Pursey's store. He and John James sometimes went hunting or fishing together. River Pete had helped John James clear the fallen trees. His final appearance in the tale came when Merriam saw him at the pump by the back door, where he was washing mud off his hands and beard.

River Pete might have known something about the bottle. He was there that day. He might have known where John James got a piece of porcelain from the *Esperanza.*

He might've, but he would be dead by now. Isabel didn't know whether he'd stayed in the area. She didn't even know his last name. It was a shame she'd never asked Merriam about it.

There might be other old-timers around who remembered him, though. People who would know, at least, whether he'd stayed around, or had children. River Pete had worked at a store, so he would have been a familiar face.

Isabel went to the phone table and found the *St. Elmo and Vicinity* directory. Pursey's store. Merriam had mentioned the store in other reminiscences. As far as Isabel knew, it didn't exist anymore. She had the impression it had been the place nearest Cape Cache to buy supplies.

She leafed through the directory. Each community was listed separately. No Purseys in St. Elmo, none on

Cape Cache, none in Westpoint. She riffled through the *P*'s in the rest of the book. Nothing, nothing, nothing, noth—jackpot. Not one, not two, but three Purseys—J.G., N.K., and L.B.—listed at Turpentine Creek.

Turpentine Creek, to Isabel's faint recollection, was a tiny community on the edge of the river swamp, at least twenty-five miles away. She probably couldn't even find it without a map.

She drummed her fingers on the open page. J. G. Pursey, N. K. Pursey, L. B. Pursey. An embarrassment of riches.

Thinking hard, she was startled when the phone rang. She heard Harry's voice and her fingers tightened on the receiver.

"I was hoping I'd catch you," he said. She heard conversation and music in the background. "Can I stop by tonight?"

"No. No, you can't."

"Listen, Isabel—" His voice dropped. "I want to talk to you."

"No, Harry."

She pressed the button to break the connection. Listening to the dial tone, she ran her finger down the page to the telephone number of J. G. Pursey.

26

BUDDY BURKE SAT ON A STUMP AT THE EDGE OF A FIELD. Twilight was descending. The field was overgrown with weeds. Junked cars rusted among them.

Another night on the road. Buddy didn't know whether he could stand it. He was so hungry, he couldn't keep track of anything besides his hunger. Buddy had done various stupid things since he'd gotten out, and he knew he'd done some of them because he hadn't had enough to eat.

Like throwing away the motorcycle. The thought of it brought tears to Buddy's eyes. Oh, if only he had kept that machine. It had gotten him past Alma before it ran out of gas. If he had been himself, he would have checked the gauge, nothing easier than checking the gauge, but he hadn't been himself, and when the cycle ran out of gas, Buddy got mad. He got the feeling the whole world was pissing on him. So what he did was to wheel it across the tall grass on the shoulder and pushed it down the culvert, all the time yelling, "*Run* out of gas, you son of a bitch!"

Buddy could still see the cycle bouncing down the incline, hear it crash at the bottom, see the helmet tumbling after it. If he'd been in his right mind, he wouldn't have done that, for two reasons: First, he could have gotten some gas and continued riding the cycle, and probably been at Cape Cache by now; second, the cycle would be found, and more than likely somebody would figure Buddy had stolen it, and they'd know which way Buddy was heading.

Losing (Buddy preferred to call it losing) the cycle had taken the heart out of Buddy somewhat. He had continued walking through the woods, miles and miles of woods. Sometimes he followed the road and sometimes the railroad tracks. He lost any sense of where he was. He had intended to head for the coast, but here he was at a junked-car field.

Buddy needed food, not the bits of this and that—candy bars and peanut butter crackers, jerky sticks and canned Vienna sausages—he'd been eating. Buddy needed a square meal, so he could think. Fried chicken, scalloped potatoes, corn bread.

Buddy stood up and plunged his hand in the pocket of his new jeans. He had gotten the jeans this afternoon, taken them off a clothesline. He'd needed to change clothes so he wouldn't fit whatever description they'd put out. He had buried his other pants, piling pine straw on the place to hide the dug-up earth. His yellow cap was gone. He wasn't sure when he'd lost it. He was almost as sorry about the cap as he was about the motorcycle.

Buddy pulled his money out and counted. Seven dollars. He started walking toward the road, keeping to the woods at the perimeter of the field. By the time he got there, it was just about dark. Several cars were coming. Buddy stepped to the roadside and stuck out his thumb.

The cars passed him by. In the lull that followed, Buddy had time to wonder why he was hitching now, whether it was a good idea, but only in a vague way. He seemed to be following an order. When the next headlights approached, he stuck his thumb out again.

The car stopped, and Buddy felt a spasm in his chest. "All right, then," he muttered, and ran to open the door.

The driver was a middle-aged woman. She wore a blouse with a bow at the neck and square glasses, and her dark hair had been teased and sprayed into immobility. At first glance, she resembled Buddy's Aunt Grace. "Guess you do need a ride, standing in the dark. What are you doing out here?" she said.

Buddy didn't even have to think hard. "Truck broke down. I got to go into—into town and get a part." What town? Buddy had no idea.

"Into Brewton?" the blessed lady, so much like Aunt Grace, said.

"Yes, ma'am. Brewton." Buddy slid down in the seat. Brewton. He hadn't strayed as far off the trail as he'd feared.

"That's where I'm going. I'll drop you at the filling station."

"Thank you, ma'am." Buddy looked at the blurred black tees skimming by. The air conditioner was on. The seat was soft. His eyes started to close.

"Tell me something," the lady said.

Buddy roused himself. "Yes, ma'am?"

"It's kind of a personal question."

Buddy tried to assemble an explanation, an apology really, for his body odor. Working hard all day, truck down, no place to take a shower. "What's that?"

The lady's face was serious. "Have you accepted Jesus as your Savior and Lord?"

Whoa. Buddy settled on what he considered to be, under the circumstances, the only possible response. "I tell you what," he said. "I have. I surely have."

The lady seemed disappointed. "Fully and completely? Without doubt and fear?"

"Well . . . mostly," Buddy said. He didn't want to get put out of the car because he was already saved.

Mollified, the lady said, "Doubts do come, don't they? What doubts do you have?"

Buddy felt the bristles on his face. He wondered what

he had done to deserve this. "It's awful hard to be good sometimes," he said after some thought.

"Yes!" That set her off. She went on to tell Buddy, giving chapter and verse, why it was so hard to be good. Buddy, heavy-lidded, nodded every now and then and bit the inside of his cheek to keep himself from falling asleep. Before she'd had a chance to check back with him about his other doubts and fears, they were entering the city limits of Brewton.

Buddy was saying, "Thanks" as the lady pulled up at the gas station, but she interrupted him by leaning on the horn and yelling out the window, "Oscar! Oscar!"

Buddy was rigid. "Don't bother to call him," he said as he opened the door.

"Oscar!"

A swarthy man emerged from the station. "Oscar, this young man needs a part from you. A part for his truck," the lady said.

Buddy was out on the concrete by now. "What do you need?" Oscar was asking while the lady looked on with interest.

Buddy couldn't think. "I got to—I got to"—his mouth had dried up—"call my brother. Find out exactly what." Buddy looked down the block. He could see a Dairy Queen. "They got a phone down there?"

"We got one here," Oscar said. He looked as if he thought Buddy might be an escaped convict.

"I'll be back," Buddy said. He bent and waved goodbye to the lady, then turned and walked energetically toward the Dairy Queen. Let them call the sheriff. At least he'd have time for a hamburger first.

As it happened, he ate three. With onions. And an order of fries. And a chocolate milk shake. He was almost out of money, but his stomach was full. He walked on, out of the city limits.

He had been too hungry to think about Joy in a while,

or Kimmie Dee and the boots, but now they returned to his mind. The thought of what he'd been through because of Joy made Buddy sweat with fury.

A few houses were clustered along the road on the outskirts of town. A pickup sat in the driveway of one of the houses, and by the porch light Buddy could see a shotgun on the rack in its cab.

Now that he'd eaten, Buddy wasn't as afraid as he'd been before. He sidled up to the truck. No dogs barked. He pressed gently on the door handle and felt it give as the door opened. Reaching into the cab, he extracted the gun from the rack and slid back out of the truck. He leaned against the door until it clicked shut again.

It's awful hard to be good sometimes. Carrying the stolen gun, Buddy left Brewton behind him.

PART THREE

27

ISABEL DROVE ALONG THE STATE ROAD, SCANNING THE horizon for the fire tower. The young man she'd talked to on the phone, one of the Purseys, had told her, "Turn at the fire tower and keep going for about ten miles. You won't have any trouble getting here unless there's a good rain tonight."

The young Pursey, whose name she never got, had answered the N. K. Pursey's phone. He had seemed unfazed by—or, more likely, uninterested in—her lurching story of trying to locate River Pete, a former Pursey employee. When she finished, he said cheerfully, "You say that was back when the store was at Cape Cache?"

"Yes."

"You ought to talk to Donna. Donna's the one keeps up with all that."

So Isabel, after a night of thinking what a waste of time it was, was on her way to talk to Donna. She pictured Donna Pursey as a blue-haired matron who spent her days studying genealogical charts and family trees.

The road was lined with cattail-choked ditches, and cattle grazed in the shade of spreading oaks. Occasionally, there was a tangled wood, half-choked by kudzu vines. A flock of blackbirds wheeled and settled on a field of half-grown corn.

She saw the fire tower up ahead. At the intersection, there was a wooden sign—TURPENTINE CREEK—with an arrow. Smaller signs appended said, LOTS AVAILABLE and BOAT LANDING. She turned off on the secondary road.

As she continued, the terrain became swampier, the

bumpy road passing stands of silver-leaved bay trees and still, murky ponds covered with lily pads and bordered with moss-hung cypresses. Sometimes the tree branches met over the road, creating a sun-splashed tunnel. The hot air rushing in the car window had a brackish smell.

When she passed a few small cabins, she began looking for the house where she'd been told to meet Donna. Its major identifying feature, according to the young man who'd given her directions, was a fence made of whitewashed truck tires.

A few miles farther along, she caught sight of the fence. The tires, half-buried, made a scalloped border around a rambling frame house set back under chinaberry trees. When she pulled up in front and got out of the car, a boy in a baseball cap appeared on the screened porch. "You the one looking for Donna?" he shouted. "She said to tell you she's down to the landing." He pointed to an extension of the road, a narrow track under a canopy of oaks. "Leave your car here, if you want."

Isabel walked along the dusty, rutted trail. She smelled rotting vegetation and heard a dog barking. She emerged from beneath the trees into a basin of red clay opening on a dark brown creek. Cars with boat trailers attached ringed the basin, and several boats were in the water, moored to a makeshift dock.

Across the basin, an open-sided pavilion made of unpainted lumber sheltered a ragged sofa, folding chairs, a trestle table with a camp stove, and a blackened coffeepot. TURPENTINE CREEK LANDING SPORTSMAN'S PARADISE was painted in crude letters on the roof of the pavilion. Back on higher ground stood a concrete-block building with a metal sign—TURPENTINE LANDING GENERAL STORE—over the door.

The place was deserted except for a large black mongrel dog with a plume of a tail standing on the bank and a figure in overalls sitting in one of the moored boats, tinkering with an outboard motor. As Isabel approached, the tinkering figure looked up and called, "Hey there! You Isabel Anders?"

It was, Isabel realized, a woman, with straight dark hair raggedly cut off at shoulder length. Under the overalls, she wore a white T-shirt with flapping sleeves. She stood and wiped her hands on a rag, which she replaced in her pocket, leaving the end trailing out. She was gaunt-faced, probably in her mid-fifties, and when she stood and jumped from the boat to the clay bank, Isabel saw she was at least six feet tall.

"Donna Pursey," the woman said, offering a smudged hand, and Isabel's vision of the blue-haired matron with the family trees vanished. As the black dog yipped and danced around them, Donna Pursey jerked her head toward the boat. "Got to get it running right before I take off up the river in the morning." She gestured at the pavilion. "Want coffee? Won't take but a second to heat it up."

The coffee was strong, and bitter as bile. Isabel's eyes watered when she took her first swallow. A boat came along the creek, motor chugging, and the dog ran to the bank and barked as it passed. The men in the boat raised hands in languid greeting and Donna waved back. Donna said, "Joey—that's my nephew—told me you want to know something about the store Granddaddy used to have down at Cape Cache."

"I'm trying to trace someone who used to do odd jobs there. Back in the twenties."

Donna leaned forward, cradling her tin mug. "The twenties? There was hardly anybody there back in those days. Cape Cache got too built-up for us after a while, though. Way too many people. One day in 1955, Daddy said, 'That's it,' and moved the whole shebang out here. Our store used to be where Margene's MiniMart is now.

Daddy and Granddaddy sold everything there—fish bait, ladies' hats, hard candy, rat poison. Not like it is now, with sorry little plastic inner tubes and suntan lotion."

"I don't know much about the person I'm trying to trace. Not even his last name."

Donna took a swig of coffee "I'll do what I can to help you. I'm the only one keeps up with the stories. They want to know something, they ask Donna. I ought to write it down, but I never do." She chuckled. "I tell them, 'What are y'all going to do when you can't ask Donna?' I ought to write it, but I'm a whole lot better at fishing than I am at writing. About to go up the river and drown some worms, once I get my motor running."

The black dog came and rested his head on Isabel's knee, gazing at her with adoring brown eyes. She settled back on the musty sofa. The second swallow of coffee went down more easily than the first.

Donna said, "See, I used to be so bad, beating up my brothers, getting in trouble, that they'd punish me by making me stay in the store with Grandma and Granddaddy instead of going out to play. I got so I liked it, sitting there listening to their tales. So then I'd get in more trouble, so I'd get to stay at the store with them. Lordy, I could get in the most mischief. One time—" She laughed and shook her head. "Never mind. What did you want to know?"

"I'm trying to trace a tramp who did odd jobs at the store in the twenties. All I know is that he was called River Pete."

"River Pete." Donna gazed out over the basin, her mug balanced on her knee. "There used to be tramps from time to time, all right. Even I remember some, from when I was little. They'd stay awhile, then go on. Maybe they were in bad with the law; maybe they drank too much, or gambled too much, or were just down on their luck. Granddaddy believed in giving a helping hand, so he'd let them work in exchange for what they needed—chewing tobacco, grits, beans, or like that."

"Did he ever mention one called River Pete?"

She shook her head. "I don't remember the names, really. I ought to write it down."

So much for that. The dog's tail thumped on the rough floorboards.

"Don't give up yet," Donna said, "This doesn't always work, but we could try asking Daddy. Seems like he's having a pretty good day." She seemed to come to a decision. "Come on up to the store. Let's see what we can do."

Isabel followed Donna and the black dog up the bank. In front of the store, another dog, this one yellow, lay sleeping in the sun in front of a Coke machine. Just inside the screen door a shriveled old man, also in overalls, sat watching a rerun of "The Brady Bunch" on a small television set on the counter. On the shelves behind him, cans of vegetables sat beside fishing tackle and shotgun shells. Behind the cash register hung a dingy oil painting of a person in overalls, possibly the same old man, standing in front of a building that was dimly recognizable as the one they had just entered. There was a smell of bug spray.

Donna touched the old man's shoulder. "Hey, Daddy?"

The old man twitched his shoulder, but his eyes didn't move from the screen.

Donna raised her voice. "This lady has a question! About when we had the store at Cape Cache!"

Mr. Pursey seemed unimpressed.

"Daddy—"

"Wait for the commercial!" snapped Mr. Pursey in a reedy voice.

Two commercial breaks came and went before Mr.

Pursey consented to give some thought to Donna's question. "River Pete!" Donna bawled. "A tramp! Do you remember?"

The old man drew back and glared at Donna. He bared yellow teeth and cried, "You remember him, girl! The twenty dollars!"

Donna sagged against the counter. "Oh my Lord," she said to Isabel. "Is he that one? If I'd known, I could've told you in the first place."

They left Mr. Pursey to the television set. Outside, they sat on a narrow bench beside the Coke machine. The yellow dog continued to sleep. The black one cavorted with delight when Isabel reappeared, jumping up to lick her hand.

Donna stretched her legs out and leaned back against the wall. "So River Pete is the twenty-dollar one. I wish I'd realized. I must've heard the story a hundred times."

The concrete wall was warm against Isabel's back. Down at the landing, a boat putted by. A dragonfly hovered briefly and darted away.

"That tramp made a big impression on my grandfather," Donna said. "He did odd jobs all right, but Granddaddy gave him credit, too. He wrote it down in the ledger, and then the tramp—Pete, I guess—would either work the amount off or go fishing and bring in a mess of fish, but some way or other he'd pay his bill. That was kind of unusual in itself, and Pete was so good about it, Granddaddy started trusting him. Then one day he went off, like they always did, and didn't come back."

"When was this?"

"Heck if I know. Long time ago." She kicked at a pebble. "Before he left, this Pete character had run up a bill of about twenty dollars, which was a lot of money in those days. Then, all of a sudden, he's gone. Granddaddy didn't worry about it much at first, because Pete had gone off before, but after a month passed, then two, and so forth, he commenced to think he'd seen the back of that tramp and lost his twenty dollars.

"Now, you didn't know my Granddaddy, but if you had, you'd know how bad that got away with him. He never wiped it off the books, because he wasn't somebody to forget being done out of twenty dollars—or twenty cents, come to that." She leaned down to scratch behind the ears of the yellow dog, and the dog heaved a slobbery sigh.

"So Pete was never heard from again?"

"Oh, yes he was. This is the good part." Donna sat up. "Five years went by. Five at least. One day in the mail, Granddaddy gets an envelope postmarked Gilead Springs. You know where that is?"

"Not far from Tallahassee?"

"Right. A hundred miles away from here, more or less. No return address on the envelope. Inside it is a twenty-dollar bill and a note—'Thanks from Pete,' or some such. 'Course, Granddaddy always said he figured after all that time Pete should've paid interest, too, but that was Granddaddy."

"You never found out what happened to Pete?"

"Not that I know of. That was the end of it. I don't know if it helps you any. Maybe Pete ended up in Gilead Springs, or maybe he just mailed the money from there."

"It would help a lot if I knew his last name."

"Shoot. I hadn't thought of that."

Inside the store, the television chattered on. The yellow dog got up, ambled a few steps into the shadow of the Coke machine, and lay down again. Another boat came into view, and the black dog scampered down to bark at it.

Donna said, "I'll bet we can find that name. Let's go look at the old books. They're back there in the office."

"The old books?"

"The records. We've got them back to 1907, when Granddaddy first opened up a store."

Donna led the way past her father, down the aisle to a door at the back. The office was dusty and disordered, the window glass smeared and the sills piled high with papers. A wildlife calendar on the wall was turned to March of 1990. Donna opened a closet door, pulled the chain on a light inside, and said, "I won't let them throw these away. I say, 'This is history, right here.' "

Isabel looked in. The floor and shelves were piled with ledger books. "I pretty much know where everything is," Donna said. "What year do you want to try?"

"Nineteen twenty-two."

"All righty. Sit down for a minute or two, why don't you?"

Isabel settled in the desk chair and Donna disappeared into the closet. Moments later, Isabel heard several thuds, and Donna said, "Damnation!"

"Can I help?"

"Nope, just give me a minute. Nineteen twenty-two. Nineteen twenty-two. It's here somewhere, you can take my word on that."

Eventually, Donna emerged, looking cobwebby, with a ledger book under her arm. She dusted the book with the rag from her pocket, shoved some of the clutter on the desk aside, and put it down in front of Isabel. "When I was a little girl, I'd look at these books for hours," she said. "It was as good as TV. There was a whole lot you could figure out from these books."

She opened the ledger. The entries were written in fading brown ink in a fastidious copperplate hand. Donna turned the pages slowly, running her finger down the columns. She tapped the page. "There's your grandma, isn't it? Polly Anders, ten pounds of cornmeal?"

"Yes, it is." Isabel thought of her grandmother, sickly Polly, cooking corn bread on a wood-burning stove.

"And here she bought some lye. See? People made their own soap. Boiled the clothes out in the backyard."

Yes, they had boiled the clothes. Isabel remembered the iron wash pot that had washed away in the storm.

"Where are you, Pete?" Donna said. She turned a page. "Here we go. Granddaddy gave him five cents worth of tobacco on credit."

The notation was: "River Pete A.—tobacco—5 cnts." "It doesn't show his last name," Isabel said, disappointed.

"Don't you worry. My Granddaddy never gave anybody twenty dollars' worth of credit without knowing his last name. We'll find it." The pages crackled. "Here's one for a sack of grits, but he just says, 'River Pete.' "

They continued through the pages. River Pete's name appeared often. Sometimes he was River Pete, sometimes River Pete A., sometimes Pete A. The last name was not noted.

"I'll tell you what let's do," Donna said. "Let's look at the last page. Maybe he made a notation at the end of the year." She turned the remaining pages over. On the inside back cover, they found it—an underlined notation in the copperplate hand: "River Pete Addison took off owing $20.00. No Further Credit."

Isabel borrowed a piece of paper and wrote down, "Pete Addison, Gilead Springs."

"If you go there, you might track him down, I reckon," said Donna. She sounded doubtful.

Isabel put the paper in her bag. At least she had a name, if she decided to pursue it. She thanked Donna and bid farewell to her admirer, the black dog. Before returning to her car, she stood under the oak canopy and looked back at the landing. Donna Pursey was in her boat, working on the motor. The black dog sat on the bank, watching Donna. In the shadow of the Coke machine, the yellow dog slept.

On the way home, Isabel thought about River Pete. He seemed more real to her now, after she had read in the ledger about his tobacco and cornmeal and soda crackers. Pete Addison. What had led him, she wondered, to send twenty dollars to settle his old debt with the Purseys? His conscience had bothered him, she supposed. He had been unusually honest, apparently, to merit getting so much credit in the first place.

She reached the fire tower and turned toward St. Elmo. It was late afternoon and the atmosphere was hazy gold. Her mind turned once again to the day after the storm. Pete and John James had spent the day sawing up trees that had been blown down. Before John James left, Merriam saw Pete washing at the pump. Soon after that, John James gave Merriam the letter and the bottle.

The thought came suddenly. Isabel braked, pulled over on the shoulder, and cut the motor off so she could concentrate.

The bottle. John James found the bottle that day, when he and Pete were clearing the dead trees. The bottle had not been washed up by the storm. The bottle had been buried.

She heard Clem's voice, saying the Spanish had often salvaged wrecks themselves. Suppose survivors from the *Esperanza* had saved some of its cargo and brought it to shore. They might bury it, mightn't they, on high ground at the base of a tree? With the intention of returning for it once they had saved their own lives?

Except they hadn't come back. Nobody ever came back, and what they had buried was undisturbed until the storm blew a tree down and Isabel's grandfather,

John James, and River Pete Addison turned up to clear the debris.

What had they found, besides the lovely Chinese porcelain bottle that John James gave his ten-year-old daughter?

Isabel was still holding on to the steering wheel. She forced her fingers to relax. John James had given Merriam the bottle and a letter. The letter was gone. The bottle remained.

Cows were grazing in a field nearby. Isabel watched them and tried not to succumb to the tantalizing thought that John James and River Pete had uncovered Spanish gold along with the bottle.

Isabel thought, after all, she would go to Gilead Springs.

The sun was setting when she reached Cape Cache. Donna Pursey would be sitting down to supper with her family, secure in her memories, her history scribbled in ledger books stacked in a closet. Tomorrow, Donna Pursey would go up the river fishing. Perhaps she would take the black dog, Isabel's special friend, with her. Isabel envied Donna Pursey.

She pulled up beside the trailer, parked, got out of the car. Unlocking the trailer door, she went into the semi-darkness.

The lame toiling of the air conditioner barely moved the tepid air. She dropped her bag on the table, kicked off her sandals, and walked barefoot into the bedroom. She would change from her sundress into shorts and think about dinner. She turned on the bedroom light.

In the corner by the closet door, something moved. Before she could focus on it, it began to undulate across the narrow strip of bare floor. She registered that it was a snake, a big one.

She jumped for the bed, and watched the snake

disappear underneath it. It was brownish green, as big around as her arm, and between three and four feet long.

She tasted blood. She must have bitten her lip or her tongue. Her body was damp, sweat collecting behind her knees, sliding between her breasts. She heard a whisper of sound as the snake rubbed past her suitcase, then nothing.

The telephone was in the living room, out of reach. Nobody would hear if she screamed. The window was too small to squeeze through. Sweat ran into her eyes and she wiped it away with her skirt.

Isabel! Listen to me, young'un! It was Merriam talking. *If you're going to live out here, you got to know a few things.*

Ten-year-old Isabel didn't want to know about snakes. Sullen and unhappy, she refused to look at Merriam.

I'm talking to you, Isabel.

Isabel hadn't seen the snake's head clearly, so she didn't know for sure, but it could've been a cottonmouth moccasin. If it was, she was in serious trouble. *Cottonmouth will surely bite you if he gets the chance, and he's full of poison.*

Merriam had killed a rattlesnake in the parlor once, broken its back with a broom handle. They'd had cottonmouths and other water snakes around the shed and even, once or twice, under the house when the weather had been especially wet and the creek rose.

It was too late to worry about how the snake had gotten in. She had to worry about how to get it out.

The snake would be afraid, too. It would hide if it could, but would surely attack if it felt threatened. If it stayed where it was, under the bed, Isabel could get across to the top of the dressing table without touching the floor. From the dresser top, she could launch herself through the bedroom door into the living room and make it outside to run for help.

A cottonmouth doesn't coil to strike like a rattlesnake, Isabel, but it will lunge at you. The trick of it is to keep distance between you and the snake.

Isabel would be happy to keep distance between herself and the snake. It was her dearest wish.

If you got to hurt it, throw something and smash the head. Or use a pole to hit it with.

She scanned the room. The bulkiest items in her reach were a hairbrush on the dressertop and a flashlight on the bedside table. As for poles, the closest one was a broom hanging on a hook on the kitchen wall. The crowbar she'd used to get into the house was back in the cabinet under the sink.

Getting from the bed to the dresser would be easy. The room was so small, there was very little space between them. The bedsprings creaked as she eased her body toward the foot of the bed.

Suddenly, the snake shot from beneath the bed and slithered through the door into the darkening living room. This time, she had a better view of it. She couldn't be positive, but she was pretty sure she hadn't seen its eyes. *A harmless snake—you look down, you can see its eyes. A cottonmouth, you can't. That's one way to know.*

Blood was beating in her neck and temples. The living room was a pool of shadow, the snake nowhere in sight. After catching her breath, she eased herself to the head of the bed and got the flashlight from the bedside table. She returned to the foot and switched the light on.

The faint beam didn't illuminate much. She could see a stretch of bare floor, the end of the sofa. No snake.

Hoping for a better view, she climbed from the foot of the bed to the dressertop and shone the beam through the door again. She could see more of the sofa this time, but still no sign of the snake.

Did snakes like to hide in dark places? She wasn't sure whether Merriam had expounded on that subject. If it wanted darkness, it could have gone behind the counter dividing the living-dining room from the darker kitchen.

Her sneakers were on the floor at the foot of the bed. They wouldn't deflect a cottonmouth's fangs, but she'd feel better wearing them. She bent down and fished them up. Still sitting on the dressertop, she put them on and double-tied them. This was no time to be stumbling over loose shoelaces.

The shoes made her feel safer and able to think more clearly. The overhead light in the living room could be controlled from two switches—one just inside the front door, one next to the bedroom door. Turning it on had to be the next step. That meant getting down from her perch and walking across the floor.

Once more, she raked the flashlight beam over the portion of the living room she could see. She slid her legs around and put her feet on the floor. Breathed. Took a step. The floor seemed flimsy, creaky. She sensed that the snake, wherever it was, could feel her every move vibrating against its body.

Another step and she was in the doorway. She reached around the corner, felt for the light switch, and turned it on. She tensed herself to jump back.

Now, she saw it. It was in a corner again, this time across the room, on the far side of the front door. If she could get the door open, it might be persuaded to leave. The door was opposite the end of the kitchen counter. She would have to get up on the counter and reach across to the doorknob. It would be a stretch, but she thought she could do it.

The snake was a still, dark form in the shadows. Her

eyes on it, Isabel moved through the doorway. In another couple of steps, she had reached the sofa. She stepped up on it and walked across the sagging cushions to the end nearest the counter. From there, she snagged a dining chair and stepped on it, then moved from the chair to the counter.

Her activity had disturbed the snake again. It was sliding up and down the floor of the kitchen, seeming to search for a way out. Isabel crawled to the end of the counter. She reached but couldn't touch the doorknob.

Her fear, while real, seemed remote. She didn't have time for it. She eased herself onto her stomach on the counter and inched forward, her outstretched fingers reaching for the doorknob and the latch beneath it. Her arm, shoulder, and the tendons in her neck ached with the effort. If she overbalanced, she would land on the floor. With her left hand, she clung to the edge of the counter.

At last, her groping fingers touched the lock, gripped it, turned it. Her fingertips slid on the smooth surface of the doorknob, but after a couple of tries she managed to turn it and pull the door open.

The agitated snake remained in the kitchen. It showed no inclination to make for the door.

There was still the broom.

The broom was hanging on the opposite wall of the kitchen, but the kitchen was only a few feet wide. Isabel got to her feet. She leaned forward until she overbalanced, then caught herself against the opposite wall. She retrieved the broom from its hook and heaved herself back to the counter.

Now, she was prepared to break the snake's back with the broom handle. Except that given her position, and the lack of space for a windup, doing such a thing was physically impossible. She would have to practice her sweeping, another talent honed under Merriam's tutelage.

Isabel clutched the broom in both hands, leaned forward, and with all her strength swept the snake toward the front door.

It moved a few feet but didn't like it. She saw the white cottony lining when its mouth opened. She swept again, harder, pushing the writhing creature toward the door. One more thrust and it was out, sailing through the air. She jumped down and slammed the door.

For reasons she couldn't explain, she climbed back onto the countertop and sat cross-legged, holding the broom. She was still there fifteen minutes later when Harry Mercer arrived.

28

HARRY BEAT ON THE DOOR UNTIL HE HEARD ISABEL SAY, "Come in. It's open." He had known what Scooter had done as soon as he found the bathroom door open and Sis gone. His chest ached with the desire to get his hands on Scooter and kill him.

Isabel was sitting cross-legged on the kitchen counter, holding a broom across her lap. Her face was milky white. She said, "Harry, a cottonmouth got in here."

Harry closed the door behind him. "Where did it go?"

"I swept it out." She waved the broom with an odd smile. "I swept the goddamned thing out. You should've seen it. You know"—she giggled—"Merriam killed one, a rattlesnake, with a broom once, but I just swept it. Like an enthusiastic housewife." She laughed again, a breathless hiccup. "What in the hell are you doing here, Harry?"

He said, "Let me get you a drink. All right? What have you got?" He walked into the kitchen, opened cabinets. He found a bottle of gin, poured some over an ice cube, and put the glass on the counter beside her. "Do you want me to help you down from there?"

Her lip curled. "No, thanks. I got up here by myself all right." She picked up the glass and drank. "Didn't I tell you not to come over?"

"That was yesterday."

She drank more gin, giving him a look he couldn't read. "So here you are."

"Yeah."

Isabel seemed to be waiting, giving him a chance to say something, but when he didn't take it, she said, "How did that snake get in here, do you think?"

He couldn't look at her. He shifted his gaze. "Got to be an opening somewhere. Around the pipes, maybe. You want me to look?"

She stayed up on the counter, drinking her gin, while he checked the pipes. After a while, he said, "I'm going to look outside. You got a screwdriver? And a flashlight?"

"The screwdriver's under the sink. The flashlight? I guess I dropped it over there, on the sofa." As he went out, she said, "Be careful. It's still out there somewhere."

He shook his head. "It's in the slough by now."

No sign of Sis outside. Harry pushed through the bushes at the back of the trailer, shining the light in front of him. Insects whirled in its beam. He found the place where the pipes led into the kitchen. The metal cladding around the opening was rusty and loose. Although the gap didn't seem large enough for a snake of any size to get through, Harry tightened the screws.

He also shone his light on a ventilation panel that was hanging loose, affording a larger opening. That's where Scooter had put Sis in. He probably brought her over in the plastic garbage can. Harry snapped the panel back in place.

When he went inside he said, "I found it. Out by the kitchen pipes. I tightened it up for you."

She climbed stiffly down from the counter. "I was thinking I might have to sleep up here."

One important thing he did have to say. "I left Kathy."

She frowned. "You what?"

"I left Kathy."

"Who's Kathy?"

"My wife."

He could tell by her face that she'd had enough. She looked ready to scream and blow her top. He rushed on. "It was going to happen sooner or later. Anyway, I wanted to tell you she's the one who wrote those letters to you."

"What?"

He should have left this for another time, but he wasn't sure there would be one. "I had told her about us, a long time ago when she and I were courting. She never forgot, and when you came back, she got worried." He had hit a snag. "She wrote the letters because she was worried—" He stopped, then tried again. "She was worried that I still loved you," he said. He wiped his mouth with the back of his hand.

She didn't say anything. After a minute, he said, "Anyway, I'm glad you're safe."

She looked right into his eyes. "Are you?" she said, and he saw in her face that Scooter was right: She had gone into the house. She knew.

Loss and desolation filled him. He said, "You take care, all right?" Lifting a hand in farewell, he left. The lock on the door clicked behind him.

29

A TRUCK WAS PARKED BESIDE THE ROAD WITH A DAY-GLO orange sign propped against it: FRESH BOILED PEANUTS. Isabel pulled over and bought a bag. Juice was already soaking through the brown paper. The barrel-shaped, almost toothless woman selling them said, "Enjoy those, you hear?" Isabel ate them one-handed, a messy process, as she drove on toward Gilead Springs.

She had left early, after a restless night during which the cottonmouth and Harry Mercer disturbed her dreams in tandem. She awoke eager to go. The idea of getting away was so appealing, she had brought an overnight bag, just in case. Although the trip was a long shot, compared with her other preoccupations, its outcome seemed admirably predictable: Either she would find some trace of River Pete Addison in Gilead Springs or she wouldn't.

At almost noon, she passed a sign announcing the Gilead Springs city limits. It was a small town, formerly a spa where people came to take the waters from warm sulfur springs. Those days were long gone, and now the town consisted of a Taco Bell, a brambly old cemetery, a few beautiful Queen Anne–style houses, a row of unimposing stores, and the Gilead Springs Lodge, a cavernous stone building dating from the glory days of Gilead Springs. The Lodge, Isabel was surprised to see, had been refurbished and was actually in business.

Across from the Lodge was the county courthouse, a two-story white stucco building. The courthouse would be as good a place as any to start looking for Pete Addison.

The high, echoing halls seemed deserted, and Isabel soon remembered it was lunchtime. She wandered until she found a door with PROPERTY RECORDS painted on it in gold. She tried it, expecting to find it locked. It wasn't. A gray-haired man in shirtsleeves sat at a desk, eating a sandwich—tuna salad, judging from the smell. When she appeared, he put it down, dusted his fingers, and listened attentively to her query about people named Addison who might have owned property in the area.

"Addison?" His forehead wrinkled. "I don't know anybody by that name, and I've been here a good long time. When would this have been?"

"I'm not sure. In the twenties maybe."

He guffawed. "Well, I don't go back quite that far. I can let you look at the records, but they're not cross-referenced and computerized yet. The money to do it got knocked out of the budget last year. If you want to dig through, you're welcome."

"Thanks. I'll give it a try."

"I'll get a batch and get you started."

Time passed. Workers in the Records office returned from lunch, chatted, went back to their tasks. After two hours, Isabel was starving, cross-eyed from studying small print, and generally discouraged. She was also relatively, but only relatively, sure that Pete Addison had not been a property owner in Gilead County.

She returned the last pile of documents to the man and thanked him. Damn it, she had been so pleased at her good luck with Donna Pursey, she had made the mistake of believing it would continue. "If I wanted to trace somebody who used to live in Gilead Springs, where else would I look?" she asked the man.

He hung his head back and studied the ceiling. "I guess you could try the graveyard," he said.

She left the courthouse and tottered, weak with hunger, to the Taco Bell. Try the graveyard? She might as well. The overgrown cemetery was only half a block away. Carrying her taco and a Diet Pepsi, Isabel picked her way through blackberry vines and dead leaves to a stone bench under a tree. The bench was mottled dull green with lichen and was surrounded by tilting tombstones.

After she finished eating, she got up to wander along the ill-kept paths and decipher the tombstones. She tried to be methodical, working her way from the front of the enclosure to the back, where a wire fence was bedecked with a profusion of yellow rambling roses. She was on the next to last row of stones, and the sun was lowering, when a voice said, "You looking for anybody in particular?"

The voice had come from behind the rose-hung fence. She looked up, to see a shrunken man wearing a straw hat with a gaudy band. Only his head was visible over the mass of roses. Isabel shaded her eyes. "Addison. Pete Addison."

The man shook his head. "He ain't there. I know every one of them stones. Lived next door to them for forty years."

"Did you ever heard of Pete Addison?"

The man shoved his hat up on his forehead. "You doing genealogy? We get a fair number doing genealogy."

"Well . . ." There was no way to explain. "Sort of."

He wagged his head. "No Pete Addison there, and I never heard of him, neither. 'Course, this ain't the only cemetery around. You got St. James, that's the Catholics, up on the highway, and Rose of Sharon, out next to the Primitive Baptist Church."

Isabel's hands went to her aching back. St. James. Rose of Sharon.

"And there's the new memorial park, too, on the coast road," the man finished triumphantly. He shook his head. "No Pete Addison in this one, I can tell you. I'd know for sure if there was."

Isabel murmured, "All right, all right" under her breath, but the man, having delivered his message, had disappeared. She wasn't about to tackle St. James, Rose of Sharon, and the new memorial park tonight. She started for the Lodge, hoping it wasn't fully booked.

30

BUDDY BURKE WAS PAST WESTPOINT, THE LAST TOWN before St. Elmo. He was damn near home.

For the first time, he got the idea that everything might work out. Maybe Joy wasn't cheating on him with Mr. S. Maybe she had bought Kimmie Dee the boots by now, and when he mentioned it she would whoop a laugh and say, "You ran off work release because of *that?*" He'd go back, then, and serve his time and be satisfied.

Buddy sure hoped it would end up that way.

Buddy was sitting on an upturned bateau back in the weeds near the Turpentine Creek landing, eating salami and soda crackers and drinking a 7-Up. His shotgun was propped beside him. Buddy could have shot something to eat, a squirrel or a rabbit, but he had discovered it was easier to steal. You didn't have to skin, gut, and cook a salami. It was hanging right there in the store for you to take. Hell, he had stolen the knife he was cutting off the bites with, too. Buddy had learned a lot on this trip, but what he'd learned most about was stealing.

Down in front of him, across the weeds and rutted clay, was the boat-launching basin. Turpentine Creek, then the river, then the canal, was the route Buddy would take to Cape Cache. He was too close now to risk hitching a ride. Too many people around here knew him. And he'd had enough walking through woods and swamps. A boat was the quickest and easiest way. Buddy had done the trip by boat many a time on hunting and fishing excursions.

There were several boats at the basin, either pulled up on the bank or moored to the dock. That was the good news. The bad news was, a white-haired man wearing a railroad engineer's cap was sitting under the pavilion, drinking coffee and looking out at the water as if he didn't have a care in the world. He was sitting there when Buddy arrived, he had sat there during the twenty minutes Buddy had been eating his lunch, and he looked likely to keep on sitting there until sundown or later. All well and fine, except Buddy didn't want to wait until sundown to take care of his business.

He watched the engineer. Retired. Not a thing in the world to do but sit and watch the creek go by. Must be nice to have nothing more than that on your mind, and to hell with other people, who had goals to accomplish.

Buddy chewed, meditating. He could go on down there. One of the boats had a motor on it; he had already spotted that. Chances were he could get it started and be on his way.

Except, he had to be sure. Once he started checking it out, the engineer would get suspicious if he had any brains at all.

Buddy finished his last bite of cracker and wiped his hands on the knees of his jeans. When he got home, he'd have a real bath, not a cold rinse from somebody's outdoor faucet. He would sit right down in a full tub and get Joy in there to scrub his back. When he was clean, he'd play with Kimmie Dee and Toby. Toby was so little, he might have forgotten his daddy already. Truthfully, Buddy had never quite cottoned to Toby the way he had to Kimmie Dee, but anyway, they'd all have a good time. It could work out all right.

As Buddy watched, the engineer emptied out the rest of his coffee on the ground. Buddy hoped this meant he was about to leave, but all he did was put the cup on the table and settle back to watch the creek some more.

Buddy couldn't wait any longer. He had to move. He picked up his shotgun and sauntered toward the basin, trying to look like he belonged here. Ripples broke on the wet clay and a rusted bait can rolled back and forth in the shallows. A cloud of gnats hung over the water.

Not looking at the engineer, Buddy stood at the edge of the basin and studied the boat he wanted. There were oars in it and a gas can. It might be the ticket, but he had to get closer to make sure. As nonchalantly as he could, Buddy got into the boat and stood still until it finished rocking. He stepped over the front seat to get to the motor. Yes, he thought he could—

"You looking for something, son?"

Buddy raised up from where he had bent over the motor. The old engineer had left his place and was standing on the bank, watching Buddy. The engineer's face was bright pink and wisps of white hair stuck out from under the cap. Buddy cleared his throat. "This is my brother's boat," he said.

The engineer didn't say anything for a minute. He pulled out a blue bandanna and wiped his neck. He said, "That boat belongs to Mr. Robert Dawkins. Mr. Dawkins is a friend of mine. His only brother died of bone cancer last year."

Now, Buddy should say, "Screw you, I was just looking." He should jump out of the boat and haul ass away from here. He'd find another boat or walk through the woods like he'd been doing. It wasn't a big deal.

Instead, he went into kind of a commando crouch, cocked his gun, and pointed it at the engineer, all in less than two seconds. He watched the engineer's face go meaty purple.

The engineer put his hands up. "I didn't say nothing."

"I heard you all right," Buddy said. He thought, *I've taken enough.*

Buddy jumped over the side of the boat into calf-deep water. His boots sank into the sludge and he felt water rushing into them. He didn't care. He strode through the shallow water to the engineer and said, "People like you ought to mind their own business."

"Yes, all right," the engineer said. His pudgy hands were shaking so fast, Buddy couldn't make out one finger from another.

Buddy jerked the engineer's bandanna out of his pocket and gagged him. The engineer made a choking sound. Buddy frog-marched the engineer into a stand of trees and shoved him down in the brush. He took off the engineer's belt and bound his hands together and tied them around a sapling. He'd probably get loose, but not until Buddy was long gone.

As Buddy was about to walk away from the grunting engineer, he took the engineer's cap and put it on. Small, but the fit wasn't too bad. He was pleased to have a cap again.

All of this had been done in what seemed no time at all, but now Buddy felt an urgent need to move. He ran back to the boat, shoved off, and paddled out into the creek. He'd get down a ways and find a place where he could work on the motor and get it started.

He was going home. In spite of everything, it might work out all right.

31

ISABEL HAD SLEPT WELL IN HER CLEAN, SPARTAN ROOM AT the Gilead Springs Lodge. Today, she had decided, was the last day of her search for River Pete. She would go to St. James, Rose of Sharon, and the memorial park. That was it.

After breakfast, armed with directions to the cemeteries, courtesy of the desk clerk, she drove out of Gilead Springs in the morning heat. The sky was such a pale blue, it was almost white. Billows of hot air rushed in the car window and tugged at her hair.

St. James, she had learned, was on the highway right outside town. She found it easily, a small, rundown white church with a packed-earth yard. The cemetery was small also, the grass lush and straggling. The place was deserted, perfectly quiet except for the occasional car whizzing past on the highway.

She walked back and forth, studying grave markers in the torrid sun. The task became so mechanical, she sometimes lost her concentration and had to retrace her steps. Even so, at the end of forty-five minutes, she was sure that no Addisons were buried at St. James Church.

According to the desk clerk, the Rose of Sharon Primitive Baptist Church was eight or nine miles out of Gilead Springs. She found the turnoff for the country road and wound past farmhouses and sun-drenched fields. She went over a rise, and in front of her was the Rose of Sharon Church. It was a large, new-looking brick building with a bright tin roof and a towering spire. Behind it, dominated by a tall cross of white stone, was the cemetery—what appeared to be several acres of treeless hillside divided by neat copings. The contrast with the other two cemeteries was all but total.

She pulled up in a gravel parking lot in front of the church and cut the motor. To proceed as she'd been doing, looking at every grave, would take days. She couldn't do it. She'd have to find somebody who could tell her who was buried here. Either that or forget it.

She got out, crossed the parking lot, and walked up the church steps to the tall front door. It was unlocked. The air inside was deliciously cold, and the tall pebbled-glass windows in the sanctuary transformed the blazing light outside into a cool, almost fluorescent glow. There was no one in sight.

There had to be an office. Isabel walked along an aisle to a side door. She found a hall with a water fountain and a small room where choir robes hung. She could hear the clatter of typing. She continued down the hall until it intersected with another and the sound of typing became more pronounced. Around a corner was an office with the door open, where a woman sat behind a desk, typing on a large manual typewriter. A burned-wood plaque beside the door read, CHURCH OFFICE. Beneath it was a smaller matching plaque: HESTER DAVIS, CHURCH SECRETARY.

The woman—Hester Davis, presumably—continued typing. She looked to be in her seventies, with ruffled gray hair and one ear plugged with a hearing aid. She wore a red wool sweater buttoned up to her neck. When Isabel was standing directly in front of her, she gave a start and said, "Goodness!" After she recovered, she continued: "What can I do for you?"

"I'm trying to trace someone who may be buried in your cemetery," Isabel said. "Is there a list of names?"

Hester Davis touched her hearing aid. "Trace what?"

Isabel raised her voice. "The cemetery! Do you have a list of people buried there?"

"Yes indeed," Hester said. "The Reverend Willis has it in his office. He's on vacation, but he'll be back a week from Saturday, if you want to check with us then."

Summoning a smile, Isabel said, "I'm from out of town. Do you think you could let me look at it now?"

The secretary shook her head adamantly. "I don't go in his office when he's not here. It's a personal rule. Avoid getting called a snoop that way." She looked as if it was a sore subject.

"I really would so much appreciate it—"

Hester shook her head again. "I'm sorry as I can be, but I can't do it."

Rows and rows of neat grave markers swam before Isabel's eyes. She couldn't face it. She turned away.

She had taken a couple of steps toward the door before Hester said, "What name were you looking for?"

Isabel turned back. "Addison."

Hester's eyes widened. "Addison! Why didn't you say so?"

Had she finally hit pay dirt? "You mean you have an Addison buried out there?"

Mention of the name Addison had entirely transformed Hester. "Goodness yes. Father of one of our church elders. I remember the old man so well, coming in for services with his wife. A fine old gentleman, so mannerly and polite." Her beaming face clouded. "The son's not well at all, I'm afraid. Did you say you're kinfolk of his?"

This was no time to get mired in tortured explanations. Isabel opted for a plain and simple lie. "I think I might be."

"Oh, he would be pleased. If you want, while you go have a look at the old man's grave, I'll phone the son and tell him you're in the neighborhood. It would do him a world of good to talk to you." She waved Isabel out. "Go on and look. The family plot is in the third row from the church building, next to the far end. You'll find it."

Isabel could hardly believe this abrupt reversal of her luck. Stammering her appreciation, she left the office while Hester was picking up the telephone.

Out in the manicured cemetery, she counted the rows of headstones, walked to the far end, and began searching. There were no Addisons. She began to suspect that Hester was simply loony. She continued to look.

After another few minutes, she saw the explanation. There were two headstones directly in front of her, surrounded by clean white pebbles and stone coping. *Mother* and *Father*. The *Father* stone was inscribed:

ADDISON BAINBRIDGE
1880–1960
BELOVED HUSBAND AND FATHER
GONE TO ETERNAL REST

Hester had sent her to someone whose first, not last, name was Addison. Isabel had tracked down the wrong man.

32

SHE SPRINTED BACK TO THE CHURCH OFFICE, BUT IT WAS too late. Hester greeted her with the news that the son of Addison Bainbridge had been delighted to hear of a visiting relation. He insisted that Isabel come right over. Hester obviously felt she had done something admirable. "I told you he hasn't been well," the secretary said, dropping her voice. "They say it's . . . serious. This will make him so happy."

Isabel didn't have the heart to tell her about the misunderstanding. She noted the directions to the Bainbridge farm, which according to Hester was only a few minutes' drive away. "He's expecting you!" Hester caroled as Isabel said good-bye.

Isabel would have to stop by and see Mr. Bainbridge, explain the mistake. What an embarrassment to have raised the sick man's hopes for a visit with a relative. As soon as she had straightened things out with him, she would be on her way.

Following Hester's directions, she took a left at the bottom of the hill. After a couple of miles, she saw the house—white frame, tree-shaded, substantial, with several outbuildings behind it. Coming up the long driveway, Isabel passed banks of camellias and azaleas, stands of fruit trees and dogwoods. Everything about the place bespoke graciousness and prosperity. A far cry from the world of River Pete, living in a driftwood shack and doing chores for the Purseys in exchange for tobacco.

She parked at the steps. As if he had been watching

for her, a man in his sixties came out on the porch. He had sparse salt-and-pepper curls and dark eyes sunk in a face with an unhealthy gray pallor. He wore a crisp white shirt, a tie knotted neatly at the neck. An aroma of after-shave made Isabel wonder whether he had dressed after he got Hester's phone call.

"I'm Addison Bainbridge," the man said. He had a deep voice, an appealing smile. "Are you my long-lost cousin?"

Isabel flushed. "Actually, I doubt it," she said. "In fact, I think there's been a mix-up."

Addison Bainbridge was not daunted. "Oh, we'll find a connection somewhere. I got out the albums. Come on in."

It wouldn't hurt her to spend half an hour with this courtly gentleman. She followed him into a parlor with chintz-covered furniture. Several ancient-looking photo albums were piled on a coffee table. "Where are you from?" Bainbridge asked.

"I grew up on Cape Cache. Near St. Elmo."

"St. Elmo." He waved an invitation to sit down. "None of our kinfolks are from that area. Not that I know of. What's your family name again?"

"Anders. My grandfather was John James Anders, and my grandmother was Polly Sheffield."

He shook his head. "Doesn't sound familiar."

Isabel tried again. "I'm sure the secretary at the church misunderstood somehow, and—"

He settled himself beside her and picked up an album. "Don't be hasty. The albums may tell us something, don't you think?"

She could see that he was set on looking at the albums and not particularly curious about who she was. She could spare the time to look at one of them before she left.

"Here's my father." Bainbridge pointed to a studio

portrait of a formidable-looking man with a mane of gray hair and a luxuriant beard. Addison Bainbridge, Sr., was dressed in a well-fitting suit, his hands folded, staring unsmiling into the camera.

"He's very striking," Isabel said.

"Oh, he was something. What a life he had," said Bainbridge with admiration. "Came to Gilead Springs with nothing but some poker winnings, bought land—" Bainbridge made a sweeping gesture to indicate the house and its surroundings, fruits of his father's labor and ingenuity.

Keeping the conversation going, Isabel asked, "When did he come to Gilead Springs?"

"He came here . . . oh, sometime in the late twenties. Look. Here's one with me."

The photo was of his father, looking no less stiff, standing next to a slight, pretty woman with a prim smile. The woman was holding a chubby baby in a lace bonnet. "That's my mother," Bainbridge said. "She was twenty-five years younger, but he outlived her. He was nearly fifty when I was born. And, oh, gracious, look at this—"

Nodding, murmuring politely, Isabel studied the Bainbridge sisters and brothers, ponies, dogs, birthdays, vacations, graduations. She was comfortable, and it seemed fine with Bainbridge if her participation was minimal. Possible connections between the families had been dropped as a topic for speculation. When the first album closed, the next one opened.

Sometime later, the last page was turned in the last album. Isabel had done her duty. She said how interesting it had been and that she'd better go.

"I have enjoyed this tremendously," Bainbridge said, and she was sure he meant it. There was a pink glow on his ashen cheeks.

"So have I." Isabel stood and offered her hand.

He took it. "I'm sorry we didn't turn up any relationship between our families. It doesn't seem likely they even knew each other. You're from the coast, and my father didn't like the ocean at all. Wouldn't go near the water and hated the taste and smell of fish."

Isabel smiled. "We'll declare ourselves honorary cousins."

He chuckled. "Let's do that. It's been lovely for me, reliving these memories."

They began a slow stroll toward the door. Bainbridge said, "You know, it's fashionable to criticize your father, isn't it, but I've always admired mine. He had a checkered career before he settled down. He was a gambler, spent time in Cuba, was pretty much a wastrel until he married my mother and joined the church. Once he did that, he never gambled again, and he swore he'd whip any of us if we ever started."

At the word *wastrel,* Isabel's ears had pricked up. She said, "He came to Gilead Spring from Cuba?"

"So I understand. He was always vague about those early days. I think he was ashamed of the way he'd lived. He said a good friend of his died of scarlet fever and that made him decide to change his life."

They were in the hall. "Let me show you something," Bainbridge said. He disappeared through a door, emerging a few minutes later with a small box of polished wood. He unfastened the catch and opened it.

The interior of the box was fitted with dark blue velvet. Lying in a round depression was a gold coin. Its edges were uneven, its worn surface carved with symbols Isabel couldn't decipher. Despite its crude look, the gold piece had an eerie beauty.

Chills rippled over Isabel's skin. She was sure—*she knew*—she was looking at a coin from the *Esperanza.*

Bainbridge caressed the coin with his forefinger. "My father told me he won several of these in a poker game in

Cuba," he said. "Spanish coins, probably pulled out of a shipwreck down there. When he came to Gilead Springs, he had four of them. He sold three to get himself started. He kept this one—for luck, and to remind him of his vow never to gamble. He had this case made up for it. See, here he is in Cuba."

A photograph was mounted in the lid of the box. It showed two men on a porch whose wrought-iron railings were nearly obscured by a flowering vine. The bearded one with his arms crossed was Addison Bainbridge. Beside Bainbridge, his face half-shadowed by a straw hat, stood John James Anders.

Isabel could not speak. Staring at John James, and it was certainly John James, she sent a silent message: *So that's what happened to you, you bastard.*

Addison Bainbridge was talking. She tried to listen. "My father made me promise never to get rid of this coin. It's in his will that I can't sell it. He was superstitious about it."

He took the box from her. The lid closed, John James vanished from view, and they were standing on the front porch saying good-bye.

Bainbridge said, "This has been a tonic for me. My wife died last year, and my children don't live close by. I haven't been well."

"I'm so sorry. I hope you'll—"

He shook his head. "No. I won't get better. But I'll hope to see you again, if you're in the neighborhood."

Isabel said good-bye to River Pete's son and started back to Cape Cache.

It was almost laughable. A few times on the way home, Isabel felt her lips pulling into a grimace.

What had happened to the sainted John James now seemed fairly clear. He and Pete had, as she guessed, dug up treasure from the *Esperanza.* Who had had the idea to go to Cuba? Pete, the footloose gambler? Or John James, the debt-ridden visionary? It was easy to imagine how they had reinforced each other.

They had found buried treasure. A person's life has to change when such a thing happens. A man doesn't go on as he has before, struggling to support a wife and children in a mockery of a house, or living on the beach and doing odd jobs. They had loaded the gold on John James's boat—no point in waiting, having word of it get around, especially to John James's creditors—and they had gone.

John James had seen fit to share his windfall by giving Merriam what was probably the least of it, the blue-and-white porcelain bottle.

And a letter. The lost letter. What had he said to excuse his defection?

A good friend of his died of scarlet fever and that made him decide to change his life. There was no way to prove it, but Isabel had to believe River Pete's dead friend had been John James Anders.

If she was right, John James had died in Cuba. River Pete Addison had come back to Florida with the last of his gold and recreated himself as Addison Bainbridge. He sold three of his remaining four gold pieces, married, joined the Primitive Baptist Church, paid his twenty-dollar debt to the Purseys. And never, ever, ate fish again.

Isabel did laugh at the thought of River Pete hating fish.

As she got closer to Cape Cache, the cottonmouth moccasin began to intrude on her thoughts. Her palms started to sweat as she saw again the flat spade-shaped head, the greenish brown form twisting along the floor of the kitchen. It couldn't come back, but what if it did?

Maybe she should try drawing the moccasin. She

thought she could do it. She had a perfect, more than vivid, mental picture of how it had looked and moved. She would try, see if she could objectify the snake, put it out there on paper instead of letting it terrorize her imagination.

Absorbed, she planned how she would render the snake, perhaps in conjunction with other local plants and animals—sandspurs and dollar weeds, grasshoppers and yellow jackets, jellyfish and pelicans. It would be a nightmare version of the illuminated manuscript effect she had worked on so hard for *The Children from the Sea.* Instead of pretty fruits and flowers, she could do a grotesque border that intruded into the picture, threatened to take it over and smother it, like kudzu vines.

She drove another mile or so, chewing at the idea, realizing that it might work.

It might even work for her book. Instead of her medieval never-never land, have Marin and Marinette, the heroic twins, shipwrecked on Cape Cache, threatened with its dangers. Instead of a stone castle, there was an old house in the midst of the weeds. Instead of classically pretty, lifeless figures for the heroes, there was—

There was Kimmie Dee Burke. Kimmie Dee wasn't the model for the evil foster sister, but for the courageous Marin and Marinette.

Isabel couldn't wait to get to her sketchbook. At least she had that. At least she could pick up her pencil and draw.

She drove up to the trailer under the lengthening shadows. Her mind full of her project, she dashed inside.

The blow came from nowhere. It caused a flash in her eyes, like staring at the sun. She had only enough time to think she shouldn't do that. She would go blind.

33

BUDDY BURKE SAT HUDDLED UNDER THE HALF-CAVED-IN roof of a shanty, waiting for night to fall. Although it was a hot evening, he was shaking like a bastard.

He was worried about the old engineer, the one he'd left tied up at the landing. Buddy was scared maybe the engineer had died.

He had gotten so worried about it, he had scuttled the boat. Doing it hadn't been easy, and Buddy was wet through.

The old man wouldn't have died. He was only tied up.

And gagged. What if he puked and choked to death? What if he had a heart attack?

Buddy pulled his legs in closer to his body.

Fears about the engineer had spoiled Buddy's home-coming mood as he rode along Turpentine Creek and out into the river. By the time he had pulled up under some bushes to sleep, he had been really spooked, almost ready to turn around and go back. He had lingered in his hiding place through this morning, paralyzed, afraid to move, until he said to himself, *Just get going.* He had gotten going and made it to the canal before fear overtook him again.

That was when he had scuttled the boat. If they found him in that boat, they'd know he had killed the engineer, if the engineer was dead. He had tossed his shotgun out on the bank and knocked a hole in the wood bottom of the boat with the propeller shaft of the motor. He had damn near drowned himself doing it and could still taste brackish water in the back of his throat. The shotgun had gotten wet, too, somehow, and he wasn't even sure it would fire.

By this time, he was pretty close to home. He had tromped through these woods, his home woods, and taken shelter in the tumbledown shanty. Buddy had only the shotgun and the clothes on his back. No food. No money. He was maybe half an hour's fast walk from the coast and his house.

There was an animal smell around, a musty aroma of droppings and decaying nests. At this point, Buddy was questioning what he had expected of his adventure. He had had a notion of waltzing up to his front door and either blowing Joy's head off or grabbing her and kissing her, depending on his mood, but he hadn't given much thought to the details. The details now seemed significant.

He had come this far. That could not be denied. He had come this far.

Since he'd been sitting here, Buddy had made an important decision: He would not go anywhere until dark. He wouldn't wander around in daylight begging them to catch him. In the dark, he could move. He knew the route home.

Yes, he was hungry and beaten-down. But he had come this far.

Keyed up as he was, Buddy managed to sleep a while, slumped against the weathered boards. When his own snoring woke him, the night was as dark as the inside of a dog.

Buddy blundered to his feet and nearly fell down again because one foot had gone to sleep. He stood shaking it, leaning on the wall. He couldn't see his hand in front of his face. He couldn't see his gun. He couldn't see jack.

On his hands and knees, he felt around until he found

the gun. He got up and struck out through the woods. He had no plan. His mind told him only, *You came this far. Now go on.* He couldn't be this close and not go home.

He put his hand to the top of his head. The engineer's cap was gone—God knows where he'd lost it. The second cap he'd lost. He would not think about whether that was a sign of bad luck. He pushed ahead.

The trip took at least an hour. Buddy could be sure he was going right only if he didn't let himself think about it. The minute he started to question the route, he was paralyzed. After a while, he came to some houses along the banks of the canal. Soon after that, he reached the culvert where the canal passed under Beach Road and then went by the Beachcomber.

Buddy had no watch. He didn't know what time it was, but he figured ten or eleven. He didn't want to risk crossing the road, so he climbed down into the culvert. He stood there catching his breath in the barrel-vaulted space.

It was not nearly as dark as before, because of the Beachcomber and the cottages. Light reflected off the water and rippled across the top of the culvert. Clutching his shotgun, Buddy inched through. On the other side, he crouched by a stand of cattails. When an inner signal told him to go, he climbed up the bank, crossed an expanse of weedy ground and plunged forward into the dunes. Sand coated his wet boots and crusted the legs of his jeans.

Keeping low, he dodged between the cottages and the road. Everything was quiet.

Finally, he got to his place—dark except for a light in the carport. Two cars there, Joy's and another one. Buddy gritted his teeth against the tears that wanted to fill his eyes. There, in front of him, was his home. His wife, his little girl, his baby son. Keeping well out of the carport light, he circled toward the water side of the house and approached slowly, slowly. He could see the windows, dark with the blinds down, and the deck. There was something in the window of Kimmie Dee's room.

After a while, he drew close enough to see what it was—a sign, in red crayon on lined school paper, was taped to the screen. The sign said, DANJUR.

Buddy knew very well, as soon as he caught on that she meant *danger,* that the sign wasn't some kiddie game. Kimmie Dee meant the sign for him, and the message was, Buddy Burke should haul ass out of here. But what was all his trouble for? What was it for if he didn't even see Kimmie Dee?

He tapped on Kimmie Dee's screen with his fingernail. If she didn't come right away, he'd leave. But it wasn't fifteen seconds before the blinds bent and her eyes peered out.

"Hey, honey," Buddy whispered The tears did come then, just a couple of them, but he wiped them away while she was letting the blind up an inch or two.

She whispered, "Hey, Daddy!"

"Hey, Kimmie Dee. Kimmie Dee, listen—"

"Daddy, didn't you see my sign?"

"I saw it, honey, but I wanted to—"

"You better be careful. Mr. Stiles is going to shoot you."

Mr. Stiles. Mr. S. "Is that who Mr. S. is? In your letter?"

"Yes, sir. Mr. Ted Stiles. He's got a—"

"Now, tell me something. Is he there now? Mr. Stiles?"

"Yes, sir."

Mr. Stiles was there, in the middle of the night, with Joy. It was all true, what he'd feared.

After a minute, Kimmie Dee said, "Daddy, can I go away with you?"

"No, honey. That wouldn't work."

"Please."

Oh God. "I can't take you with me, Kimmie Dee." There was something else. "Kimmie Dee, you wrote to me about some boots—"

She shook her head. "Never mind. Isabel got me a pair." She waved a hand. "You better *go.*"

Isabel? Who the hell was Isabel? Buddy was shaking from head to foot. Kimmie Dee was right. He had to get out of here. "I'll see you, honey," he said.

He blew her a kiss and backed away from the house as the blind swung back into place. He couldn't feel his feet on the ground.

He had taken only a couple of steps when the tall man appeared underneath the carport. Buddy saw him clear as anything, a lean man with curly hair. A gun in his hand. Mr. Ted Stiles, Buddy was willing to bet.

"Hold on, Buddy," Ted Stiles said.

Fury flooded Buddy's gut. "Don't tell *me* to hold on," he said. He swung the shotgun up, aimed, and pulled the trigger. The wet son of a bitch did not fire.

Buddy saw Ted Stiles raise his gun. Next thing, there was a boom. Something hit him hard and he was falling, his mouth making sounds that didn't mean a thing.

34

ISABEL YEARNED FOR LIGHT. IT SEEMED THAT IF SHE HAD light, the throbbing in her head would subside, and if the throbbing subsided, she would be cooler, and if—

Round and round it went. All she had were heat, darkness, pain.

She had awakened only minutes ago, although she had a memory of being carried and a notion that she had been outside.

Where was she now? In a hot, dark, painful place. She squeezed her eyes closed and opened them wide. Blackness. Had she really gone blind?

She began to be aware of the position of her body. Her wrists and ankles were tied, her hands behind her. She was lying on her side on a wood floor. Her mouth was gagged.

The atmosphere was airless.

Her former unconsciousness now seemed like bliss. She closed her eyes and let herself spin downward, trying to return to it.

She couldn't. Her head ached with every beat of her pulse; her hands and shoulders threatened to cramp. She was straining against her bonds, which made it worse. She forced her muscles to relax.

She lay without thinking. Who had done this to her, and why, seemed irrelevant. Nothing mattered except continuing, taking one searing breath after another.

After a long time, she thought she might try to sit up. A powerful part of her argued against it. She was hurting, at the mercy of whatever force had visited this on her. Sitting up would be a waste of energy, an exercise in futility.

Except that sitting up was what human beings did. Lying here aching, choked on dust and heat, was for times when you couldn't do better. If you had an inkling that you might be able to sit up, you sat.

Pulling herself upright was hellishly difficult, because she couldn't separate her ankles to lever herself. The attempt became, in its way, diverting as she tried to figure out which muscle groups were available to her.

The way to do it, she found, was to roll over on her back. She could do this by pulling with her top knee, which dragged the other leg up. Once on her back, she rocked upright and was rewarded with dizziness and nausea. She leaned forward and rested her forehead on her bent knees, willing it to pass. Her head seemed to be cracking open. The random thought came to her that she might die.

When the worst passed, she was bathed in sweat. She turned her head, rested her cheek on her knees, and tried to breathe evenly. It took all the courage she could muster to raise her head again.

This time, the reaction wasn't as bad. When the wooziness subsided, she began inching herself backward on her buttocks. Before long, her bound hands came in contact with something—a wall. Although most of the feeling was gone from her fingers, she could tell it was a wooden wall. She managed, awkwardly, to lean back against it.

Wood floor, wood wall. She wondered—

She heard footsteps. The sound was muffled. The steps were closed off from her, or she from them, but somebody was there, nearby. Her heart drummed, but whether from hope or dread, she didn't know. She listened hard, put all her strength into listening.

The steps stopped, and just then she heard another

sound. Far off, a siren was wailing. A fire truck or an ambulance. She hadn't heard a siren, not one, since she'd arrived at Cape Cache. She used to hear them all the time in New York. For a moment, she entertained the crazed notion that her captor had somehow transported her to New York.

The siren continued. Even in the enclosed space where she was, it grew fairly loud. Something was happening close by. Could it be a fire? Was she—had she been left in a place that was on fire? She felt her lips push against the cloth of her gag as she tried to scream, but the incipient groans died in her throat and she thought, *Breathe. Breathe. Do you smell smoke?*

She breathed. She smelled dust and a faint, familiar, almost medicinal smell, but no smoke. The heat was intense, but it wasn't getting worse. She decided this place was not, after all, on fire.

The siren cut off. She could see nothing, hear nothing. No more footsteps. What was the smell, though? The very, very faint smell? She knew what it was, but it was so faint, and her nose was full of dust. She rested her head against the wall and forgot about it.

Not much later, the siren began again. Loud, louder, loudest, and then fading away.

She wished it would come back. Frightening as the sound was, it meant help. An ambulance or fire truck carried help to those in need, and right now Isabel counted herself among the needy.

She heard footsteps again, briefly. When they stopped, there was only silence.

Hours passed. She didn't sleep but lapsed into a suspended, semiconscious state. Dreamlike visions passed through her mind—Merriam twirled a baton and sang "He's Got the Whole World in His Hands"; on a Cuban balcony, John James Anders smelled a blossom on a flowering vine; Isabel herself ran down an endless staircase to meet Ben Raboski.

Isabel saw a pale gray line. She blinked, and it was still there. She kept her eyes fixed on the line to see what it would do.

Gradually, the line brightened, modulating from gray to pale yellow. She heard movement, shuffling, soft footsteps. She kept her eyes on the line.

She had forgotten the smell, but now it came back to her. The line had brightened enough so she could see a little. Wooden walls loomed around her, a small, familiar enclosure, and she thought, *Mothballs. Mothballs.* She was in the house, a captive in the closet in her old bedroom.

The sounds from the bedroom continued. Was it Harry out there? The thought that it might be Harry filled her with anguish.

Forget it. Harry cared only about protecting the treasure he'd found. He must have guessed that Isabel had come in the house, maybe noticed her clumsy attempt to refasten the boards over the back door.

She felt helpless, and despised the feeling. She sat with her back against the wall, listening to the sounds in the room—her room.

Then the sounds stopped and footsteps moved toward the door. She waited, wondering whether the person out there had gone away.

He could have left, or he could be standing outside the door. She listened.

She was certain he would come back.

The line of light under the door had brightened until she could see the floorboards. She could see her feet in sandals, her ankles tied with nylon rope. She tested herself. Her fingers were too numb even to wiggle. She couldn't begin to stand up. She could creep along on her butt, rocking from one side to another. She could turn her head. And if she could get the right balance, she was pretty sure she could kick, lying on her back and striking out with her feet.

It wouldn't be stealthy. If her captor was in the house, he would hear. Yet she believed trying something was better than waiting to see what he had in mind for her.

She maneuvered herself into position. Her arms and hands, which she had thought were deadened by lack of circulation, proved able to register intense pain when she rocked back against them.

Her first attempt was pathetic. She had imagined a powerful thrust but had misjudged the distance, so her feet only grazed the door and slid to the floor with a feeble thud. Now, any listener was alerted. She moved closer and tried again.

Her feet were asleep, and she barely felt the impact at first, until the pins and needles started. Still, the door shivered in its frame. She was reasonably sure it wasn't locked. Her closet door had never locked. She kicked out again, this time connecting solidly under the knob with the soles of her feet. She wished she was wearing thicker shoes, but never mind.

She stopped to listen. No returning footsteps. She kicked again, gathering power, her breath exploding from her chest.

John James had built his house of the finest wood, all solid. When it was new, the floors must have been straight, the doors securely hung. But the years, wood worms, and moist air had done their work. Straight lines were warped, connections loosened. When she kicked again, she heard splintering. With the next kick, the door gave and opened an inch or so, and she saw it outlined with daylight.

It wouldn't open wider. Further kicks were futile. Something was braced against it from the outside.

She wasn't stopping now. She sat up, edged her body around, and pressed her face against the crack in the door.

He had put a board, one of the shelves where the artifacts had been, under the doorknob. Her efforts had knocked it askew.

She jiggled her body against the unfastened door, trying to set up a vibration and dislodge it. This took more energy than kicking and was at first less successful. The door would open a crack but no farther. The door rattled, the sound invading her head until she couldn't remember other sounds.

Nothing was happening. Nothing was happening.

Without warning, the board fell free.

The door swung open suddenly and she toppled out. She lay on the floor a few seconds, then struggled to sit up again.

The room was practically empty. The diving equipment was gone. So was the ice chest, the gasoline can, the tackle box, and the sleeping bag. The shelves had been dismantled. The cannonballs still lay in the middle of the floor, and few bottles of chemicals were pushed against the wall. The sounds she had heard must have been her captor packing.

Isabel became aware of her raging thirst. She had never been so tortured by the need for water. Her lips felt swollen against the cloth of her gag, and her mouth and throat were burning. Thirst dragged at her, making it difficult to think what to do next.

But she had to think. Her captor might be returning right now. He might be approaching, in sight of the house.

The thought sent her lurching to the nearest window. It was open, the tattered shade pulled down. She edged the shade aside with her head. Through the bowed-out rusty screen, she could see the trailer. And on the concrete-block front step of the trailer sat the small, disconsolate-looking figure of Kimmie Dee Burke.

35

BUDDY BURKE WAS STRAINING TO WAKE UP. HE SAW RED and orange on the inside of his eyelids, but his eyes wouldn't open. He remembered he was in a hospital, and he had the spooky feeling that maybe his eyes had been sewn shut. A doctor could sew your eyes closed if he took a notion. He could sew your eyes closed to punish you, and Buddy reckoned he was going to be punished six ways from Sunday.

Buddy moved his head back and forth and heard himself making an *Mmmm* noise as he continued to try to open his eyes. His neck hurt—he hurt all over the goddamn place, not even to mention the shoulder he was shot in, but right now the eye situation bothered him the worst. He was trembling on the verge of a yell by the time he screwed his face up and one of his eyes popped open at last and piercing white light poured in. The other eye was crusted shut. Buddy must have done some crying in the night. He thought he probably had.

With both eyes open at last, he studied his hospital room. It was too damn bright. Light bounced off the white walls and shone from a neon coil in the ceiling. Buddy studied the coil for a while before he let his gaze drift toward the door, where a burly young man in a County Sheriff's Department uniform was sitting in a chair reading *People* magazine. Buddy watched him wet a finger and turn a page. Buddy cleared his throat and said, "Hey, bro."

The deputy looked up. "Mr. Burke."

"I got to pee."

The deputy didn't reply. Keeping his finger in his place in the magazine, he stood up and put his head outside the door for a short chat with somebody. After a minute or two, a nurse, a cute freckled thing, came in with a contraption kind of like a pitcher that she seemed to think Buddy would be willing to pee into.

Buddy squirmed. "Can't I use the toilet?"

"You're not supposed to be out of bed."

He nodded at the deputy. "Make him leave, anyway."

The deputy, standing by the door, didn't move. The nurse said, "He has to stay. Come on now."

Buddy closed his eyes so he wouldn't have to look at the nurse or the deputy. He was going to be punished six ways from Sunday. This was only the beginning.

After that, they sponged his face and gave him breakfast. As the memory of the previous night returned in detail, Buddy felt more and more downcast.

The deputy stayed in the chair, reading his magazine, while the nurses came and went. Buddy kept his eye on the door, trying to see what might be going on in the hall, and when the nurse pushed out with a cart, he got a glimpse of somebody. He got a glimpse of a tall rat bastard with curly hair, the same rat bastard who had stood under Buddy's carport last night and shot him in the shoulder.

Buddy started violently and yelled, "Yo!"

The deputy dropped the magazine. "What is it?"

Gesturing wildly with his good arm, Buddy roared, "What is that son of a bitch doing here!"

The deputy glanced around. "Who?"

"The one who shot me! Out there! By God—"

Buddy was trying to climb out of bed, but the deputy got to him and held him down, and the nurse and a couple of other people, including Sheriff Turl, rushed into the room when the deputy yelled.

"Goddamn it, Buddy," Sheriff Turl said.

"He's out there, Mr. Turl!"

"Shut up. I've had enough aggravation from you."

"He's out there!"

"So is your mama. Now shut up."

At the mention of his mother, Buddy shut up. He lay back and felt the deputy let him go. "Get the son of a bitch away from me," he said weakly.

The sheriff said, "To tell the truth, he wants to talk to you."

This is a nightmare, Buddy thought. A man screws my wife, he shoots me, and then he wants to talk to me. "I don't want to talk to him."

"I think maybe you should, Buddy."

Buddy heard something in the sheriff's tone. "He shot me," he said.

"Well, hell. You were fixing to shoot him, weren't you?"

Buddy didn't answer. Maybe this was a good time to ask for a lawyer, but he didn't have the energy. He turned his face away.

"He seems to think he can help you," the sheriff said.

Buddy gave a soft, derisive hoot. When the sheriff didn't continue, he said, "Help me how?"

"I can't say. But the situation you're in, I think if a lawman wants to help you, you should listen to him."

Maybe he hadn't heard right. Buddy turned toward the sheriff. "What do you mean, a lawman?"

"He's Marine Patrol."

Buddy worked at keeping his face a blank while his mind went clicking over. The rat bastard was Marine Patrol. "Want me to tell him to come in?" the sheriff asked.

In a minute, everybody except the deputy had left and Ted Stiles was standing within a couple of feet of

Buddy's bed. He pulled out an ID and wagged it in front of Buddy's face.

Buddy looked at the ID. Theodore Stiles. *I don't like Mr. S.* "Remember me?" Stiles said.

"You shot me, you son of a bitch."

Stiles pursed his lips. He said, "Reckon they don't allow smoking in here."

"Go ahead and smoke. I don't care." Buddy studied Stiles. He must be fifty at least, broken veins alongside his nose, leathery wrinkles, limp gray-blond curls. Buddy pictured him with Joy.

Stiles looked around and said, "No ashtray." There was a jug of water and some glasses on Buddy's bedside table. Stiles poured himself a drink and said, "Does the name Darryl Kelly mean anything to you? Patrolman Darryl Kelly?"

Buddy rolled his eyes up. Now he had a hint of what this was about. "Sure it does. He's the one who arrested me last time."

Stiles nodded. "Caught you hauling marijuana in your boat. Right?"

"I reckon you know that's right."

"Have you heard what happened to Darryl not long after that?"

Buddy chewed his lip, staring at the starched sheet that covered his body. "I heard he went missing."

"Got eaten by a shark."

Buddy nodded. "I didn't have nothing to do with it. I was in jail by that time."

Hands in his pockets, Stiles bounced on his heels. "I know you were in jail by that time. But I'm not sure you had nothing to do with it. Is there any little thing you could tell me about what went on between you and Darryl Kelly?"

Buddy hated Ted Stiles. He hated Ted Stiles more

than anybody he'd ever hated, except maybe Joy. "No, there isn't."

"Give it some thought. Maybe you'll change your mind," Stiles said.

Buddy didn't have to lie here and let this rat bastard jerk him around. "I haven't changed my mind about shooting your dick off when I get a chance."

Ted Stiles actually laughed. "You ought to talk to me," Stiles said. "The situation is different now. You see that, Buddy." He fumbled in his breast pocket and brought out a cigarette. He placed it between his lips but didn't light it. "Before, you could look forward to getting out pretty soon," he said. The cigarette bobbled with every syllable.

Buddy closed his eyes.

"Now, with this stunt you've pulled, your situation isn't as favorable as it was. You escaped from jail, assaulted a man, stole a boat, tried to shoot me. A lot of folks are mad with you, Buddy."

Buddy had also stolen a motorcycle, but he decided not to mention it. When he opened his eyes, Stiles was looking at his watch, a fancy digital job. "Don't let me hold you up," Buddy said.

Stiles smiled. "I'm saying it plain. You help me out, I'll try to help you out."

Buddy smelled a food smell, as if somewhere in the hospital they had started to serve lunch. He thought, *Why did the day come when I had to deal with this?* "You screwed my wife," he said.

Stiles shook his head, but Buddy couldn't tell if he meant to deny it. Stiles said, "I was trying to find out whether you'd told her anything. Looking for leads on Darryl Kelly. Unofficially."

"I don't believe you."

Stiles took the cigarette out of his mouth and studied

it. "Believe what you want to. It doesn't make any difference to the fix you're in now."

It did make a difference, though. It made a big difference to Buddy.

"Think about it," Stiles said.

Buddy sneered, "Go to hell," but unfortunately, he knew he would have to think about it.

Ted Stiles walked away, a cigarette lighter in his hand. On his way out the door, he said, "I'll be close around if you want to talk." Then he left and Buddy's mama came in.

36

THE SUN SHONE BRIGHTLY ON KIMMIE DEE'S BLOND HEAD. Her back was bent, her chin resting on her hands. If Isabel, at the window, could cry out, she could tell Kimmie Dee to run and get help. She so much longed to scream at Kimmie Dee that she felt the tendons in her neck straining, but the gag stayed in place.

Isabel had to get Kimmie Dee's attention. She didn't have time to work out niceties and refinements. Bracing herself against the wall, she inched her body up to the level of the window. She gathered her strength. She hurled herself against the rusted screen, rebounded like a pinball, and fell to the floor. The screen made a faint twang. She struggled back to the window. Kimmie Dee hadn't even looked up.

Try again. She repeated the process, throwing herself against the screen as hard as she could. This time, it ripped away from the frame. Isabel tumbled out the window and landed with a jarring thump on the floor of the upstairs veranda. Gasping, she dragged herself to the railing and looked out through the carved banisters.

Kimmie Dee had heard. She was standing, looking up at the house, frowning into the sun. Isabel struggled to her knees. Kimmie Dee called, "Isabel?"

Isabel stared at Kimmie Dee, willing the girl to comprehend what was going on and do something.

Kimmie Dee came closer, picking her way through the weeds. "Isabel?" she called again.

Isabel nodded vigorously.

When Kimmie Dee reached the house, she said, "What's wrong? What's that on your mouth?"

Help. Go get help, Isabel bid her silently

The girl said, "Mr. Stiles shot my daddy, Isabel. Just like I said he would."

Oh no. Isabel would have to deal with that later. *Go get help, Kimmie Dee.*

"I better come up and help you," Kimmie Dee said.

No! Don't come up here!

Kimmie Dee was walking around the side of the house.

Isabel gritted her teeth. She didn't know whether Kimmie Dee would be able to get in. She should have left the girl alone, not lured her over here and put her in danger.

After what seemed a long time, she heard light footfalls in the bedroom. Kimmie Dee's head appeared at the window. The girl said, "Do you want me to untie you?"

Isabel nodded. Yes, she wanted Kimmie Dee to untie her.

Kimmie Dee tugged at the gag and pulled it down around Isabel's neck. She said, "Now you can talk if you want to."

Tears rushed to Isabel's eyes. She ran her dry tongue over her swollen lips. After a few moments, she was able to croak, "Thanks, Kimmie Dee."

"All right. You want me to do your hands now?"

"Yes. Hurry. We're in a lot of trouble."

Kimmie Dee moved to Isabel's back and began picking at the rope. Every twitch hurt. The girl said, "Whoever tied this tied it tight."

"Just keep trying." Isabel bit her lip to keep herself from crying out. She said, "How did you get in?"

"The back door was open. Isabel, did you hear what I said about my daddy?"

"Yes. What happened?"

"He came back, and Mr. Stiles shot him. He's in the hospital. I told him to go away, but he waited too long."

"Is he going to be all right?"

"I think so. My mama keeps crying and crying. Looka there! I got one."

When the first knot was undone, the others came more easily. In a few minutes, Isabel's arms were loosened. She groaned as she moved her shoulders forward. The blood rushing into her hands was agony.

She tried to help Kimmie Dee free her ankles, fumbling with the knots with paralyzed fingers. She said, "Kimmie Dee, you should go now. Go and get help. Tell your mother to call the police."

Kimmie Dee shook her head. "I want to stay with you."

"I mean it. Go on. Tell your mother—"

"She won't do it. She wouldn't believe me."

Isabel gave up. They pulled at the final knot, and Isabel's legs were free.

She tried to stand, clutching at the railing, but at first her legs wouldn't hold her. When at last she could stay shakily on her feet, she said, "Let's go." She picked up the ropes that had bound her and the two of them climbed back in the window.

Isabel limping, they hurried out of the bedroom. They were halfway down the stairs when Isabel heard footsteps on the back porch. Beside her, Kimmie Dee had heard them, too. Isabel felt the girl pulling back. She hissed, "Keep going! Go in the room at the foot of the stairs! Don't make any noise!"

The two of them scrambled downward as the back door opened. They rounded the corner into the small sitting room across the hall from the parlor. This was where the radio had been, where Isabel did her homework and Merriam sat in the evenings crocheting afghans. It was empty now, dust curls in the corners. Isabel pushed Kimmie Dee against the wall and flattened herself beside the girl. The footsteps were in the kitchen now—and now crossing the dining room.

Isabel breathed shallowly through her mouth. She had forgotten about being thirsty, forgotten about aching ankles and wrists.

The steps were coming closer. The tread was measured, neither slow nor hurried. It was not the hesitant step of the explorer. The person in the hall knew where he was going.

He was at the foot of the stairs, only a few feet from them. He started to climb.

They had to cross the hall and go out the back. When he reached the top of the stairs, they were poised in the doorway.

Kimmie Dee was clinging to Isabel's hand. Isabel whispered, *"Now,"* and they skittered across the hall, through the dining room, and into the kitchen.

A clattering noise came from upstairs and the steps started again, coming fast this time.

Isabel and Kimmie Dee flew through the kitchen and out the back door. The steps were coming down the stairs. *He'll see us.* The words rushed into Isabel's head as they ran out the back door. She dragged Kimmie Dee down the steps and the two of them, in desperate concert, crawled past the sagging lattice guard fence and took refuge under the house.

They lay on their stomachs in the dirt, panting. The footsteps thundered through the kitchen and across the porch, the floorboards rattling above their heads. The feet descended the steps and passed within less than a yard of Isabel's face. She had every opportunity to recognize the worn deck shoes and khaki trousers. It was Harry Mercer.

Isabel and Kimmie Dee watched Harry's feet as they

pounded away from the house, around the corner of the shed, and into the woods. Isabel could hear him crashing toward the slough.

Something was pressing painfully against Isabel's rib cage. She shifted positions and looked down. There was a hard semicircular ridge in the earth.

Kimmie Dee whispered, "Is he gone?"

Isabel eased herself forward to look, scraping her ribs again. She said, "I think so." She listened a moment more. "Kimmie Dee, run for help. Make your mother listen, or call the police yourself. I mean it this time."

Kimmie Dee did not argue. She slid out beside the steps and took off. Isabel saw Kimmie Dee's bare legs flash as she rounded the corner of the house. Then she clambered out and struggled to her feet. Her adrenaline was pumping. She started after Harry. She wasn't going to let him get away.

37

I WANT TO SEE JOY," BUDDY BURKE SAID.

Ted Stiles nodded.

"Kimmie Dee, too. I want to see Kimmie Dee. And Toby." Buddy blinked cigarette smoke out of his eyes. Stiles had gotten the nurse to put Buddy in a wheelchair and wheel him to a lounge down the hall. The room was closed, nobody sitting on the green Naugahyde-and-stainless-steel furniture except Stiles. The windows looked out on pine trees. Across the room, the deputy studied the offerings of a soft-drink machine.

"Hey, bro," Buddy called to the deputy. "Hey, lawman."

The deputy turned.

"Bring me a Co'Cola, hey?"

Not until Stiles gave him the high sign did the deputy start feeding change into the machine.

Tapping ash into a Styrofoam cup, Stiles said, "I'm not sure how Mrs. Burke would feel about it, but I could—"

"You stay away from her."

"I was going to say, I could have somebody talk to her."

Buddy looked at Stiles and thought, *This chain-smoking sucker has got me by the balls.*

The deputy brought the Coke over. When he handed it to Buddy, he said, "Get you something, Mr. Stiles?"

Stiles shook his head and the deputy returned to his post by the machines. "I'm willing to explore the possibility of letting you see your family right away, providing you're willing to help me out," Stiles said.

Buddy swigged his drink. "What the hell else are we talking about?"

Twin streams of smoke poured from Stiles's nostrils. Man looked like a goddamn dragon. "All right, then," Stiles said.

"Don't forget the other, either," Buddy said. "The taking into consideration part."

"Remember I haven't made you any promises."

"Damn it, you said—"

Ted Stiles didn't even blink. "I said I'd see what I could do. And I will."

Buddy slumped in his wheelchair. He was sick and tired. That summed it up: sick and tired. "I never wanted to hurt nobody," he said. "I'm a lover, not a fighter. All I did was, a couple of times I hauled in some weed. A fellow over at Westpoint and his cousin was growing it. I told about that when I got arrested."

"Right." Stiles tapped out his cigarette. He opened a tan briefcase and pulled out a yellow pad with scribbling on it.

"I never hurt a solitary soul," Buddy said. "All I wanted was to make money for my family, and—"

"Cut the crap," Stiles said.

Buddy was miffed. What was the point if he couldn't tell it his way? Stiles kept studying his scribbles, and after a while Buddy continued. "You know, I had this boat. Your people confiscated it. I was berthing it at the Beachcomber. What ever happened to it, by the way?"

"Sent to South Florida."

Buddy mourned for his boat a second or two. Another good thing gone to hell. "In the berth next to mine was the *Miss Kathy*. Owned by a dive captain named Harry Mercer. You know him?"

Stiles, writing on his pad, didn't answer.

"Harry's a charter captain, takes out dive parties, fishing parties. Well, I was in and out of there a lot, going to and from Westpoint, and I noticed that Harry and his deckhand kept taking the boat out by themselves, no paying customers on board. I started to wonder what they was up to."

Stiles grunted. "You figured they were cutting in on your trade?"

"I reckon so." It seemed long ago, those days when Buddy was free. "Anyway, I started to keep an eye out. Sure enough, I saw them come in and carry off ice chests and stuff and put them in Harry's truck. Now, you take a few cold drinks when you go out fishing, but this was different. So what I did—" Buddy stopped. "You aren't going to get me for this, too, are you?"

Ted Stiles waved at him to go on.

"I waited till they left one evening and I sneaked onto Harry's boat. One thing that interested me was a big old tank they had built on deck. I wanted to know what they had in there. It was fastened with a lock and chain, but there was enough slack so I could pull the top up and shine a flashlight down in there. You know what I saw?"

"Bales of marijuana?"

"No siree." It was a true pleasure to get one up on Ted Stiles. "The thing was half full of water, and in that water was some cannonballs, and part of something that looked like a musket. That's what was in there."

Buddy didn't want to spoil his own surprise, so he went on: "Those boys had found a wreck and was hauling stuff out of it. And they was keeping it such a secret, you can bet your bobtail there was more in it than a few cannonballs."

The veins in Ted Stiles's nose glowed brighter. "Gold, you mean?"

"That's what I was figuring."

"So what did you do?"

"Do? Nothing." Buddy hadn't had a chance to do anything. Ted Stiles hadn't asked what he'd *intended* to do.

"You didn't try to persuade them to let you in on it?"

"No!" Buddy acted like the idea had never occurred to him.

"Why not? Darryl Kelly arrested you before you got around to it?

Stiles obviously never gave anybody the benefit of the doubt. Although, in truth, it had been only a couple of days later that Kelly had caught Buddy and Buddy's present difficulties commenced.

Buddy's shoulder hurt. Now he really was tired. "Your friend Kelly pulled me in. I didn't want to go to jail, you know? I cooperated right off the bat. But he told me I'd have to go, anyway."

"It was your third offense. It's the law."

"Yeah, that's what he said. But I thought if I could give him something good, they might make an exception, so I told him about Harry Mercer and the wreck. Taking stuff out of a wreck is illegal, too, unless you've got the permits."

Stiles's face was serious now. "What did Darryl say when you told him?"

"Laughed in my face." The memory of it galled Buddy even now. "He thought I was making it up."

"He must have decided to check it out, though," Stiles said slowly.

"I told him, if they arrested somebody, I ought to get part of the treasure for turning them in. He laughed at that, too."

"In the end, it didn't turn out so funny." Stiles closed his pad. "Harry Mercer, you said?"

"Yeah," Buddy said. "I want to see Joy. And Kimmie Dee, and Toby."

"I'll work on it." Stiles signaled the deputy to wheel Buddy back to his room.

38

PROPELLED BY FURY, HARRY CHARGED THROUGH THE woods. The thought of the empty upstairs room made his legs pump like machinery. He barely felt the sweat coursing down his body, the hot breath whistling through his lungs.

I'll find you, Scooter. If you're not at the dock, I'll—

But Scooter was at the dock, pulling a tarp over a pile of stuff—the treasure, Harry's treasure—that he'd loaded in the skiff with the putt-putt motor.

Scooter had heard Harry coming. His head was turned Harry's way, and when Harry burst out of the swamp, Scooter let go of the tarp.

Harry jumped at Scooter with an inarticulate cry of rage. His only desire in the world was to make Scooter suffer and then kill him. He actually prayed, for a split second, to be able to do just that.

Scooter was ready. His wiry body uncoiled at Harry, and Harry felt Scooter's fingers around his throat. Harry said, "You son of a bitch—" and, a lucky shot, kneed Scooter in the balls.

Scooter howled and let go. When he bent forward, Harry kicked him in the ribs, but instead of falling down, Scooter, still bent double, sprang back at him. They wrestled on the uneven turf, neither with an advantage.

"Don't you run out on me, you son of a bitch," Harry wheezed.

Scooter's fist drove into Harry's gut. Harry's breath rocketed out of him, and he felt his mouth opening and closing like the mouth of a beached fish. He reached out blindly and grabbed a handful of Scooter's hair. Scooter, flailing, caught Harry's nose hard with his bony knuckles. Harry felt a sharp jolt of pain and tasted blood. He fell to his knees in the mud and long grass, with blood sliding out of his nose and dripping down his chin.

Scooter, standing over him, said, "You're a fool, you know that, Harry? A small-time fool."

"The wreck—"

"The wreck is tapped out, haven't you realized that? There isn't any more gold down there. Somebody else got it. Where do you think that bottle came from? Somebody took most of the gold out long ago."

Harry was choking on desperation and his own blood. "You've got to give me my share, anyway," he rasped.

"Your share! When you fucked us up every possible way? Go let your girlfriend out of the closet. She's your share."

Harry was holding his arm to his bleeding nose. "What closet?"

"The closet in the house, sucker, where I put her so she wouldn't get in the way. She's been there since last night, so she'll be plenty glad to see you. Maybe she'll even let you—"

Harry stumbled to his feet and swung at Scooter. He put more behind it that he thought he could, and although Scooter ducked, he didn't completely avoid the blow. Harry caught him on the ear and knocked him off balance.

Then something strange happened.

Isabel—yes, it was Isabel, Scooter must have been lying about the closet—rocketed out of the undergrowth and grabbed Scooter from behind. Now even more off balance, and dragged by Isabel's weight, Scooter dropped to one knee as he clawed at Isabel's arms.

Wondering if he was hallucinating, Harry shambled

forward on spongy legs and fell on Scooter, knocking him flat. As Scooter writhed beneath him, Harry shouted, "Rope! In the boat!" and moments later Isabel was back with a handful of nylon twine.

Scooter spit in Harry's face as they struggled to tie him up. Feeling the spittle on his cheek gave Harry the impetus to crack Scooter on the side of the head with all his strength. Scooter's eyes rolled up and his body went limp. They trussed his legs and arms and stretched him out in the long grass, and Harry waded into the brown water and rinsed his face. To Isabel he said, "I'm glad you showed up."

She was sitting on the bank, looking battered and filthy. She said, "He put me in the closet. Kimmie Dee let me out. She's gone for the police."

Harry was sick, deep within himself, to think of what she had suffered because of him. "Isabel, I'm sorry."

"I thought it was you," Isabel said dully.

"No." He blotted his nose some more. It had almost stopped bleeding. "You know what we've been up to, don't you?"

"Why don't you tell me?"

He told her. He told her how Scooter had found the wreck when they came to help Clem Davenant when his son drowned, how they decided to salvage it and set up a base in the house because it was out of the way. "Miss Merriam never even knew we were there, I promise you," he said.

Her eyes narrowed. "Are you sure?"

"I'm sure. If she'd known, she wouldn't have kept it to herself."

"What about the Marine Patrolman, then? Darryl Kelly?"

Harry didn't understand. "The one that had the accident? What did he have to do with us?"

"I thought maybe he caught you."

It took a while before Harry saw what she meant. She believed he was the kind of person who would kill two people in cold blood, one of them an old lady he'd known for years. When he'd finished protesting, she said, "You can't answer for Scooter, though."

That was true. He couldn't answer for Scooter.

While they talked, Harry's eyes had been on the loaded skiff. He had made a decision. "Isabel, if I were to leave, would you come with me?"

"Leave?"

"Right now. Take the skiff. Take off and go, before the law gets here."

She looked startled, but not horrified. She said, "No, thanks. I've done that already. And I feel bound to tell you it doesn't solve anything."

"I know that's what they say, but I never tried it." Harry stood up. In spite of all the pain from Scooter's battering, he was feeling much better. Much, much better. "I'm not going to stay here and let my life be eaten up by the law."

He reached out a hand and helped her to her feet. She said, "They'll come after you."

"Maybe they won't find me. I know the coast pretty good." He was walking toward the boat now. He lifted a flap of the tarpaulin. Yes, there was some of his diving gear. And the tackle box with the coins in it, and some of the other stuff. No shards of blue-and-white porcelain, though. Scooter must not have thought they were worth saving. He straightened, turned to Isabel. "Come with me."

She shook her head.

In the distance, a siren howled. Conscious of his bloody nose and dirty shirt, Harry didn't try to embrace her. He held on to her shoulders for a minute, then jumped into the boat and said, "Cast off, would you?"

She untied the mooring rope and tossed it in the boat.

He cranked the motor, settled himself by the tiller, and waggled his hand in farewell. *Now it's my turn to go,* he thought, and, filled with exhilaration, he watched the prow of the skiff cut through the brown water as he went deeper into the swamp.

39

THE SOUND OF HARRY'S MOTOR THROBBED IN THE DIStance for so long, Isabel was not quite sure when she ceased to hear it. She stood on the dock, watching Scooter's motionless body, half hidden by grass. After a while, she realized that his eyes were open. He stared at her, unblinking.

The sirens had stopped. The police would be on their way. They would go to the house first. If she didn't hear them soon, she'd go find them.

Scooter's pale blue eyes were on her.

She said, "Did the Marine Patrolman catch you taking something from the wreck?"

No answer.

"My aunt saw what happened to him. She was murdered, too."

The blue eyes glared.

"You were right about the wreck. The treasure isn't there," Isabel said. "The treasure hasn't been there for centuries. My great-grandfather found it, buried under a tree behind the house. And then he took it, and—"

"I didn't kill anybody," Scooter said. "You aren't saying I killed somebody. Harry must have done it. Where's Harry?" He thrashed from side to side. *"Harry!"*

Isabel heard voices in the woods now. Coming closer. She said, "Harry's gone."

She was shocked to see Scooter's eyes redden. "Harry was my partner," he said. "None of it was your business. Nobody needed you."

"Harry's gone," Isabel repeated.

"They'll catch him, the dumb fuck," Scooter said. His voice was hoarse.

"Hello!" the voices called. *"Where are you? Isabel?"*

She cupped hands around her mouth. "Here! This way!" To Scooter she said, "Are you the man in the hood?"

A disdainful look again. "Do you think I'm a monk or something?"

"You wear a diving hood, don't you? Isn't that something divers wear?"

"Some do. Not me." The subject didn't seem to interest him. "They'll catch him," he said. "He won't even make it out of the county."

Then they were surrounded by people and voices.

40

I WAS SO ALONE. OH, BUDDY." JOY BURKE SOBBED.

"I know, Joy. I know." Buddy patted his wife's back. This was what he had wanted, wasn't it? Yes, it was.

Over his wife's head, his eyes met Kimmie Dee's. Kimmie Dee looked cute today in a polka-dot dress and her hair in a ponytail. Buddy was as proud of that child as he could be. As far as he could tell, she wasn't too impressed about people gushing over what a brave girl she was.

Kimmie Dee said, "Daddy, will you be able to come see me in the talent contest on July Fourth?"

Buddy shook his head. Joy's face was buried in his neck and he could feel her tears wetting the collar of his pajamas. "I got to go back to jail for a while, honey. I won't be out in time for that. Maybe somebody will make a video for me."

"So alone," Joy said. He patted her back some more.

Toby, seeing his mother crying so hard, started to wail. Kimmie Dee pulled on his chubby arm and said, "Hush, Toby! Be sweet for Daddy."

After a minute, Toby's face unscrewed. He said, "Dee." Buddy thought he would burst. What a fine little fellow.

Joy pulled back and got a tissue out of her bag. She blotted her eyes and said, "I would have come to visit you up there more, but it seemed like there was so much to do around here."

"I know, sugar."

"We'll come now. Nothing else matters."

"All right."

A nurse came in and pointed to her watch. Buddy said, "Looks like time's up." He beckoned. "Come here, Kimmie Dee."

She came up and stood by the arm of his wheelchair. He squeezed her shoulders. "Kimmie Dee, while I'm gone you help your mama, hear?"

Kimmie Dee looked as if she thought that was a dumb thing to tell her. "I will."

"I'm so proud of you, honey. I'm going to come home as soon as I can."

"Won't that be fine?" Joy chimed in. "Having Daddy back home?"

Kimmie Dee leaned on the arm of the chair. She said, "What about Mr. Stiles?"

Joy's eyes narrowed. "That bastard," she said.

Buddy took Kimmie Dee's chin in his hand. "We aren't going to worry about Mr. Stiles anymore," he said. "He's history. Over and done with. Okay?"

"Okay."

Buddy gave her a hug and kiss and then Joy held Toby up and Toby gave Buddy a wet little smack. Then it was Joy's turn, and then they were all at the door, waving. Kimmie Dee waved one last time and her eyes met Buddy's again. It occurred to Buddy, briefly, that he would never really know what went on in her head, and then the doorway was empty and he heard them talking to one another as they walked down the hall.

41

THEY RECKON SCOOTER KILLED THE MARINE PATROLMAN," Clem Davenant said. "It's a matter of finding more evidence. In the meantime, there's plenty to hold him on."

"Good," Isabel said. After a night in the hospital she was back in the trailer, propped on pillows on the sofa. Clem had brought her home and stayed to tell her the story. "Knowing how much Scooter hated me, I wouldn't want to stay here if he were let go."

"He won't be."

"And . . . what about Harry?"

"They haven't caught him yet, but nobody doubts they're going to. It's just a matter of time."

Clem's confident tone was irritating. Isabel thought of Harry in his bloody shirt, gliding through the swamp in the skiff.

Clem stood up. "I'll be on my way." He stopped to look at the blue-and-white bottle on its stand under John James's photograph. "To think this came from the *Esperanza,*" he said. "The ship Edward found. Those two salvaging that wreck—it's like robbing his grave."

Feeling argumentative, Isabel said, "The bottle hadn't been on the *Esperanza* in years. It was buried out back of here with the rest of the treasure John James and River Pete found and took to Cuba."

Clem's eyes were still on the bottle. "Edward worked so hard. He never knew what a good job he did." At the door he said, "Your bruises are healing?"

"Yes." Isabel displayed her wrists, reddish purple

and flecked with scabs. her ankles looked much the same. "My ribs are still sore, but that's about all."

"Your ribs? What happened to them?"

Isabel could barely remember. She had a curved bruise on her ribs. "I'm not sure. I think—" It came back to her. "Oh, right. I was hiding under the house, lying pressed against a raised ridge, a kind of semicircular—" She stopped. She hadn't thought about it before.

"A semicircular what?" Clem asked.

Isabel wanted him to go, wanted to consider her idea alone. "I don't know. A ridge of hardened dirt, probably." Except she didn't really think it was hardened dirt.

She went to the window and watched Clem's car pull out of the drive. Then she changed into jeans, sneakers, a long-sleeved shirt. She tied a bandanna around her hair to keep the cobwebs out. Under the sink with the other household tools she found a gardening trowel.

The afternoon heat was sultry and invaded her too-heavy clothes as soon as she stepped outside. The heat, and perhaps a leftover emotional kick, made her woozy as she walked toward the house, and she stood by the back steps a few minutes, gathering her determination. Then she got down on her hands and knees and maneuvered herself through the opening between the sagging lattice barrier and the back steps, into the dim space where she and Kimmie Dee had lain. The dirt, the spider webs, the buzzing of insects—all were as they had been.

Stretched on her belly, she ran her fingers lightly across the dirt. *This was the place,* she thought. *Here, or maybe a little more to the right. . . .*

There it was, the semicircular ridge. It was definitely not dirt. It was hard, metal. It wasn't surprising that her ribs had been bruised by pressing against it.

She began scraping with the trowel.

At first the dirt moved easily, but a few inches down it

was packed firm. She continued to dig. The ridge, she saw, was not a semicircle at all. It was a circle, of about the same diameter as she could make with her curved arms.

By the time she had dug down a foot, it was clear that she had found a cast-iron wash pot. She remembered that a cast-iron pot had been lost, presumably washed away, in the storm of 1922. If it had merely been tumbled under the house by the water, surely it would have been found. Enough note had been made of its absence so that Merriam remembered it.

Isabel scraped at the packed dirt. Her hands and clothes were filthy. She worked doggedly, hacking away, until a particularly stubborn and immovable patch of dirt wasn't dirt at all, but ragged burlap.

She peered into the pot's black interior. The burlap was half-disintegrated. She pulled at it and a strip gave way, exposing more burlap. She pulled at that. As rotten as the first piece, it tore.

Gold gleamed underneath.

She was cold. Her teeth chattering, she reached out and touched a gold coin, a thick coin with uneven edges like the one she had seen at Addison Bainbridge's house. The coin, with what appeared to be quite a few others like it, was wrapped in a burlap packet.

Feverishly, she dug with her fingers to loosen the packet. Her fingers touched burlap again. There were other packets underneath.

Tears filled her eyes as she looked down at the pile of coins in its tattered wrapping. John James hadn't taken the treasure to Cuba with him after all. John James had given Merriam a letter, and Merriam had lost it. Now, Isabel could imagine what the letter had said: *I must go away, but if you dig behind the back steps—* Had he planned to return? *I urge you to maintain secrecy, so it doesn't benefit only my creditors—* She would never know.

Her cheeks wet, she gathered up the opened packet of coins and, holding it close, edged out from under the house, inching forward on her elbows.

If only Merriam had known. If only she had known, everything would have been different. Resentment at Merriam's death vibrated in her.

The man in the hood.

Scooter had told her he never wore a hood when he was diving.

She sat on the back steps and put the coins in her lap. They were as bright and beautiful as if they just been minted. She freed them from the disintegrating burlap and counted.

Twenty. Twenty gold pieces were lying on her shirt-tail. There were more still in the wash pot.

Why should I believe what Scooter said? She did believe him. She believed him because he hadn't known why she was asking. He hadn't known Merriam had talked about a man in a hood.

She doubted he had even known where Merriam was staying. But others had.

The coins clinked when she stood, holding the bottom of her shirt to form a bag. She started to run, jingling at every step. She had to get to the telephone. She had to—

"You found it, I see," a voice said.

She whirled. Ted Stiles was leaning against the corner of the house, grinning, his hands in his pockets. He said, "You sure were occupied. I could have ridden down here on an elephant." He took a step toward her. "From what Scooter is telling down at the jailhouse, I gathered Harry Mercer didn't get away with the whole shebang. Some story about a porcelain bottle, and stuff buried on the property. Seemed worth keeping an eye on the activities around here."

"Go to hell," Isabel said. Ted Stiles. Absurdly, Kimmie Dee's letter came into her mind: *I don't like Mr. S.*

"Naw, really," Stiles said. "This is the best time there is. Not a soul in the world knows it's been found except you and me."

When he took his right hand out of his pocket, she saw that he held a gun.

Fighting to keep her breathing even, Isabel said, "I thought you were some kind of investigator, working undercover. That's what Clem told me."

Stiles chuckled. "I am. And when you're talking about Spanish gold, that's something worth investigating."

They were face to face, Isabel clutching her shirttails. He reached down and picked up a coin. He turned it in his fingers, studying it, then slipped it in his pocket. "I tell you what, Miss Isabel. You're coming along with me." He pulled a folded handkerchief from his pocket, shook it out, and handed it to her. "Tie those coins up first."

Isabel knelt and spread the handkerchief on the ground. Constantly aware of the gun pointed at her head, she piled the coins on the handkerchief, twisted it and tied two of the ends together to make a pouch.

"Nice," Stiles said. He took the bundle from her. "Now, what we're going to do is, we're going to walk down to the lighthouse. Stroll down, like we wanted some fresh air before dinner." He gestured with the gun. "This is going to be in my pocket, pointed at you. Let's go."

The day was waning. They walked up the drive under the rustling palms and turned toward the lighthouse. There were no houses along here, only the dense palmetto woods, with overhanging live oaks and towering pines. Along the shore, the waves boomed.

"You knew where Merriam was. You kept asking about her," Isabel said.

He didn't answer. Their steps scraped rhythmically.

"You knew Scooter and Harry were salvaging. Clem said Buddy Burke told Darryl Kelly, trying to make a deal. Darryl Kelly must have told you."

"He thought it was a joke," Stiles said. "If it was such a damn joke, why was he checking it out? My guess is that he wanted it, too."

"He caught you, so you killed him. Merriam saw you."

"I hadn't found anything that day but a couple of cannonballs. Knocked him a-winding with them. I would've just as soon nobody had to get hurt, but it didn't work out that way."

The intensity of her anger demolished Isabel's fear. "You didn't want to hurt anybody? You tracked down a helpless, sick old woman and murdered her!"

"She saw me," Stiles said. "I wish she hadn't, but she did. I quit after that. Let Harry Mercer and his deck-hand take it out, and I'd get it later."

"That's right," Isabel said. "What would they do? Call the law?"

They reached the barrier, climbed over it, and skirted the sandy knoll where the lighthouse stood. Laboring through the dunes, they came out on the opposite side of the peninsula. In a small, hidden inlet a blue boat with a ragged canvas roof was pulled up on the sand.

Stiles said, "Now, what you're going to do, Isabel, is push this boat out into the water. I'd be a gentleman and do it myself, but I've got to keep an eye on you."

Push the boat out, so he can take me out and kill me. Dump my body on the shoals. The gun was out of his pocket again. "Go on, now." She pushed the boat's bow. It scraped along the sand and floated out into the surf. Stiles waded after it, heedless of his shoes and pants legs. He tossed the coins in the boat and jumped in himself. "Keep pushing," he said. "Take it out about waist deep."

The water was warm. Waves broke around Isabel's body, soaking her sneakers and jeans. She pushed the boat as Stiles watched her over the side, following her with the gun. When the water had reached her waist, he said, "That's good. Deep enough to let the motor down. Get in." He extended his free hand, and she clambered over the side. The boat had crosswise, benchlike seats. Stiles was sitting in the stern, beside the motor.

This, Isabel knew, was the only time she had to do something. Stiles had to let the motor down and get it started. After that, there would be no more distractions until they were far enough away from shore for him to shoot her without anyone hearing.

Stiles, in the back, was lowering the motor. Under the seat between the two of them lay the bundle of Spanish coins, where they had fallen when Stiles tossed them in the boat.

Isabel bent over and put her head on her knees.

"Sit up," Stiles commanded. He had put the gun down on the seat beside him while he adjusted the motor.

"I'm sick," Isabel said.

"If you're going to puke, do it over the side."

Not a bad idea. Clutching her stomach, Isabel slid off the seat and, on her knees, struggled to the side of the boat making retching sounds. She was now in a position to reach the coins, and Stiles was in her peripheral vision. When she saw him turn back to the motor, she slumped and grabbed the bundle. Her fingers closed around the knot.

Isabel sat on the middle seat and swung her legs over. She was aware of Stiles's head turning as she jumped toward him. She drew back the bundle of coins and smashed it into his temple.

He gave a wheezing gasp. She could smell him, smell sweat and tobacco. She drew back and hit him again. His face dark red, he slipped sideways off the seat.

Isabel lunged forward. Her fingers closed on the gun.

42

HIS SECOND DAY OUT, HARRY GOT A JOB AS A DECKHAND on a boat called the *Carina.* Rich people on vacation. The guy they'd had before got drunk once too often. They were planning to end up in Key West after a while. Once Harry got there, he was going to be a dive bum. Maybe that's what he was meant to be all along.

He had the coins with him, still in the tackle box. The rest of the stuff he'd stashed in a safe place.

Treasure diving was what Harry really wanted to do. He was planning to hook up with an outfit in South Florida. Quite a bit of it went on down there, from what he had heard.

After a while, when he got himself in order, Harry would go back to Cape Cache, sneak back and see Isabel. She'd be sick of the place by that time and ready to come with him. Harry imagined a house down in the Keys, a simple place on the water, with a deck. He could see Isabel on that deck, her feet up, her sketch pad on her knees. She would be concentrating so hard, she wouldn't hear Harry coming up next to her, wouldn't know he was there until he touched her. Then she'd smile and put her drawing away. They'd sit in the dusk, watching the sun set far out over the water.

This was Harry's new life. Across the way, Harry could see the lights on shore, bright points marking places he didn't have to go to, where he wasn't expected or known. He had a tackle box full of gold coins, and all the time in the world.

epilogue

IT WAS MIDAFTERNOON ON THE FOURTH OF JULY. ON A wooden platform in the St. Elmo Municipal Park, a man was playing "My Darling Clementine" on the harmonica. The bleachers were packed, and the smell of grilling hot dogs wafted from an open barbecue where men in aprons sweated. Behind the bleachers, children and dogs chased one another. From the top row, Isabel Anders and Clem Davenant watched the talent show.

The wash pot had contained two hundred gold coins. All of them were legally Isabel's, since they had been found on her property. The coins were worth about half a million dollars, which would allow Isabel to keep and restore the house.

She was, she had found, incapable of letting it go.

Ted Stiles was a fixture in her nightmares. Often, she dreamed she had shot him and woke up wishing it were true. In life, she had brought him in with monumental calm, having been pushed to a place beyond emotion. In her sleep, she screamed obscenities at him and slashed at his eyes with her fingernails.

Working on *The Children from the Sea* had helped during the past days. She was almost finished with it. She thought it was macabre enough to please most children.

Harry was still at large. The police continued to claim he would be caught any day.

The last plaintive sounds of "My Darling

Clementine" faded and the audience broke into applause. Isabel realized she was tense. She craned to see the skinny figure in the red leotard and white boots at the foot of the steps leading to the stage.

The man with the harmonica took his last bow. When the clapping ended, the master of ceremonies moved to the mike and began to talk about "a little lady whose bravery has impressed us all, and who needs no introduction." Kimmie Dee was climbing the steps. She stood at the back of the platform until he said her name, then stepped forward smartly. She stood in position, waiting for the music to begin.

MICKEY FRIEDMAN grew up in the Florida panhandle and now lives with her husband in New York City. A full-time writer, she is the author of six previous mysteries, most recently *A Temporary Ghost* (Viking, 1989).

HarperPaperbacks *By Mail*

MYSTERIES TO DIE FOR

THE WOLF PATH
by Judith Van Gieson

Low-rent, downtown Albuquerque lawyer Neil Hamel has a taste for tequila and a penchant for clients who get her into deadly trouble. *Entertainment Weekly* calls Hamel's fourth outing "Van Gieson's best book yet — crisp, taut and utterly compelling."

THE RED, WHITE, AND BLUES
by Rob Kantner

From the Shamus Award-winning author of THE QUICK AND THE DEAD. P.I. Ben Perkins takes on a case that strikes too close to home. When babies begin to mysteriously disappear from the very hospital where his own daughter was born, Ben embarks on a macabre trail of corruption, conspiracy and horror.

PORTRAIT IN SMOKE/ THE TOOTH AND THE NAIL
by Bill S. Ballinger

HarperPaperbacks is proud to bring back into print, after thirty years a special two-in-one edition from the Edgar Allan Poe Award-winning author the *New York Times* dubbed "a major virtuoso of mystery technique." In PORTRAIT IN SMOKE, second-rate businessman Danny April is haunted by a beautiful woman. So is magician Lew Mountain in THE TOOTH AND THE NAIL. And both are involved in mysteries that seem impossible to solve.

RUNNING MATES
by John Feinstein

From the *New York Times* bestselling author. Investigative reporter Bobby Kelleher has just about given up the hope of ever landing the "big hit" —the story that will make him a star. Then the governor of Maryland is assassinated and things start to change—quickly and violently.

EVERY CROOKED NANNY
by Kathy Hogan Trocheck

In this high-caliber debut, Trocheck introduces Julia Callahan Garrity, a former cop who now runs a cleaning service in Atlanta. Sue Grafton calls this novel "dust-busting entertainment," and *The Drood Review* picked it as a 1992 Editor's Choice selection.

BLOOD SUGAR
by Jim DeFilippi

In the tradition of the movie BODY HEAT, this gripping suspense novel has just the right touch of sex and a spectacularly twisty ending. Long Island detective Joe LaLuna thinks he knows what to expect when he's sent to interview the widow of a murder victim. Another routine investigation. What he gets is the shock of his life. The widow is none other than his childhood sweetheart, and now, he must defend her innocence despite the contrary evidence.

COMING SOON FROM HARPERPAPERBACKS

For Fastest Service— Visa and MasterCard Holders Call 1-800-331-3761

refer to offer HO661

MAIL TO: **Harper Collins Publishers**
P. O. Box 588 Dunmore, PA 18512-0588
OR CALL: (800) 331-3761 (Visa/MasterCard)

Yes, please send me the books I have checked:

- ☐ THE WOLF PATH (0-06-109139-1) $4.50
- ☐ THE RED, WHITE, AND BLUES (0-06-104128-9) $4.99
- ☐ PORTRAIT IN SMOKE/THE TOOTH AND THE NAIL (0-06-104255-2) $5.99
- ☐ RUNNING MATES (0-06-104248-X) $4.50
- ☐ EVERY CROOKED NANNY (0-06-109170-7) $4.50
- ☐ BLOOD SUGAR (0-06-109106-5) $4.50

SUBTOTAL .... $________
POSTAGE AND HANDLING .... $ $2.00
SALES TAX (Add applicable sales tax) .... $________
TOTAL: $________

*FREE POSTAGE/HANDLING IF YOU BUY FOUR OR MORE BOOKS!
Orders of less than 4 books, please include $2.00 p/h. Remit in US funds, do not send cash.

Name ________________________________

Address ________________________________

City ________________________________

State ________ Zip ____________ Allow up to 6 weeks for delivery. Prices subject to change.

(Valid only in the US & Canada) HO661